ROGER TORRAWAY HAD BEEN . . . CHANGED.

Inside the great white cube of the project building Roger Torraway lay spread-eagled on a fluidized bed. Prosthetic and surgical teams had done things to him that had never been done to any human being before. His entire nervous system was revised and all the major pathways connected to a computer backpack. To power it, great jet-black solar panels that resembled the wings of a bat hung from his arms. His skin was smooth, black and featureless, his internal organs compact and efficient. His eyes were gleaming red, faceted jewels. He was a masterpiece of twenty-first-century science, the best of man and machine: a cybernetic organism—a cyborg.

But was he still *human*?

D1412288

BOOKS BY FREDERIK POHL

The Heechee Saga
Gateway
Beyond the Blue Event Horizon*
Heechee Rendezvous
The Annals of the Heechee
The Gateway Trip
The Boy Who Would Live Forever*

The Eschaton Sequence
The Other End of Time*
The Siege of Eternity*
The Far Shore of Time*

The Age of the Pussyfoot
Drunkard's Walk
Black Star Rising
The Cool War
Homegoing
Mining the Oort
Narabedla Ltd.
Pohlstars
Starburst
The World at the End of Time
Jem
Midas World
The Merchants' War
The Coming of the Quantum
     Cats
Man Plus*
Chernobyl
The Day the Martians Came
Stopping at Slowyear
The Voices of Heaven*
O Pioneer!*

Platinum Pohl* (story collection)
All the Lives He Led*

With Jack Williamson
The Starchild Trilogy

Undersea City
Undersea Quest
Undersea Fleet

Wall Around a Star
Farthest Star
Land's End*
The Singers of Time

With Lester del Rey
Preferred Risk

With C. M. Kornbluth
The Space Merchants

With Sir Arthur C. Clarke
The Last Theorem

The Best of Frederik Pohl
(edited by Lester del Rey)
The Best of C. M. Kornbluth (editor)

Nonfiction
The Way the Future Was
Chasing Science*
Our Angry Earth* (with Issac Asimov)

*DENOTES A TOM DOHERTY
ASSOCIATES BOOK

Man Plus

Frederik Pohl

A TOM DOHERTY ASSOCIATES BOOK

NEW YORK

This is a work of fiction. All of the characters, organizations, and events portrayed in this novel are either products of the author's imagination or are used fictitiously.

MAN PLUS

Copyright © 1976 by Frederik Pohl; © renewed 2004.

Originally published by Random House

All rights reserved.

An Orb Book
Published by Tom Doherty Associates, LLC
175 Fifth Avenue
New York, NY 10010

www.tor-forge.com

ISBN 978-0-7653-2178-7

First Orb Trade Paperback Edition: May 2011

Printed in the United States of America

0 9 8 7 6 5 4 3 2 1

CONTENTS

Man Plus

1

An Astronaut and His World

It is necessary to tell you about Roger Torraway. One human being does not seem particularly important, when there are eight billion alive. Not more important than, for example, a single microchip in a memory store. But a single chip can be decisive when it carries an essential bit, and Torraway was important in just that way.

He was a good-looking man, as people go. Famous, too. Or had been.

There had been a time when Roger Torraway hung in the sky for two months and three weeks, along with five other astronauts. They were all dirty, horny and mostly bored. That wasn't what made him famous. That was just "people in the news" stuff, fit for two sentences on the seven o'clock wrap-up on a dull night.

But he did get famous. In Bechuanaland and Baluchistan and Buffalo, people knew his name. *Time* gave him its cover. He didn't have it all to himself. He had to share it with the rest of his team in the orbiting lab, because they were the ones who got lucky and rescued the Soviet bunch that came back to Earth with no steering jets.

So they were all famous men overnight. Torraway was twenty-eight years old when that happened, and had just married a green-eyed, black-haired teacher of ceramic sculpture. Dorrie on Earth was what made him yearn, and Rog in orbit was what made Dorrie a celebrity herself, which she loved.

It took something special to make an astronaut's wife news-worthy. There were so many of them. They looked so much alike. The newspersons used to think that NASA picked the astronauts' wives out of the entries in Miss Georgia contests. They all had that look, as though as soon as they changed out of their bathing suits they would show you some baton-twirling or would recite "The Female of the Species." Dorrie Torraway was a little too intelligent-looking for that, although she was also definitely pretty enough for that. She was the only one of the astronaut wives to get major space in both *Ladies' Home Journal* ("Twelve Christmas Gifts You Can Bake in Your Kiln") and *Ms.* ("Children Would Spoil My Marriage").

Rog was all for the nonfamily. He was all for everything Dorrie wanted, because he was for Dorrie very much.

In that respect, he was a little less like his fellows, who had mostly discovered fine female fringe benefits from the space program. In other ways he was just like them. Bright, healthy, smart, personable, technically trained. The newspersons thought for a while that the astronauts themselves also came from an assembly line somewhere. They were available in a range of twenty centimeters in height and about a dozen years in age, and came in a choice of four shades of skin color, from milk chocolate to Viking. Their hobbies were chess, swimming, hunting, flying, skydiving, fishing and golf. They mingled easily with senators and ambassadors. When they retired from the space program, they found jobs with aerospace companies or with lost causes needing a new publicity image. These jobs paid very well. Astronauts were valuable products. They were not only prized by the publicity media and the Man in the Street. We valued them very highly too.

What the astronauts represented was a dream. The dream was priceless to the Man in the Street, especially if it was a dank, stinking Calcutta street where families slept on the sidewalk and roused themselves at dawn to queue for the one free bowl of food. It was a gritty, grimy world, and space gave it a little bit of beauty and excitement. Not much, but better than none at all.

The astronauts formed a tight little community, all around Tonka, Oklahoma, like baseball families. When each man flew his first mission he joined the major leagues. From then on they were rivals and teammates. They fought one another to get into the line-up, and coached one another from the baselines. It was the dichotomy of the professional athlete. No aging knuckle-baller sitting on the bench and staring at the latest rifle-armed kid felt more sick and angry envy than the back-up man to a planetary landing felt when he watched his Number One suit up.

Rog and Dorrie fit nicely into that community. They made friends easily. They were just oddball enough to be distinctive, not odd enough to worry anyone. If Dorrie didn't want to have children herself, she was nice to the children of the other wives. When Vic Samuelson was out of radio contact for five days on the far side of the sun and Verna Samuelson came taken down with early labor pains, Dorrie took Verna's three infants into her own home. None of them was over five years old. Two of them were still in diapers, and she changed them uncomplainingly while other wives took care of Verna's house and Verna took care of giving birth to her fourth in the NASA hospital. At the Christmas parties Rog and Dorrie never got the drunkest, nor were they ever the first to leave.

They were a nice couple.

They lived in a nice world.

In that they were, they knew, lucky. The rest of the world wasn't all that nice. The little wars chased themselves all over Asia and Africa and Latin America. Western Europe was sometimes strangled by strikes and often crippled by shortages, and when winter came it usually shivered. People were hungry, and a lot of them were angry, and there were very few cities a person would want to walk in alone at night. But Tonka kept itself unpermissive and pretty safe, and astronauts (and cosmonauts and sinonauts) visited Mercury and Mars as well as the moon, swam into the halos of comets and hung in orbit around gas giants.

Torraway himself had flown five major missions. First he flew in one of the shuttle flights to replenish Spacelab, back in the early days after the freeze, when the space program was just getting on its feet again.

Then he spent eighty-one days in the second-generation space station. This was his big moment, the one that got him the cover of *Time*. The Russkis had fired off a manned mission to Mercury, and it had got there all right and landed all right and taken off for the return trip all right; but nothing after that was all right. The Russians had always had trouble with their stabilizing thrusters—several of the early cosmonauts had set themselves spinning, had not been able to stop, and had vomited helplessly all over the insides of their spacecrafts. This time they had trouble again and used up their attitude-correction reserves.

So they managed to get themselves into a wide-assed elliptical orbit around Earth, but they had no way to get out of it safely. Or to stay in it safely, either. Their control was only approximate by then, and the periterran point was low enough inside the ionosphere of Earth's atmosphere to heat them up pretty badly.

But Roger and the other five Americans were sitting there in a spacecraft designed for tug duty, with fuel hoarded for half a dozen more missions. That wasn't any too much, but they made it do: they matched course and velocity with the *Avrora Dva*, linked up and got the cosmonauts out. What a spectacle of free-fall bear hugs and bristly kisses! Back in the space tug with what the Russians had grabbed up to bring with them, they had a party—currant juice toasting Tang, pâté traded for cheese-burgers. And two orbits later the *Avrora* meteored in. "Like a bright exhalation in the evening," said Yuli Bronin, the cosmo-naut who had gone to Oxford, and kissed his rescuers again.

When they got back down to Earth, belted in two to a ham-mock, closer than lovers, they were all heroes, and they were all adored, even Roger, even by Dorrie.

But that was long ago.

Since then Roger Torraway had done two circumlunar flights, tending ship while the radio-telescope crews conducted their orbital tests on the big new hundred-kilometer radio mirror on the farside. And finally he was on the aborted Mars lander, an-other time when they were lucky to get everyone back on Earth in one piece. But by then the glamour was gone once more. It had just been bad luck and mechanical failures, nothing dra-matic.

So most of Roger's work since then had been, well, diplo-matic. He played golf with senators on the space committee and commuted to the Eurospace installations in Zurich and Munich and Trieste. He had a modest sale with his memoirs. He served as back-up on an occasional mission. As the space program declined rapidly from national priority to contingency-planning exercises, he had less and less that mattered to do.

Still, he was backing up a mission now, although he didn't talk about it when he was wooing political support for the agency.

He wasn't allowed to. This new manned mission, which looked as though it would actually be approved sooner or later, was the first one in the space program that had been classified Top Secret.

We expected a great deal from Roger Torraway, although he was not much different from any of the other astronauts: a little overtrained, a lot underemployed, a good deal discontented with what was happening in their jobs, but very much unwilling to trade them for any others as long as there was still a chance to be great again. They were all like that, even the one that was a monster.

2

What the President Wanted

The man who was a monster was on Torraway's mind a lot. Roger had a special interest.

He was sitting in the co-pilot's seat at twenty-four thousand meters over Kansas, watching a blip on the IDF radar slide smoothly off the screen. "Shit," said the pilot. The blip was a Soviet Concordski III; their CB-5 had been racing it ever since they had picked it up over the Garrison Dam Reservoir.

Torraway grinned and throttled back another tiny increment. With the boost in relative speed, the Concordski blip picked up a momentum. "We were losing him," the pilot said glumly. "Where do you reckon he's going? Venezuela, maybe?"

"He better be," said Torraway, "considering how much fuel the both of you were burning up."

"Yeah, well," said the pilot, not at all embarrassed at the fact that he had been well over the international treaty limit of 1.5 Mach, "what's happening at Tulsa? Usually they let us come straight in, with a V.I.P. like you."

"Probably some bigger V.I.P. landing now," said Roger. It

wasn't a guess, because he knew who the V.I.P. was, and they didn't come any bigger than the President of the United States.

"You fly this thing pretty good," offered the pilot generously. "Want to land it—I mean, when they let us do that thing?"

"Thanks, no. I'd better go back and sort out my junk." But he stayed in the seat, looking down. They had begun the descent, and the patchy field of L-1 cumulus was just below them; they could feel the bumps from the updrafts over the clouds. Torraway took his hands off the controls as the pilot took over. They would be passing over Tonka pretty soon, off to the right. He wondered how the monster was getting along.

The pilot was still feeling generous. "You don't do much flying any more, do you?"

"Only when somebody like you lets me."

"No sweat. What do you do, anyway, if you don't mind my asking? I mean, besides V.I.P.ing it around."

Torraway had an answer all ready for that. "Administration," he said. He always said that, when people asked what he did. Sometimes the people who asked had proper security clearance, not only with the government but with the private radar in his own mind that told him to trust one person and not another. Then he said, "I make monsters." If what they said next indicated that they too were in the know, he might go a sentence or two farther.

There was no secret about the Exomedicine Project. Everyone knew that what they did in Tonka was prepare astronauts to live on Mars. What was secret was how they did it: the monster. If Torraway had said too much he would have jeopardized both his freedom and his job. And Roger liked his job. It supported his pretty wife in her pottery shop. It gave him the feeling of doing something that people would remember, and it took him to interesting places. Back when he was an active astronaut he had been to even more interesting places, but they were out in space and kind of lonely. He liked better the places he went to in private jets, with flattering diplomats and impressionable cocktail-party women to greet him when he got there. Of course, there was the monster to think about, but he didn't really worry about that. Much.

They came in over the Cimarron River, or the crooked red gully that would be the river when it rained again, bent the jet flow to almost straight down, cut back on the power and eased gently in.

"Thanks," Roger said to the pilot, and went back to collect his gear from the V.I.P. cabin.

This time it had been Beirut, Rome, Seville and Saskatoon before he got back to Oklahoma, each place hotter than the place before. Because they were expected at the ceremonial briefing for the President, Dorrie met him at the airport motel. He changed swiftly into the clothes she had brought him. He was glad to be home, glad to be getting back to making monsters and glad to be back with his wife. While he was getting out of the shower he had a swift and powerful erotic impulse. He had a clock inside his head that kept track of what pieces of time were available, so he did not need to check his watch: there was time. It would not matter if they were a few minutes late. But Dorrie wasn't in the chair where he had left her; the TV was going, her cigarette was burning out in the ashtray, but she was gone. Roger sat on the edge of the bed with a towel wrapped around him until the clock in his head said there was not enough time left to matter. Then he began to dress. He was tying his tie when Dorrie rapped on the door. "Sorry," she said when he opened for her. "I couldn't find the coke machine. One for you and one for me."

Dorrie was almost as tall as Roger, brunette by choice,

green-eyed by nature. She took a brush from her bag and touched up the back and sleeves of his jacket, then touched coke cans with him and drank. "We'd better go," she said. "You look gorgeous."

"You look screwable," he said, putting his hand on her shoulder.

"I just put lipstick on," she said, turning her lips away and allowing him to kiss her cheek. "But I'm glad to see the señoritas didn't use you all up."

He chuckled good-humoredly; it was their joke that he slept with a different girl in every city. He liked the joke. It wasn't true. His couple of generally unsatisfactory experiments at adultery had been more shabby and troublesome than rewarding, but he liked thinking of himself as the sort of man whose wife had to worry about the attentions of other women. "Let's not keep the President waiting," he said. "I'll check out while you get the car."

They did not in fact keep the President waiting; they had more than two hours to get through before they even saw him.

Roger was familiar with the general process of being screened, since it had happened to him before. It wasn't just the President of the United States who was taking 200 percent overlap precautions against assassins these days. Roger had been a whole day getting to see the Pope, and even so there had been a Swiss guard holding a Biretta standing right behind him every minute he was in the papal chamber.

Half of the top brass of the lab was here for the briefing. The senior lounge had been cleaned and polished for the occasion and did not look like its familiar coffee-drinking self. Even the blackboards and the paper napkins that were used for scratch paper were tucked away out of sight. Folding screens had been set up in the corners and the shades of the nearest windows discreetly pulled down; that was for the physical search, Roger knew. After that, they would have their interviews with the psychiatrists. Then if everyone passed, if no lethal hypodermic turned up in a hatpin or murderous obsession turned up in a head, they would all go to the auditorium, and there the President would join them.

Four Secret Service men participated in the process of searching, frisking, magnetometering and identifying the male guests, though only two of the men physically took part. The other two just stood there, presumably ready to draw and fire at need. Female Secret Service personnel (they were called "secretaries," but Roger could see that they carried guns) searched the wives and Kathleen Doughty. The women were searched behind one of the shoulder-high screens, but Roger could read from the expressions on his wife's face the progress of the patting, probing hands. Dorrie did not like being touched by strangers. There were times when she did not like being touched at all, but above all not by strangers.

When Roger's own turn came, he understood some of the cold anger he had seen on his wife's face. They were being unusually thorough. His armpits were investigated. His belt was loosened and the cleft of his buttocks probed. His testicles were palpated. Everything in his pockets came out; the handkerchief at his breast was shaken open and swiftly refolded, neater than before. His belt buckle and watchband were studied through a loupe.

Everyone had the same treatment, even the director, who gazed around the room with good-natured resignation while fingers combed the kinky hair under his arms. The only exception was Don Kayman, who had worn his cassock in view of the formality of the occasion, and after some whispered discussion, was escorted into another room to take it off. "Sorry, Father," said the guard, "but you know how it is."

Don shrugged, left with the man, and came back looking annoyed. Roger was beginning to feel annoyed too. It would have been sensible, he thought, for them to have passed some of the people on to the shrinks as soon as they had had their search completed. After all, these were high-powered types, and their time was worth money. But the Secret Service had its own system and operated by stages. It was not until everyone had been searched that the first group of three was conducted to the typist rooms, evacuated specially to make room for the interviews.

Roger's shrink was black by courtesy, actually a sort of coffee-cream color by complexion. They sat in facing straight-backed chairs, with eighteen inches between their knees. The psychiatrist said, "I'll make this as short and painless as I can. Are your parents both alive?"

"No, actually neither of them is. My father died two years ago, my mother when I was in college."

"What sort of work did your father do?"

"Rented fishing boats in Florida." With half his mind Roger described the old man's Key Largo boat livery, while with the other half he maintained his twenty-four-hour-a-day surveillance of himself. Was he showing enough annoyance at being questioned like this? Not too much? Was he relaxed enough? More relaxed than enough?

"I've seen your wife," said the psychiatrist. "A very sexy-looking woman. Do you mind my saying that?"

"Not at all," said Roger, bristling.

"Some white people would not like to hear that from me. How do you feel about it?"

"I know she's sexy," Roger snapped. "That's what made me want to marry her."

"Would you mind if I went a step further and asked how the screwing is?"

"No, of course not—well, hell. Yes, I mind," said Roger savagely. "It's about like anybody else's, I guess. After being married a few years."

The psychiatrist leaned back, looking thoughtfully at Roger. He said, "In your case, Dr. Torraway, this interview is pretty much a formality. You've had quarterly checks for the last seven years and profiled well within the normal range every time. There's nothing violent or unstable in your history. Let me just ask you if you feel uneasy about meeting the President."

"A little awed, maybe," said Roger, shifting gears.

"That's natural enough. Did you vote for Dash?"

"Sure—wait the hell a minute. That's none of your business!"

"Right, Dr. Torraway. You can go back to the briefing room now."

They didn't actually let him go back in the same room, but in one of the smaller conference chambers. Kathleen Doughty joined him almost at once. They had worked together for two and a half years, but she was still formal. "Looks like we've passed, Mr. Dr. Colonel Torraway, sir," she said, her eyes focused as usual on a point over his left shoulder, the cigarette held between her face and him. "Ah, good, a little libation," she said, and reached out past him.

A liveried waiter—no, Roger reminded himself, a Secret Service man wearing a waiter's uniform—was standing there with a tray of drinks. Roger took a whiskey and soda, the big prosthesiologist accepted a small glass of dry sherry. "Be sure you drink it all," she whispered to his shoulder. "They put something in it, I think."

"Something what?"

"To calm you down. If you don't drink it all, they put an armed guard behind you."

To humor her Roger drank his whiskey straight down, but he wondered how someone with her delusions and fears had passed the psychiatric clearance so readily. His five minutes with the shrink had reinforced his self-observing stance, and he was busily analyzing with one part of his mind. Why did he feel uneasy in this woman's presence? Not just because she was wiggy in her mannerisms. He wondered if the trouble was that she admired his courage so much. He had tried to explain to her that being an astronaut no longer took much courage, no more than flying a transport, probably less than driving a cab. Of course, as a back-up for Man Plus there was a very real danger. But only if the men ahead of him in line all dropped out, and that was not a chance to cause much worry. Nevertheless, she went on regarding him with that intensity that in some lights seemed to be admiration, and in others pity.

With the other part of his mind, as always, he was alert for his wife. When she finally came in she was angry, and, for her, disheveled. The hair she had spent an hour putting up was now down. It hung waist-length, a fine frothy fall of black that made her look like a Tenniel drawing of Alice, if Tenniel had been working for *Playboy* at the time. Roger hurried over to soothe her, a job which took so much of his attention that he was caught off-guard when he felt a sudden stir and heard someone say, not very loud or formally, "Ladies and gentlemen, the President of the United States."

Fitz-James Deshatine came grinning and nodding into the room, looking exactly like himself on television, only shorter. Without prompting the lab people sorted themselves into a semicircle, and the President went around it, shaking every hand, with the project director at his side making the introductions. Deshatine had been beautifully briefed. He had the politician's trick of catching every name and making some sort of personal response. To Kathleen Doughty it was "Glad to see some Irish in this crew, Dr. Doughty." To Roger it was "We met once before, Colonel Torraway. After that fine job with the Russians. Let's see, that must be seven years ago, when I was chairman of the Senate committee. Perhaps you remember." Certainly Roger remembered—and was flattered, and knew he was being flattered, that the President remembered. To Dorrie it was "Good heavens, Mrs. Torraway, how come a pretty girl like you wastes herself on one of these scientific Johnnies?" Roger stiffened a little when he heard that. It was not so much that it was downputting to him, it was the kind of empty compliment Dorrie always disdained. But she was not disdaining it. Coming from the President of the United States, it brought a sparkle to her eyes. "What a beautiful man," she whispered, following his progress as he made the circle.

When he had finished going around the semicircle, he hopped to the little platform and said, "Well, friends, I came here to look and listen, not to talk. But I do want to thank every one of you for putting up with the nonsense they make you go through to have me around. I'm sorry about that. It isn't my idea. They just tell me it's necessary, as long as there are so many wacks around. And as long as the enemies of the Free World are what they are, and we're the kind of open, trusting people *we* are." He grinned directly at Dorrie. "Tell me, did they make you soak your fingernails before they let you in?"

Dorrie laughed musically, startling her husband. (She had been complaining with vicious anger that her nail polish had been ruined.) "They certainly did, Mr. President. Just like my manicurist," she called.

"Sorry about that. They say that's to make sure that you don't have any secret bio-chem-i-cal poisons to scratch me with when we shake hands. Well, you got to do what the man says, I guess. Anyway"—he chuckled—"if you think it's a nuisance for you pretty ladies, you should see how my old cat acts when they do it to her. Good thing she didn't really have poison on her claws last time they did it. She scored on three Secret Service men, my nephew and two of her own kittens before she was through." He laughed, and Roger was a little surprised to find that he and Dorrie and the rest were joining in.

"Anyway," said the President, coming to the point, "I'm grateful for your courtesy. And I am one thousand times more grateful for the way you're pushing the Man Plus project through. I don't have to tell you what it means to the Free World. There's Mars out there, the only piece of real estate around that's worth having, apart from the one we're all standing on right now. By the end of this decade it's going to belong to somebody. There are only two choices. It will belong to them, or it will belong to us. And I want it to be us. You people are the ones that are going to make sure that happens, because you're going to give us the Man Plus that will live on Mars. I want to thank you deeply and sincerely, from the bottom of my heart, in the name of every living human being in the Free World democratic lands, for making this dream possible. And now," he said, smothering an attempt at a round of polite applause, "I think it's time I stopped talking and started listening. I want to see what's happening with our Man Plus. General Scanyon, it's all yours."

"Right, Mr. President."

Vern Scanyon was director of the laboratory division of the Grissom Memorial Institute of Space Medicine. He was also a retired two-star general and acted it. He checked his watch, glanced at his executive assistant (he sometimes called him his executive officer) for confirmation and said, "We have a few minutes before Commander Hartnett finishes his warm-up tests. Suppose we look in on him on the closed circuit for a minute. Then I'll try to tell you what's going to happen today."

The room darkened.

A TV projection screen lighted up behind the platform. There was a scrape as one of the "waiters" moved a chair for the President to sit in. He muttered something. The chair was moved back, and the President nodded, shadowy in the flicker from the projection screen, and looked up.

The screen showed a man.

He did not look like a man. His name was Will Hartnett. He was an astronaut, a Democrat, a Methodist, a husband, a father, an amateur tympanist, a beautifully smooth ballroom dancer; but to the eye he was none of those things. To the eye he was a monster.

He did not look human at all. His eyes were glowing, red-faceted globes. His nostrils flared in flesh folds, like the snout of a star-nosed mole. His skin was artificial; its color was normal heavy sun tan, but its texture was that of a rhinoceros's hide. Nothing that could be seen about him was of the appearance he had been born with. Eyes, ears, lungs, nose, mouth, circulatory system, perceptual centers, heart, skin—all had been replaced or augmented. The changes that were visible were only the iceberg's tip. What had been done inside him was far more complex and far more important. He had been rebuilt for the single purpose of fitting him to stay alive, without external artificial aids, on the surface of the planet Mars.

He was a cyborg—a cybernetic organism. He was part man and part machine, the two disparate sections fused together so that even Will Hartnett, looking at himself in the mirror on the occasions when he was permitted to see a mirror, did not know what of him was him and what had been added.

In spite of the fact that nearly everyone in the room had actually played a part in creating the cyborg, in spite of the familiarity all of them had had with his photos, TV image and his person itself, there was a muffled gasp. As the TV camera caught him he was doing endless effortless push-ups. The view was from a yard or so from the top of his strangely formed head, and as Hartnett locked himself up on his arms his eyes came level with the camera, glinting from the facets that gave him multiple scanning of the environment.

He looked very strange. Roger, remembering the old movies of his childhood hours before the TV, thought that his good old buddy looked a lot weirder than any animated carrot or magnified beetle on the horror shows. Hartnett had been born in Danbury, Connecticut. Every visible artifact he wore had been manufactured in California, Oklahoma, Alabama or New York. But none of it looked human or even terrestrial. He looked *Martian*.

In the sense that form follows function, Martian he was. He was shaped for Mars. In a sense, too, he was there already. Grissom Labs had the finest Mars-normal tanks in the world, and Hartnett's push-ups were on iron oxide sands, in a pressure chamber where the weight of gas had been dropped to ten millibars, only 1 percent of the thrust on the outside of the double glass walls. The temperature of the sparse gas molecules around him was held at forty-five degrees below zero, Celsius. Batteries of high-ultraviolet lamps flooded the scene with the exact spectrum of sunlight on a Martian winter day.

If the place where Hartnett was was not truly Mars, it was

close enough to fool even a Martian—if there had ever been such things as Martians—in every respect but one. In all but that one respect, a Ras Thavas or a Wellsian mollusk might have emerged from sleep, looked about him and decided that he was indeed on Mars, on a late fall day in the middle latitudes, shortly after sunrise.

The one anomaly simply could not be helped. He was subject to standard Earth gravity instead of the fractional attraction that would be proper for the surface of Mars. The engineers had gone so far as to calculate the cost of flying the entire Mars-normal tank in a jet conversion, dropping it along a calculated parabola to simulate, at least for ten or twenty minutes at a time, the proper Martian weights. They had decided against it on the grounds of cost, and pondering, they had estimated, allowed for and finally dismissed the effects of the one anomaly.

The one thing no one feared might go wrong with Hartnett's new body was that it might be too weak for any stresses that might be placed on it. He was already lifting five-hundred-pound weights. When he really reached Mars, he would be able to carry more than half a ton.

In a sense Hartnett on Earth was more hideous than he would be on Mars, because his telemetry equipment was as monstrous as himself. Pulse, temperature and skin resistance sensor pads clung to his shoulders and head. Probes reached under the tough artificial skin to measure his internal flows and resistances. Transmitter antennae fanned out like a peasant's broom from his backpack. Everything that was going on in his system was being continually measured, encoded and transmitted to the 100-meter-per-second broad-band recording tapes.

The President was whispering something. Roger Torraway found himself leaning forward to catch the end of it: ". . . he hear what we say in here?"

"Not until I cycle us through his communications net," said General Scanyon.

"Uh-huh," said the President slowly, but whatever it had been that he intended to say if the cyborg couldn't hear him, he didn't say it. Roger felt a twinge of sympathy. He himself still had to select what he said when the cyborg could hear, and censored what he said even when old Hartnett wasn't around. It was simply not right that anything that had drunk a beer and fathered a child should be so ugly. All the words that were relevant were invidious.

The cyborg appeared willing to keep up his metronome exercising forever, but someone who had been counting cadence— "one and two, one and two"—came to a halt, and the cyborg stopped too. He stood up, methodically and rather slowly, as though it were a new dance step he was practicing. With a reflex action that no longer had a function, he rubbed the back of a thick-skinned hand against his plastic-smooth and browless forehead.

In the darkness Roger Torraway shifted position so that he could see better, past the famous craggy profile of the President. Even in outline Roger could see that the President was frowning slightly. Roger put his arm around his wife's waist and thought about what it must be like to be the President of three hundred million Americans in a touchy and treacherous world. The power that flowed through the man in the darkness ahead of him could throw fusion bombs into every hidden corner of the world in ninety minutes' time. It was power of war, power of punishment, power of money. Presidential power had brought the Man Plus project into being in the first place. Congress had never debated the funding, knew only in the most general terms what was going on: the enabling act had been called "A Bill to Provide Supplementary Space Exploration Facilities at Presidential Discretion."

General Scanyon said, "Mr. President, Commander Hartnett would be glad to show you some of the capacities of his prostheses. Weight-lifting, high jump. Whatever you like."

"Oh, he's worked hard enough for one day," smiled the President.

"Right. Then we'll go ahead, sir." He spoke softly into the communicator microphone and then turned back to the President. "Today's test is to disassemble and repair a short in the com unit under field conditions. We'll estimate seven minutes for the job. A panel of our own shop repairmen, operating with all their tools in their own workshops, averaged about five minutes, so if Commander Hartnett makes it in the optimal time that is pretty good evidence of close motor control."

"Yes, I see that," said the President. "What's he doing now?"

"Just waiting, sir. We're going to cycle him up to one hundred and fifty millibars so he can hear and talk a little more easily."

The President said acutely, "I thought you had equipment to talk to him in total vacuum."

"Well, ah, yes, sir, we do. We've had a little trouble with that. At present our basic communication facility at Mars-normal conditions is visual, but we expect to have the voice system functioning shortly."

"Yes, I hope so," said the President.

At the level of the tank, thirty meters into the ground under the room they were in, a graduate student functioning as a lab assistant responded to a cue and opened a valve—not to the external atmosphere, but to the tanks of Mars-normal gas that were mixed and ready in the pressure sink. Gradually the pressure built up to a thin, deepening whistle. The adding on of pressure to the 150-millibar level did not benefit Hartnett's functioning in any way. His redesigned body ignored most environmental factors. It could equally well tolerate Arctic winds, total vacuum or a muggy day at the Earth's equator, with the air at 1,080 millibars and soggy with damp. One was as comfortable to him as another. Or as uncomfortable, for Hartnett had reported that his new body ached, tweaked and chafed. They could just as easily have opened the valves and let the ambient air rush in, but then it would all have had to be pumped out again for the next test.

At last the whistle stopped and they heard the cyborg's voice. It was doll-shrill. "Thanksss. Hold eet dere, weel you?" The low pressure played tricks with his diction, especially as he no longer had a proper trachea and larynx to work with. After a month as a cyborg, speaking was becoming strange to him, for he was getting out of the habit of breathing anyway.

From behind Roger, the lab's expert in vision systems said glumly, "They know those eyes aren't made to stand sudden pressure changes. Serve them right if one of them cracks on them." Roger winced, with the fantasied pain of a faceted crystalline eyeball splintering in his socket. His wife laughed.

"Have a seat, Brad," she said, pulling away from Roger's arm. Absently Roger made room, staring up at the screen. The cadence-counting voice was saying, "On the tick. Five. Four. Three. Two. One. Start sequence."

The cyborg squatted clumsily over the entry plate of a black-finished metal canister. Without haste he slid a blade-thin screwdriver into a nearly invisible slot, made a precise quarter turn, repeated the movement again in another place and lifted off the plate. The thick fingers sorted carefully through the multicolored spaghetti of the internal wiring, found a charred red-and-white-candy-striped strand, detached it, shortened it to remove the burned insulation, stripped it down by simply pinching it through the nails, and held it to a terminal. The longest part of the operation was waiting for the fluxing iron to heat;

that took more than a minute. Then the new joint was brazed, the spaghetti stuffed back inside, the plate replaced, and the cyborg stood up.

"Six minutes, eleven and two-fifths seconds," reported the counting voice.

The project director led a round of applause. He then stood up and delivered a short address. He told the President that the purpose of the Man Plus project was to so modify a human body that it could survive on the surface of Mars as readily and safely as a normal man could walk across a Kansas wheat field. He reviewed the manned space program from suborbital flight through space station and deep probe. He listed some of the significant data about Mars: land area actually greater than Earth's, in spite of its smaller diameter, because there were no seas to waste surface. Temperature range, suitable for life—suitably modified, to be sure. Potential wealth, incalculable. The President listened attentively, although, to be sure, he knew every word.

Then he said, "Thanks, General Scanyon. Just let me say one thing."

He climbed nimbly up to the platform and smiled thoughtfully down at the scientists. "When I was a boy," he began, "the world was simpler. The big problem was how to help the emerging free nations of Earth enter the community of civilized countries. Those were the Iron Curtain days. It was them on their side, locked in, quarantined. And all the rest of us on ours.

"Well," he went on, "things have changed. The Free World has had bad times. Once you get off our own North American continent, what have you got? Collectivist dictatorships everywhere you look, bar one or two holdouts like Sweden and Israel. I'm not here to rake up ancient history. What's done is done, and there's no point blaming anybody. Everybody knows who lost China and gave Cuba to the other side. We know what administration let England and Pakistan fall. We don't have to talk about those things. We're just looking toward the future.

"And I tell you, ladies and gentlemen," he said earnestly, "the future of the free human race lies with you. Maybe we've had some setbacks here on our own planet. That's over and done with. We can look out into space. We look, and what do we see? We see another Earth. The planet Mars. As the distinguished director of your project, General Scanyon, just said, it's a bigger planet than the one we were born on, in the ways that are important. And it can be ours.

"That's where the future of freedom is, and it's up to you to give it to us. I know you will. I'm counting on every one of you."

He looked thoughtfully around the room, meeting every eye. The old Dash charisma was making itself felt all over the room.

Then he smiled suddenly, said "Thank you," and was gone in a wave of Secret Service men.

3

Man Becoming Martian

Time was when the planet Mars looked like another Earth. The astronomer Schiaparelli, peering through his Milanese telescope at the celebrated conjunction of 1877, saw what he thought were "channels," announced them as "canali" and had them understood as "canals" by half the literate population of Earth. Including nearly all the astronomers, who promptly turned their telescopes in the same direction and discovered more.

Canals? Then they must have been dug for a purpose. What purpose? To hold water—there was no other explanation that saved the facts.

The logic of the syllogism was compelling, and by the turn of the century there was hardly a doubter in the world. It was accepted as lore that Mars held an older, wiser culture than our own. If only we could somehow speak to them, what marvels we would learn! Percival Lowell mused over a sketching pad and came up with a first attempt. Draw great Euclidean shapes on the Sahara Desert, he said. Line them with brushwood, or dig them as trenches and fill them with oil. Then on some moonless night when Mars is high in the African heavens, set them afire. Those alien Martian eyes that he took to be fixed firmly to their alien Martian telescopes would see. They would recognize the squares and triangles. They would understand that communication was intended, and out of their older wisdom they would find a way to respond.

Not everybody believed quite as much quite so firmly as Lowell. Some said that Mars was too small and too cold ever to harbor a hugely intelligent race. Dig canals? Oh, yes, that was a simple enough peasant skill, and a race that was dying of thirst could well manage to scratch out ditches, even enormous ditches visible across interplanetary space, to keep itself alive. But beyond that, the environment was simply too harsh. A race living there would be like the Eskimos, forever trapped on the threshold of civilization because the world outside their ice huts was too hostile to grant them leisure to learn abstractions. No doubt when our telescopes were able to resolve the individual Martian face we would see only a brutish mask, stolid and stunned, brother to the ox; able to move soil and to plant crops, yes, but not to aspire to a life of the mind.

But, wise or brutal, Martians were there—or so thought the best opinion of the times.

Then better telescopes were built, and better ways were found to understand what they disclosed. To the lens and the mirror were added the spectroscope and the camera. In the eyes and understanding of astronomers Mars swam a little closer every day. At every step, as the image of the planet itself grew more sharp and clear, the vision of its putative inhabitants became more cloudy and less real. There was too little air. There was too little water. It was too cold. The canals broke up, under better resolution, into irregular blotches of surface markings. The cities that should have marked their junctions were not there.

By the time of the first Mariner fly-bys the Martian race, which had never lived except in the imagination of human beings, was irrevocably dead.

It still seemed that life of a sort could exist, perhaps lowly plants, even a rude sort of amphibian. But nothing like a man. On the surface of Mars an air-breathing, water-based creature like a human being could not survive for a quarter of an hour.

It would be the lack of air that would kill him most quickly. His death would not be from simple strangulation. He would not live long enough for that to happen. In the 10-millibar pressure of the surface of Mars his blood would boil away and he would die in agony of something like the bends. If he somehow survived that, then he would die of lack of air to breathe. If he survived both of those—given air in a backpack, and a face mask fed with a mixture of gases that did not contain nitrogen, at some intermediate pressure level between Earth- and Mars-normal—he would still die. He would die from exposure to unshielded solar radiation. He would die from the extremes of Martian temperature—at its best, a warmish spring day; at its coldest, worse than Antarctic polar night. He would die from thirst. And if he could somehow survive all of those, he would die more slowly, but surely, from hunger, since there was nowhere on the surface of Mars one morsel that a human being could eat.

But there is another kind of argument that contradicts the conclusions drawn from objective facts. Man is not bound by objective facts. If they inconvenience him, he changes them, or makes an end run around them.

Man cannot survive on Mars. However, man cannot survive in the Antarctic, either. But he does.

Man survives in places where he ought to die, by bringing a kinder environment with him. He carries what he needs. His first invention along those lines was clothing. His second, storable food, like dried meat and parched grain. His third, fire. His most recent, the whole series of devices and systems that gave him access to the sea bottoms and to space.

The first alien planet men walked on was the moon. It was even more hostile than Mars, in that the vital supplies of which Mars had very little—air, water and food—did not, on the moon, exist at all. Yet as early as the 1960s men visited the moon, carrying with them air and water and everything else they needed in life-support systems mounted on their spacesuits or built into their landing modules. From there it was no trick to build the systems bigger. It was not easy because of the magnitudes involved. But it was straightforward scaling up, to the point of semi-permanent and not far from self-sustaining closed-cycle colonies. The first problem of support was purely logistic. For each man you needed tons of supplies; for each pound of cargo blasted into space you spent a million dollars' worth of fuel and hardware. But it could be done.

Mars is orders of magnitude more remote. The moon circles the Earth only a quarter of a million miles out. At its very closest, a few times in a century, Mars is more than a hundred times as far.

Mars is not only distant from the Earth, it is farther than Earth from the sun. Whereas the moon receives as much energy per square inch as the Earth does, Mars, by the law of inverse squares, gets only half as much.

From some point on Earth, a rocket can be sent to the moon at any hour of any day. But Mars and Earth do not circle each other; both circle the sun, and as they do so at different speeds they are sometimes not very close and sometimes very far. It is only when they are at minimal travel distances that a rocket can efficiently be sent from one to another, and those times occur only once in every period of two years, for one month and some weeks.

Even the factors in Mars's makeup which make it more like the Earth work against maintaining a colony there. It is bigger than the moon, and thus its gravity is more like Earth's. But because it is bigger and pulls harder a rocket needs more fuel to land on it, and more fuel to take off again.

What it all comes down to is that colony on the moon can be supported from Earth. A colony on Mars cannot.

At least a colony of human beings cannot.

But what if one reshapes a human being?

Suppose one takes the standard human frame and alters some of the optional equipment. There's nothing to breathe on Mars. So take the lungs out of the human frame, replace them with micro-miniaturized oxygen regeneration cat-cracking systems. One needs power for that, but power flows down from the distant sun.

The blood in the standard human frame would boil; all right, eliminate the blood, at least from the extremities and the surface areas—build arms and legs that are served by motors instead of muscles—and reserve the blood supply only for the warm, protected brain. A normal human body needs food, but if the major musculature is replaced by machines, the food requirement drops. It is only the brain that must be fed every minute of every day, and fortunately, in terms of energy requirements the brain is the least demanding of human accessories. A slice of toast a day will keep it fed.

Water? It is no longer necessary, except for engineering losses—like adding hydraulic fluid to a car's braking system every few thousand miles. Once the body has become a closed system, no water needs to be flushed through it in the cycle of drink, circulate, excrete or perspire.

Radiation? A two-edged problem. At unpredictable times there are solar flares, and then even on Mars there is too much of it for health; the body must therefore be clothed with an artificial skin. The rest of the time there is only the normal visible and ultraviolet light from the sun. It is not enough to maintain heat, and not quite enough even for good vision; so more surface must be provided to gather energy—hence the great bat-eared receptors on the cyborg—and, to make vision as good as it can be made, the eyes are replaced with mechanical structures.

If one does all these things to a human being, what is left is no longer precisely a human being. It is a man plus large elements of hardware.

The man has become a cybernetic organism: a cyborg.

The first man to be made into a cyborg was probably Willy Hartnett. There was some doubt. There were persistent rumors of a Chicom experiment that had succeeded for a while and then failed. But it was pretty clear that Hartnett was at least the only one alive at this particular moment. He had been born in the regular human way and had worn the regular human shape for thirty-seven years. It was only in the last eighteen months that he had begun to change.

At first the changes were minor and temporary.

His heart was not removed. It was only bypassed now and then by a swift soft-plastic impeller that he wore for a week at a time strapped on a shoulder.

His eyes were not removed either . . . then. They were only sealed closed with a sort of gummy blindfold, while he practiced recognizing the perplexing shapes of the world as they were revealed to him through a shrilly buzzing electronic camera that was surgically linked to his optic nerve.

One by one the separate systems that would make him a Martian were tested. It was only when each component had been tested and adjusted and found satisfactory that the first permanent changes had been made.

They were not *really* permanent. That was a promise that Hartnett clung to. The surgeons had made it to Hartnett, and Hartnett had made it to his wife. All the changes could be reversed and would be. When the mission was over and he was safely back, they would remove the hardware and replace it with soft human tissue again, and he would be returned to purely human shape.

It would not, he understood, be exactly the shape he had started out with. They could not preserve his own organs and tissues. They could only replace them with equivalents. Organ transplants and plastic surgery would do all they could to make him look like himself again, but there was small chance he would ever again be able to travel on his old passport photo.

He did not greatly mind that. He had never considered himself a handsome man. He was content to know that he would have human eyes again—not his own, of course. But the doctors had promised they would be blue, and that lids and lashes would cover them again, and with any luck at all, they thought, the eyes could even weep. (With joy, he foresaw.) His heart would again be a lump of muscle the size of a fist. It would pump red human blood to all the ends of limb and body. His lung muscles would take air into his chest, and there natural human alveoli would absorb oxygen and release CO_2. The great photoreceptor bat-ears (that gave so much trouble, because their support strength was up to the demands of Martian gravitation but not terrestrial, so that they were constantly being detached and returned to the shop) would be dismantled and gone. The skin that had been so painfully constructed and fitted to him would be equally painfully flayed off again, and replaced with human skin that sweated and grew hair. (His own skin was still there under the skin-tight artificial covering, but he did not expect it would survive the experiment. It had had to be discouraged from carrying on its normal functions during the time it was buried under the artificial hide. Almost surely it would have lost the capacity for them and would have to be replaced.)

Hartnett's wife had exacted one promise from him. She had made him swear that as long as he wore the Halloween mask of the cyborg, he would keep out of the sight of his children. Fortunately the children were little enough to be biddable, and teachers, friends, neighbors, parents of schoolmates and all had been made cooperative by hints of stories of jungle rot and skin ailments. They had been curious, but the story had worked, and no one had urged Terry's father to come to a PTA meeting or Brenda's husband to join her at their backyard barbecue.

Brenda Hartnett herself had tried not to see her husband, but in the long run curiosity drove out fear. She had herself smuggled into the tank room one day while Willy was practicing a coordination test, riding a bicycle around the reddish sands with a basin of water balanced on the handlebars. Don Kayman had stayed with her, fully expecting her to faint or scream or perhaps be sick to her stomach. She did none of those things, surprising herself as much as the priest. The cyborg looked too much like a Japanese horror film to be taken seriously. It was only that night that she really related the bat-eared, crystal-eyed creature on the bike with the father of her children. The next day she went to the project's medical director and told him that Willy must be getting starved for screwing by then and she didn't see why she couldn't accommodate him. The doctor had to explain to her what Willy had not been able to bring himself to say, that in the present state of the art those functions had had to be regarded as superfluous and therefore had been temporarily, uh, disconnected.

Meanwhile the cyborg toiled away at his tests and awaited each next installment of pain.

His world was in three parts. The first part was a suite of rooms kept at a pressure equivalent to about 7,500 feet of altitude so that the project staff could go in and out with only mild inconvenience when they had to. This was where he slept, when he could, and ate what little he was given. He was always hungry, always. They'd tried, but they hadn't been able to disconnect the cravings of his senses. The second part was the Mars-normal tank in which he did his gymnastics and performed his tests so that the architects of his new body could observe their creation at work. And the third part was a low-pressure chamber on wheels that rolled him from his private suite to his public test arena, or wherever else he, rarely, had any occasion to go.

The Mars-normal tank was like a zoo cage in which he was always on display. The rolling tank offered him nothing but waiting to be moved into something else.

It was only the little two-room suite that was officially his home that gave him any comfort at all. There he had his TV set, his stereo, his telephone, his books. Sometimes one of the graduate students or a fellow astronaut would visit with him there, playing chess or trying to talk a conversation while their chests labored and lungs pumped fruitlessly at the 7,500-foot pressure. These visits he looked forward to and tried to prolong. When no one was with him he was on his own resources. Infrequently he read. Sometimes he sat before the TV, regardless of what was being shown on it. Most often he "rested." That was how he described it to his overseers, by which he meant sitting or lying with his vision system in stand-by. It was like having one's eyes closed but remaining awake. A bright enough light would register on his senses, as it will even through a sleeper's closed lids; a sound would penetrate at once. In those times his brain raced; conjuring up thoughts of sex, food, jealousy, sex, anger, children, nostalgia, love . . . until he pleaded for relief and was given a course in self-hypnosis which let him wash his mind empty. After that in "rest" mode he did almost nothing that was conscious, while his nervous system groomed and prepared itself for the next sensations of pain and his brain counted the seconds until his flight would be over and his normal human body given back to him.

There were a lot of those seconds. He had multiplied them out often enough. Seven months in orbit to Mars. Seven months coming back. A few weeks at both ends, getting ready for the launch and then debriefing before they would start the process of restoring him to his own body. A few months—no one would tell him exactly how many—while the surgery took place and the replaced parts healed.

The number of seconds, close as he could guess it, was some forty-five million. Give or take as much as ten million. He felt each one of them arrive and linger and reluctantly slip past.

The psychologists had tried to avoid all this by planning every moment for him. He refused the plans. They tried to understand him with devious tests and pattern-scanning. He let them pry, but inside himself he kept a citadel of privacy that he would not let them invade. Hartnett had never thought of himself as an introspective man; he knew that he was a mile wide and an inch deep, and that he led an unexamined life: He liked it that way.

But now that he had nothing left but the interior of his mind that was his own, he guarded that.

He wished sometimes that he did know how to examine his life. He wished he could understand his reasons for doing what he did.

Why had he volunteered for the mission? Sometimes he tried to remember, and then decided he had never known. Was it because the Free World needed Martian living space? Because he wanted the glamour of being the first Martian? For the money? For the scholarships and favors it would mean for the kids? To make Brenda love him?

It probably was in among those reasons somewhere, but he couldn't remember. If he had ever known.

In any case he was committed. The thing he *was* sure of was that he had no way to back out now.

He would let them do whatever savage, sadistic torturing they wanted of his body. He would board the spaceship that would take him to Mars. He would endure the seven endless months in orbit. He would go down to the surface, explore, stake claims, take samples, photograph, test. He would rise up again from the Martian surface and live somehow through the seven-month return, and he would give them all the information they wanted. He would accept the medals and the applause and the lecture tours and the television interviews and the contracts for books.

And then he would present himself to the surgeons to be put back the way he was supposed to be.

All of those things he had made his mind up to, and he was sure he would carry them out.

There was only one question in his mind to which he had not yet worked out an answer. It had to do with a contingency he was not prepared to meet. When he first volunteered for the program, they had told him very openly and honestly that the medical problems were complex and not fully understood. They would have to learn how to deal with some of them on him. It was possible that some of the answers would be hard to find or wrong. It was possible that returning him to his own shape would be, well, difficult. They told him that very clearly, at the very beginning, and then they never said it again.

But he remembered. The problem he had not resolved was what he would do if for any reason, when the whole mission was over, they could not put him back together right away. What he couldn't decide was whether he would then simply kill himself or at the same time kill as many as possible of his friends, superiors and colleagues as well.

4

Group of Probable Pallbearers

Roger Torraway, Col. (Ret.) USAF, B.A., M.A., D.Sc. (Hon.). At the time he woke up in the morning, the night shift finished bench-running the cyborg's photoreceptors. There had been an unidentified voltage drop caught on the monitors when they were last in use on the cyborg, but nothing showed in the bench test, and nothing had been visible when they were stripped. They were certified serviceable.

Roger had slept badly. It was a terrible responsibility, being custodian of mankind's last forlorn hope for freedom and decency. When he woke up it was with that thought in mind; there was a part of Roger Torraway—it showed itself most commonly in dreams—that was about nine years old. It took all the things the President said at face value, although Roger himself, doubling as diplomat and mission head, world traveler, familiar of a dozen capitals, really did not think in his conscious mind that the "Free World" existed.

He dressed, his mind in the familiar occupation of resolving a dichotomy. Let's assume Dash is on the level, and occupying Mars means salvation for humanity, he thought. Can we cut it?

He thought of Willy Hartnett—good-looking (or he had been, till the prosthesiologists got at him). Amiable. Good with his hands. But also a little bit of a lightweight, when you came to look at him honestly. Likely to take a drink too many at the club on a Saturday night. Not to be trusted in the kitchen with another man's wife at a party.

He was not a hero, by any measure Roger could find. But who was? He cast his mind down the list of back-ups to the cyborg. Number One, Vic Freibart, currently off on a ceremonial tour with the Vice President and temporarily removed from the order of succession. Number Two, Carl Mazzini, on sick leave while the leg he had broken at Mount Snow healed up. Number Three: Him.

There was no Valley Forge quality in any of them.

He made his breakfast without waking Dorrie, got the car out and left it puffing on its skirts while he picked up the morning paper, threw it into the garage and closed the door. His next-door neighbor, walking toward his car pool, hailed him. "See the news this morning? I see Dash was in town last night. Some high-level conference."

Roger said automatically, "No, I haven't put on the TV this morning." But I did see Dash, he thought, and I could take the wind out of *your* sails. It annoyed him not to be able to say it. Security was a confounded nuisance. Half of his recent trouble with Dorrie, he was sure, came from the fact that in the neighborhood wives' morning block conference and coffee binge she was allowed to mention her husband only as a formerly active astronaut, now in administrative work. Even his trips abroad had to be played down—"out of town," "business trip," anything but "Well, *my* husband is meeting with the Chiefs of Staff of the Basutoland Air Force this week." She had resisted. She still resisted, or at least complained to Roger about it often enough.

But as far as he knew, she had not broken security. Since at least three of the wives were known to report to the Lab intelligence officer, he undoubtedly would have known.

As Roger got into the car he remembered that he had not kissed Dorrie goodbye.

He told himself that it did not matter. She would not wake up and therefore would not know; if by any chance she did wake up, she would complain at being wakened. But he did not like to give up a ritual. While he thought about it, however, he was automatically putting the car into Drive and keying his code number for the Lab; the car began to move. He sighed, snapped on the TV and watched the *Today Show* all the way to work.

Fr. Donnelly S. Kayman, A.B., M.A., Ph.D., S.J. As he began celebrating the Mass in the Lady Chapel of St. Jude's, three miles away, on the other side of Tonka, the cyborg was greedily swallowing the one meal he would get that day. Chewing was difficult because lack of practice had made his gums sore, and the saliva didn't seem to flow as freely as it should any more. But the cyborg ate with enthusiasm, not even thinking about the test program for the day, and when he had finished he gazed sadly at the empty plate.

Don Kayman was thirty-one years old and the world's most authoritative areologist (which is to say, specialist in the planet Mars)—at least in the Free World. (Kayman would have admitted that old Parnov at the Shklovskii Institute in Novosibirsk also knew a thing or two.) He was also a Jesuit priest. He did not think of himself as being one thing first and the other with what part of him was left over; his work was areology, his person was the priesthood. Meticulously and with joy he elevated the Host, drank the wine, said the final *redempit,* glanced at his watch and whistled. He was running late. He shed his robes in record time. He aimed a slap at the Chicano altar boy, who grinned and opened the door for him. They liked each other; Kayman even thought that the boy might himself become both priest and scientist one day.

Now in sports shirt and slacks, Kayman jumped into his convertible. It was a classic, wheels instead of hoverskirts; it could even be driven off the guided highways. But where was there to go off the highways? He dialed the laboratories, switched on the main batteries and opened his newspaper. Without attention the little car nosed into the freeway, found a gap in the traffic, leaped to fill it and bore him at eighty miles an hour to his job.

The news in the newspaper was, as usual, mostly bad.

In Paris the MFP had issued another blast at the Chandrigar peace talks. Israel had refused to vacate Cairo and Damascus. New York City's martial law, now in its fifteenth month, had failed to prevent the ambush of a Tenth Mountain Division convoy trying to sneak across the Bronx-Whitestone Bridge to the relief of the garrison in Shea Stadium; fifteen soldiers were dead, and the convoy had returned to the Bronx.

Kayman dropped the paper sadly. He tilted the rearview mirror back, raised the side windows to deflect some of the wind and began to brush his shoulder-length hair. Twenty-five strokes on each side—it was almost as much a ritual with him as the Mass. He would brush it again that day, because he had a lunch date with Sister Clotilda. She was already half convinced that she wanted to apply for relief from certain of her vows, and Kayman wanted to resume the discussion with her as soon, and as often and as long, as suitable.

Because he had less distance to travel, Kayman arrived at the laboratories just behind Roger Torraway. They got out together, turned their cars over to the parking system and went up to the briefing room in the same elevator.

Deputy Director T. Gamble de Bell. As he prepared to juice up key personnel at the morning briefing, the cyborg was thirty meters away, spread-eagled face down and nude. On Mars he would eat only low-residue food and not much of that. On Earth it was thought necessary to keep his eliminatory system at least minimally functional, in spite of the difficulties the changes in skin and metabolism produced. Hartnett was glad for the food, but hated the enemas.

The project director was a general. The science chief was a distinguished biophysicist who had worked with Wilkins and Pauling; twenty years back he had stopped doing science and started doing figureheading, because that was where the rewards were. Neither had much to do with the work of the labs themselves, only with liaison between the operating people and those shadowy outside figures who worked the money switch.

For the nitty-gritty of daily routine, it was the deputy director who did the work. This early in the morning, he already had a sheaf of notes and reports, and he had read them.

"Scramble the picture," he ordered from the lectern, not looking up. On the monitor above him Willy Hartnett's grotesque profile broke up into a jackstraw bundle of lines, then turned into snow, then rebuilt itself into its proper features. (Only the head showed. The people in the briefing room could not see what indignity Willy was suffering, though most of them knew well enough. It was on the daily sked sheet.) The picture was no longer in color. The scan was coarser now, and the image less steady. But it was now security-safe (on the chance that some spy had tapped the closed circuit), and in portraying Hartnett the quality of the picture made, after all, very little difference.

"All right," said the deputy director harshly, "you heard Dash last night. He didn't come here to get your votes, he wants action. So do I. I don't want any more screw-ups like the photoreceptor crap."

He turned a page. "Morning progress report," he read. "Commander Hartnett is functioning well in all systems, with three exceptions. First, the artificial heart does not respond well to prolonged exercise at low temperatures. Second, the CAV system receives poorly in frequencies higher than medium blue— I'm disappointed in that one, Brad," he interpolated, looking up at Alexander Bradley, the expert in the perceptual systems of the eye. "You know we're locked into UV capability on that. Third, communications links. We had to admit to that one in front of the President last night. He didn't like it, and *I* didn't like it. That throat mike doesn't work. Effectively we don't have voice link at Mars-normal pressure, and if we don't come up with a solve we'll have to go back to plain visual systems. Eighteen months down the drain."

He glanced around the room and settled on the heart man. "All right. What about the circulation?"

"It's the heat build-up," Fineman said defensively. "The heart is functioning perfectly. You want me to design it for ridiculous conditions? I could, but it would be eight feet high. Fix up the thermal balance. The skin closes up at low temperatures and won't transmit. Naturally the oxygen level in the blood drops, and naturally the heart speeds up. That's what it's supposed to do. What do you want? Otherwise he'll go into syncope, maybe short-change the brain on O_2. Then what've you got?"

From high on the wall of the room the cyborg's face looked on impassively. He had changed position (the enema was over, the bedpan had been removed, he was now sitting). Roger Torraway, not very interested in a discussion that did not in any way involve his specialty, was gazing at the cyborg thoughtfully. He wondered what old Willy thought, hearing himself talked about that way. Roger had gone to the trouble of requisitioning the private psychological studies on Hartnett because of curiosity on that point, but they hadn't been very informative. Roger was pretty sure he knew why. All of them had been so tested and retested that they had acquired considerable skill in answering test questions the way the examiners wanted them answered. By now nearly everyone in the labs must have come to do that, either by design or simply as a trained-in reflex. They would make marvelous poker players, he thought; smiling, he remembered poker games with Willy. Covertly he winked at the cyborg and gave him a thumbs-up. Hartnett did not respond. It was impossible to tell, from those faceted ruby eyes, what he saw.

"—we can't change the skin again," the integuments man was arguing. "There's already a weight penalty. If we put in any more sensor-actors he'll feel like he's wearing a wet-suit all the time."

Surprisingly, a rumble from the monitor. The cyborg spoke: "What theee hell do you think it feeeelsss layk now?"

A beat of silence, as everyone in the room remembered it was a living person they were talking about. Then the skin man insisted: "All the more reason. We'd like to fine it down, simplify it, get some of the weight off. Not complicate it."

The deputy director raised his hand. "You two get together," he ordered the opponents. "Don't tell me what you can't do— I'm telling you what we have to do. Now you, Brad. What about that vision cutoff?"

Alex Bradley said cheerily, "Under control. I can fix. But listen, Will, I'm sorry, but it means another implant. I see what's wrong. It's in the retinal mediation system; it's filtering the extra frequencies. The system's all right, but—"

"Then make it work," said the deputy director, glancing at the clock. "How about the communications foul-up?"

"Talk to respiration," said the hardware man. "If they give us a little more retained air, Hartnett can get some voice. The electronics systems are fine, there's just nothing for them to carry."

"Impossible!" shouted the lung man. "You've only left us five hundred ec's of space now! He uses that in ten minutes. I've gone over the drill with him a hundred times to practice conserving it—"

"Can't he just whisper?" asked the deputy director. Then, as the communications man began hauling out frequency-response curves, he added, "Work it out, will you? All the rest of you, looks good. But don't let up." He closed the notes into their plastic folder and handed it to his assistant. "That's that," he said. "Now let me get to the important part."

He waited for them to settle down. "The reason the President was here last night is that a launch target has been approved. Friends, we are now on real time."

"When?" cried a voice.

The deputy went on: "A.S.A.P. We've got to complete this job—and by that, friends, I mean complete it: get Hartnett up to optimum performance so that he can actually live on Mars—no back to the workshops if something goes wrong—in time for the launch window next month. Launch time is set for oh eight hundred hours on twelve November. That gives us forty-three days, twenty-two hours and some odd minutes. No more."

There was a second's pause, then a rush of voices. Even the cyborg's expression visibly changed, though no one could have said in what direction.

The deputy director continued: "That's only part of it. The date is fixed, it can't be changed, we have to meet it; now I want to tell you why. Lights, please."

The chamber lights dimmed down, and the deputy's deputy, without waiting for a signal, projected a slide on the end wall of the room where all could see it, even the cyborg in his distant cell. It displayed a crosshatched chart, with a broad black line growing diagonally upward toward a red bar. In bright orange letters at the top it was marked MOST SECRET, EYES ONLY.

"Let me explain what you're looking at," said the deputy director. "The black diagonal is a composite of twenty-two trends and indices, ranging from the international credit balance to the incidence of harassment of American tourists by government officials abroad. The measure is of probability of war. The red bar at the top is marked 'O.H.,' which I can tell you stands for 'Outbreak of Hostilities.' It is not certainty. But the statistics people tell us that when the upper limit is reached there is a point-nine probability of war within six hours, and as you can see, we are moving toward it."

The noise had stopped. The room was crypt-still. Finally one voice inquired, "What's the time scale?"

"The back data covers thirty-five years," said the deputy director. There was some easing—at least the white space at the top would have to be some months, not minutes.

Then Kathleen Doughty asked, "Does it say anywhere in there who it is we're going to be at war with?"

The deputy director hesitated, then said carefully, "No, that is not included in the chart, but I think we can all form our own guesses. I don't mind giving you mine. If you've been reading the papers you know that the Chicoms have been talking about the wonders of increased food production they could bring the world by applying Sinkiang Province farming techniques to the Australian outback. Well, no matter what that quisling bunch in Canberra are willing to agree to, I feel pretty sure that this administration is not going to let the Chinks move in. Not if they want to keep my vote, anyway." After a moment, he added, "That's just personal opinion, off the record; do not include it in the minutes of this meeting. I don't know any official answer, and I wouldn't tell you if I did. All I know is what you know now. The trendline forecasts look pretty sour. Now they show nuclear escalation probabilities peaking pretty fast. We've got a date for it. The curve continued shows the point-nine probability in less than seven years.

"Which means," he added, "that if we don't have a viable Mars colony by then, we may not live to have it ever."

Alexander Bradley, B.Sc., E.E., M.D., D.Sc., Lt. Col. USMCR (Ret.). While Bradley was leaving the conference and changing from the expression of concern he had worn for the briefing to the more natural open-faced jollity he showed the world, the cyborg was down-pressuring for the Mars-normal tank. His monitors were somewhat concerned. Although they could not read emotion from his face, they could from his heart, breath and vital signs, as telemetered constantly to them, and it appeared to them that he was in some sort of up-tight state. They proposed delaying the test, but he refused angrily. "Don't you know there'sss a war on, almosssst?" he demanded in shrill tones, and would not answer when they spoke to him again. They decided to continue with the tests, but to recheck his psych profile as soon as they were completed.

When Alexander Bradley was ten years old he lost his father and his left eye. The Sunday after Thanksgiving, the family was driving back from church. It had turned cold. The morning dew had frozen, impalpably thin and slick, in a film on the road. Brad's father was driving with great care, but there were cars in front of him, cars behind him, cars in the other half of the two-lane road going in the other direction; he was constrained to keep to a certain speed, and he was short in his answers when the rest of the family said anything to him. He was concerned, but he was not concerned enough. When the disaster came he could do nothing to avert it. To Brad, sitting beside his father in the front seat, it looked as though a station wagon coming toward them a hundred yards away turned out, slowly and calmly, as though it were making a left turn. But there was no road there for it to turn into. Brad's father stepped on the brake and held it. Their car slowed and slid. And for some seconds the boy sat watching the other car sliding sidewise toward them, themselves skidding gently and inevitably toward it. It was stately and deliberate, and inevitable. No one said anything, not Brad, not his father, not Brad's mother in the back seat. No one did anything, except to hold their rigid poses as though they were actors in a National Traffic Council tableau. The father sat silent and erect at the wheel, staring concentratedly at the other car. The driver of the other vehicle looked wide-eyed and inquiringly toward them over his shoulder. Neither moved until they hit. Even on the ice the friction was slowing them, and they could not have been moving at a combined velocity of much more than twenty-five miles an hour. It was enough. Both drivers were killed—Brad's father impaled, the other man decapitated. Brad and his mother, though they were wearing their safety belts, suffered fractures, cuts and bruises as well as internal injuries; and she lost the flexure of her left wrist forever, while her son lost his eye.

Twenty-three years later Brad still dreamed about it as though it had just happened. In his sleep it scared him witless, and he awakened sweaty and crying and gasping for breath.

It was not all loss. He had discovered that considerable advantages had been bought at the cost of an eye. Item, there was the

insurance, on the life of his father and on the maiming of everyone concerned. Item, the injury had kept him out of the Army,
and had permitted him to join the Marine Corps in an essentially
civilian capacity when he wanted field experience in his specialty. Item, it had given him an acceptable excuse for avoiding
the stupider risks and more tiresome obligations of adolescence.
He never had to prove his courage in violent sports and always
was excused from whatever parts of gym he most detested.

Biggest item of all, it gave him an education. Under the Aid
to Handicapped Children provisions of his state's welfare system, it had paid his way through school, college and graduate
school. It had given him four degrees and turned him into one
of the world's greatest experts on the perceptual systems of the
eye. On balance, it was a favorable transaction. Even adding
in the negative factor of a mother who had spent the remaining
ten years of her life in some pain and a good deal of shortness of
temper, it was worthwhile.

Brad had wound up on the Man Plus project because he was
the best they could get. He had chosen to work for the Marine
Corps, because nowhere better could one find experimental
subjects prepared by shell, claymore and bolo than in the field
hospitals of Tanzania, Borneo and Ceylon. That work had been
noted in high echelons of the military. They had not accepted
Brad, they had drafted him.

What he was not sure of was that Man Plus was the best *he*
could get. Other recruits had been dragged into the space program by glamour or appeals to duty. It wasn't at all like that
with Bradley. As soon as he had grasped what the man from
Washington was driving at, the implications and opportunities
spread out before him. It was a new track. It meant abandoning
some plans, deferring others. But he could see where it would
lead: say, three years helping to develop the optic systems of the

cyborg. A world reputation coming out of it. Then he could quit the program and enter the limitless lush pastures of private practice. One hundred and eight Americans per hundred thousand had essentially total loss of function in one or both eyes. It added up to better than three hundred thousand prospective patients, every one of whom would want the best man in the field to treat him.

Working on the Man Plus program would stamp him the best man in his field at once. He could have a clinic of his own before he was forty. Not big. Just big enough to be supervised personally in every detail by him, and run by a staff of juniors trained by him and working under his direction. It would run to, oh, maybe five or six hundred patients a year—a fraction of 1 percent of the prospects. Which fraction of 1 percent would he accept? At least half of them would come from those most solvent and most willing to pay. Also, of course, charity cases. At least a hundred of them a year, everything free, even their bedside phones. While the several hundred who could pay would pay a lot. The Bradley Clinic (already it sounded as time-honored and proper as "Menninger" in his ears) would be a model for medical services all over the world, and it would make him one hell of a lot of money.

It was not Bradley's fault that the three years had extended themselves past five. It wasn't even his part of the program that caused the delays. Or not most of them, anyway. In any event, he was still young. He would leave the program with thirty good working years ahead of him—unless he chose to retire earlier, perhaps keeping a consultancy and a stock arrangement at the Bradley Clinic. And there were other advantages to working in the space program, in that so many of his associates had married such attractive women. Bradley had no interest in getting married, but he very much liked having wives.

Back in the seven-room laboratory suite where he ruled, Brad kicked ass on enough of his subordinates to insure that the new retinal mediation link would be ready for transplant within the week, and glanced at his watch. It was not yet eleven. He dialed Roger Torraway on the intercom and got him after a delay. "How about lunch, Rog? I want to go over this new implant with you."

"Oh, too bad, Brad. I wish I could. But I'm going to be in the tank with Will Hartnett for at least the next three hours. Maybe tomorrow."

"Talk to you then," said Brad cheerfully, and hung up. He was not surprised; he had already checked Torraway's schedule. But he was pleased. He told his secretary that he would be leaving for an outside conference and then lunch, and would be back after two, then ordered his car. He fed it the coordinates for the corner of the block where Roger Torraway lived. Where Dorrie Torraway lived.

5

Monster Becoming Mortal Again

As Brad left, whistling, his car radio was full of news of the world. The Tenth Mountain Division had recoiled back to a fortified area in Riverdale. A typhoon had wrecked the rice crop in Southeast Asia. President Deshatine had ordered the U.S. delegation to walk out of the United Nations debate on sharing scarce resources.

There was much news that was not on the sound-only radio, because the newscasters either didn't know about it or didn't think it was important. For example, not one word was said about two Chinese gentlemen on a mission in Australia, or about the results of certain secret popularity polls the President kept locked in his safe, or about the tests being run on Willy Hartnett. So Brad didn't hear about any of these things. If he had, and had understood their importance, he would have cared. He was not an uncaring man. He was not an evil one, either. He was just not a particularly good one.

Sometimes that question came up—for instance when it was time to get rid of a girl or drop a friend who had been helpful on the way up. Sometimes there were recriminations. Then Brad would smile and shrug and point out that it wasn't a fair world. Lancelot didn't win all the tournaments. Sometimes the evil black knight dumped him on the ground. Bobby Fischer wasn't the most lovable chess player in the world, merely the best. And so on.

And so Brad would confess that he was not a model man by social standards. Indeed he wasn't. Something had gone wrong in his childhood. The bump of ego on his skull had swollen large, so he saw the whole world in terms of what it could give him. War with China? Well, let's see, calculated Brad, there's sure to be a lot of surgery; perhaps I'll get to head my own hospital. A world depression? His money was in farmland; people would always eat.

He was not admirable. All the same, he was the best person alive to do what the cyborg needed—namely, to provide Willy Hartnett with mediation between stimulus and interpretation. Which is a way of saying that somewhere between the external object the cyborg saw and the conclusions the cyborg's brain drew from it, there had to be a stage where unnecessary information was filtered out. Otherwise the cyborg would simply go mad.

To understand why this is so, consider the frog.

Think of a frog as a functional machine designed to produce baby frogs. This is the Darwinian view, and is really what evolution is all about. In order to succeed, the frog has to stay alive long enough to grow up and get pregnant or get some female frog pregnant. That means it has to do two things. It has to eat. And it has to avoid being eaten.

As vertebrates go, the frog is a dull and simple kind of creature. It has a brain, but not a big one or a very sophisticated one. There's not much excess capacity in the frog brain to play around with, so that one doesn't want to waste any of it on non-essentials. Evolution is always economical. Male frogs do not write poems or torture themselves with fears that their female frogs may be unfaithful. Nor do they want to think about things which do not directly concern staying alive.

The frog's eye is simple, too. In human eyes there are complexities frogs know not. Suppose a human comes into a room containing a table which bears an order of steak and French fries; even if he cannot hear, cannot taste and has lost the power of smell, he is drawn to the food. His eye turns to the steak. There is a spot on the eye called the "fovea," the part of the eye with which a person sees best, and it is that spot that directs itself toward the target. The frog doesn't do that; one part of its eye is as good as another. Or as bad. Because the interesting thing about a frog's-eye view of what for a frog is the equivalent of a steak—namely, a bug big enough to be worth swallowing but small enough not to try to swallow back—is that the frog is blind to food unless the food *behaves* like food. Surround the frog with the most nutritious chopped insect paté you can devise. It will starve to death—unless a ladybug wanders by.

If one thinks about how a frog eats, this strange behavior begins to make sense. The frog fits a very neat ecological niche. In a state of nature, no one fills that niche with minced food. The frog eats insects, so insects are what he sees. If something passes through his field of vision which is the right size for an insect, and moves at the proper speed for an insect, the frog does not debate whether he is hungry or not or which insects taste best. He eats it. Then he goes back to waiting for the next one.

In the laboratory this is an antisurvival trait. You can trick a frog with a piece of cloth, a bit of wood on a string, anything that moves properly and is the right size. He will eat them and starve. But in nature there are no such tricks. In nature only bugs move like bugs, and every bug is frog dinner.

This principle is not difficult to understand. Say this to a naïve friend and he will say, "Oh, yes, I see. The frog just ignores anything that doesn't look like a bug." Wrong! The frog doesn't do anything of the kind. He does not ignore non-bug objects. He simply never sees them in the first place. Tap a frog's optic nerve and drag a marble slowly past—too big, too slow—and no instrument can pick up a nerve impulse. There is none. The eye does not bother to "see" what the frog does not want to know about. But swing a dead fly past, and your meter dials flick over, the nerve transmits a message, the frog's tongue licks out and grabs.

And so we come to the cyborg. What Bradley had done was to provide a mediation stage between the ruby complex eyes and the aching human brain of Willy Hartnett which filtered, interpreted and generally prepackaged all of the cyborg's visual inputs. The "eye" saw everything, even in the UV part of the spectrum, even in the infrared. The brain could not deal with so vast a flow of inputs. Bradley's mediation stage edited out the unimportant bits.

The stage was a triumph of design, because Bradley was indeed extremely good at the one thing he was good at. But he was not there to install it. And so because Brad had a date, and also because the President of the United States had to go to the bathroom and two Chinese named Sing and Sun wanted to try a pizza, the history of the world changed.

Jerry Weidner, who was Brad's principal assistant, supervised the slow laborious process of resetting the cyborg's vision systems. It was a fussy, niggling sort of job. Like nearly all of the things that had to be done to Willy Hartnett, it was attended with maximum discomfort for him. The sensitive nerves of the eyelid had long since been dissected out; otherwise they would have been shrieking pain at him day and night. But he could feel what was happening—if not as pain, then as a psychically disturbing knowledge that somebody was sliding edged instruments around in a very touchy part of his anatomy. His actual vision was kept on stand-by mode, so he "saw" only dim moving shadows. It was enough. He hated it.

He lay there for an hour or more while Weidner and the others tinkered with changes in potentials, noted readings, talked to each other in the numbers that are the language of technologists. When they were finally satisfied with the field strength of his perceptual system and allowed him to stand, without warning he almost toppled. "Sheesssst," he snarled. "Dizzzzy again."

Worried and resigned, Weidner said, "All right, we better ask for vertigo checks." So there was another thirty-minute delay while the balance teams checked his reflexes until he burst out, "Chrisst, cut it out. I can ssstand on one foot for the nexssst twenty hours, ssso what doesss it prove?" But they kept him on one foot anyhow, measuring how close he could get his fingertips to touching with his vision in stand-by mode.

The balance teams then declared themselves satisfied, but Jerry Weidner was not. The dizziness had happened before, and it had never been satisfactorily tracked down, either to the built-in mechanical horizon or to the crude natural stirrup-and-anvil bones in his ear. Weidner did not know that it stemmed from the mediation system that was his own special responsibility, but he didn't know that it did not, either. He wished Brad would get the hell back from his long lunch.

At that time, halfway around the world, there were these two

Chinese named Sing and Sun. They were not characters in a dirty joke. Those were their names. Sing's great-grandfather had died at the mouth of a Russian cannon after the failure of the Righteous Harmony Fists to expel the white devils from China. His father had conceived him on the Long March, and died before he was born, in combat against the soldiers of a war lord allied to Chiang Kai-shek. Sing himself was nearly ninety years old. He had shaken the hand of Comrade Mao, and diverted the Yellow River for Mao's successors and was now supervising the greatest hydraulic engineering project of his career in an Australian town called Fitzroy Crossing. It was his first pro-longed trip outside the territory of New People's Asia. He had three ambitions for it: to see an uncensored pornographic film, to drink a bottle of Scotch that came from Scotland rather than the People's Province of Honshu, and to taste a pizza. With his colleague Sun he had made a good start on the Scotch, had found out where to accomplish the viewing of the film and was now desirous of tasting the pizza.

Sun was much younger—not yet forty—and in spite of every-thing, suffering from respect for his associate's age. There was also the fact that Sun was several echelons lower in social status than the older man, although he was obviously a coming man in the techo-industrial wing of the Party. Sun had just returned from a year of leading a mapping team through all of the Great Sandy Desert. It was not only sand. It was soil—good, arable, productive soil—lacking only a few trace elements and water. What Sun had mapped had been the soil chemistry of a mil-lion square miles. When Sun's soil map and Sing's great uphill aqueduct, with its fourteen great batteries of nuclear-driven pumps, came together, they would equal a new kind of life for those million miles of desert. Chemical supplements + sun-distilled water from the distant seacoast = ten crops a year with which to feed a hundred million ethnically Chinese New Australians.

The project had been carefully studied and contained only one flaw. The Old New Australians, descendants of the populating drives of the post–World War II period, did not want New New Australians coming in to farm that land. They wanted it for themselves. As Sun and Sing entered Danny's Pizza Hut on Fitzroy Crossing's main street, two Old New Australians, one named Koschanko and one named Gradechek, were just leaving the bar, and unfortunately recognized Sing from his newspaper pictures. Words passed. The Chinese recognized the smell of stale beer and took the truculence to be only drink; they tried to pass, and Koschanko and Gradechek pushed them out of the street door. Bellicosity began swinging, and the ninety-year-old skull of Sing Hsi-chin split itself open against a curbstone.

At this point Sun drew a pistol he was not authorized to be carrying, and shot the two assailants dead.

It was only a drunken brawl. The police of Fitzroy Crossing had handled thousands of more dramatic crimes, and could have handled this one if they had been allowed to. But it did not stop there, because one of the barmaids was herself a New New Australian of Honanese extraction, recognized Sun, discovered who Sing was, picked up the phone and called the New China News Agency bureau in Lagrange Mission, down on the coast, to say that one of China's most famous scientists had been brutally murdered.

Within ten minutes the satellite network had carried a factually shaky but very colorful version of the story all over the world.

Before an hour was out, the New People's Asian mission to Canberra had requested an appointment with the Foreign Minister to deliver its protest, spontaneous demonstrations were in full blast in Shanghai, Saigon, Hiroshima and a dozen other NPA cities, and half a dozen observation satellites were being nudged out of their orbits to pass over Northwest Australia and the Sunda Islands seas. Two miles outside the harbor of Melbourne a great gray shape swam to the surface of the sea and floated there, offering no signals and responding to none for more than twenty minutes. Then it declared itself the NPA nuclear submarine *The East Is Red* on a routine diplomatic visit to a friendly port. The news was received in time to cancel the RAAF air strike that had been ordered against the unknown intruder, but only just.

Under Pueblo, Colorado, the President of the United States was interrupted in his after-lunch nap. He was sitting on the edge of his bed, distastefully sipping a cup of black coffee, when the DOD liaison aide came in with a sitrep and the news that a condition red alert had been declared, in accordance with the prepared responses long since programmed into the North American Defense Command Net. He already had the satellite reports and an on-the-scene account from a military mission to Fitzroy Crossing; he knew about the appearance of the submarine *The East Is Red*, but did not yet know that the air strike had been called off. Summarizing the information, he said to the President, "So it's go or no-go, sir. NADCOM recommends a launch with abort options in fifty minutes."

The President snarled, "I don't feel good. What the hell did they put in that soup?" Dash was not in a mood to think about China just at that moment; he had been dreaming about a private poll which showed his popularity down to 17 percent, including both the "excellent" and "satisfactory" ratings, with 61 percent calling his administration "poor" or "very unsatisfactory." It had not been a dream. That was what the morning's political briefing had shown him.

He pushed the coffee cup away and glumly contemplated the decision he, alone in all the world, was now required to make. To launch missiles against the major cities of New People's Asia was in theory a reversible choice: they could be aborted at any time before reentry, defused, falling harmlessly into the sea. But in practice the NPA posts would detect the launch, and who knew what those crazy Chinese bastards would do? His belly felt as though he were in the last minutes of pregnancy, and there seemed to be a good chance that he would throw up. His number one secretary said chidingly, "Dr. Stassen did advise you not to eat any more cabbage, sir. Perhaps we should instruct the chef not to make that soup any more."

The President said, "I don't want lectures right now. All right, look. We'll hold at the present state of readiness until further orders from me. No launch. No retaliation. Understood?"

"Yes, sir," said the DOD man regretfully. "Sir? I have several specific queries, from NADCOM, from the Man Plus project, from the admiral commanding SWEPAC—"

"You heard me! No retaliation. Everything else, keep going."

His number one secretary clarified the point for him. "Our official position," he said, "is this affair in Australia is a domestic matter and not a national concern for the United States. Our action stance does not change. We keep all systems go, but take no action. Is that right, Mr. President?"

"Right," said Dash thickly. "Now you can get along without me for ten minutes. I got to go to the john."

Brad did think of phoning in to see how the recalibration was going, but he really liked showering with a girl, with all the fun involved in soaping each other, and the Chero-Strip bathroom armorarium included bath oil beads, bubbles and marvelous thick towels. It was three o'clock before he decided to think about going back to work.

By that time it was pretty much too late. Weidner had tried to get permission to postpone testing from the deputy director, who wouldn't do it on his own authority but bucked it to Washington, who queried the President's office and received the reply: "No, you cannot, positively cannot, repeat not, postpone this or any other test." The man giving the reply was the President's number one secretary, who was looking at the "risk of war" projection on the wall of the President's most private study while he spoke. Even as he was talking the broad black bar was bending itself still more steeply up toward the red line.

So they went ahead with the test, Weidner tight-lipped and frowning. It went well enough until it began to go very badly indeed. Roger Torraway's mind was far away until he heard the cyborg call him. He locked in and stood, in skin suit and breathing mask, on the ruddy sands. "What's the matter, Willy?" he demanded.

The great ruby eyes turned toward him. "I—I can't ssssee you, Roger!" the cyborg shrilled. "I—I—"

And he toppled and fell. It was as quick as that. Roger did not even move toward him until he felt a great thundering hammer of air beat in on him, sending him stumbling toward the recumbent monster form.

From the 7,500-foot equivalent outside the Mars-normal chamber Don Kayman came desperately running in. He had not waited to lock. He had thrown both doors open. He was no longer a scientist. He was a priest; he dropped to his knees beside the contorted form of what had been Willy Hartnett.

Roger stared while Don Kayman touched the ruby eyes, traced a cross on the synthetic flesh, whispering what Roger could not hear. He did not want to hear. He knew what was happening.

The first candidate for cyborg was now receiving Extreme Unction in front of his eyes.

The lead backup was Vic Freibart, taken off the list by presidential order.

The number two alternate was Carl Mazzini, ruled out because of his broken leg.

The third alternate, and the new champion, was him.

6

Mortal in Mortal Fear

It is not an easy thing for a flesh-and-blood human being to come to terms with the knowledge that some of his flesh is going to be ripped from him and replaced with steel, copper, silver, plastic, aluminum and glass. We could see that Torraway was not behaving very rationally. He went blundering down the hall away from the Mars-normal tank in great urgency, as though he had a most pressing errand. He had no errand except to get away. The hall seemed like a trap to him. He felt he could not stand to have one person come up to him and say he was sorry about Willy Hartnett, or acknowledge Torraway's own new status. He passed a men's room, stopped, looked around—no one was watching him—and entered to stand at the urinal, eyes glazed, fixed to the shiny chrome. When the door pushed open, Torraway made a great show of zipping and flushing, but it was only a boy from the typing pool who looked at him incuriously and headed for a booth.

Outside the men's room the deputy director caught him. "Goddamn lousy thing," he said. "I guess you know you're—"

"I know," said Torraway, pleased that his voice was so calm.

"We're going to have to find out what happened *fast*. I'm having a meeting in my office in ninety minutes. We'll have the first autopsy reports. I want you there."

Roger nodded, glanced at his wrist watch and turned smartly away. The important thing, he thought, was to keep moving as though he were too busy to interrupt. Unfortunately he couldn't think of a single thing he had to do, or even that he could pretend to be doing, to keep conversation away. No, he recognized, not conversation. It was thought he wanted to keep away, thinking about himself. He wasn't afraid. He wasn't furious at fate. He just wasn't prepared to look into the personal consequences of Willy Hartnett's death, not right at that moment—

He looked up; someone had been calling his name.

It was Jon Freeling, Brad's surgical assistant in perceptual systems, looking for Brad.

"Why, no," said Torraway, glad to be talking about something other than Willy's death or his own future, "I don't know where he is. Went to lunch, I think."

"Two hours ago. His tail's going to be in a crack if I can't find him before the DD's meeting. I'm not sure I can field all the questions—and I can't go looking for him, they're bringing the cyborg into my lab now, and I've got to—"

"I'll find him for you," Torraway said hastily. "I'll call him at home."

"Tried it. No dice. And he didn't leave a number where he could be reached."

Torraway winked, suddenly feeling relieved, delighted to have a challenge he could respond to. "You know Brad," he said. "You have to remember there's a lot of tomcat in that boy. I'll find him." And he took the elevator to the administrative floor, turned two corners and rapped on the door marked *Administrative Statistics*.

The function of the people inside that door had very little to do with statistics. The door didn't open at once; instead, a spyhole opened and a blue eye looked out at him. "I'm Colonel Torraway, and it's an emergency."

"One moment," said a girl's voice; there was a sound of clattering and scraping, and then the door unlocked and she let Torraway in. There were four other people in the room, all of them in civilian clothes and looking rather undistinguished, as they were meant to do. Each had an old-fashioned rolltop desk, of a kind one did not usually expect to see in a modern space-agency office. The tops could be pulled down to conceal what was on the desks at a moment's notice; they were down now.

"It's Dr. Alexander Bradley," Roger said. "He's needed urgently in about an hour and his department can't find him. Commander Hartnett is dead, and—"

The girl said, "We know about Commander Hartnett. Do you want us to find Dr. Bradley for you?"

"No, I'll do it. But I expect you can tell me where to start looking. I know you keep tabs on all of us, extracurricular activities and all." He did not actually wink at her too, but he heard the sound of a wink in his voice.

The girl looked at him steadily for a moment. "He's probably at—"

"Hold it," called the man at the desk behind her, his voice surprisingly angry.

She shook her head, overruling him without looking at him. "Try the Chero-Strip Hover Hotel," she said. "He usually uses the name of Beckwith. I'd suggest you telephone. Maybe it would be better if we did it for you, at that—"

"Oh, no," said Torraway easily, resolute to keep this chore for himself. "It's important I talk to him myself."

The young man said strongly, "Dr. Torraway, I really suggest you let us handle—"

But he was already backing out of the door, nodding, not listening any more. He had made up his mind not to bother telephoning but to drive to the motel; it was a valid reason to get out of the lab while he collected his thoughts.

Outside the air-controlled laboratory buildings Tonka had been getting hotter and hotter. The sun penetrated even the tinted windshield, filling Torraway's car with heat that defied the cooling system. He drove inexpertly on manual, taking the curves so sloppily that the guidance wheels skidded. The motel was fifteen stories tall and solid glass; it seemed to aim the sunlight directly at him, like Archimedes's warriors defending Syracuse. He was glad to get out in the underground parking lot and take the moving stairs up to the lobby.

The lobby itself was as tall as the building, completely enclosed, with the rooms racked around it and flying bridges and galleries crisscrossing overhead. The clerk had never heard of Dr. Alexander Bradley.

"Try Beckwith," suggested Torraway, offering a bill. "He sometimes has trouble remembering his name."

But it was no use, the clerk either couldn't place Brad or wouldn't. Roger drove out of the parking space, paused in the heat of the sunshine and considered what to do next. He stared unseeing into the reflecting pool that doubled as the motel's air-conditioning heat sink. Probably he should try phoning Brad at his apartment, he thought. Should have done it while he was in the lobby; he didn't much want to turn around and go back in. Or call from the car, for that matter; the car phone was broadcast radio, and the conversation would be better private. He could go home and call from there, he planned; it was not more than a five-minute run—

At which point it first registered on Roger that he really ought to tell his wife what had happened.

It was not a duty he looked forward to. Telling Dorrie unfortunately implied spelling it all out to himself. But Roger had a good attitude toward inevitable things, even if unpleasant, and keeping his mind in neutral, he turned the car toward home and Dorrie.

Unfortunately Dorrie wasn't there.

He called to her in the hallway, peered into the dining room, looked at the swimming pool in the back, checked both bathrooms. No Dorrie. Out shopping, no doubt. It was annoying, but it couldn't be helped, and he was just about to leave a note for her, staring out the window while he tried to think how to phrase the note, when he saw her driving up in her micromidget two-seater.

He had the door open for her before she got to it.

He expected she would be surprised. He had not expected that she would just stand there, her pretty eyebrows raised and motionless, her expression showing no movement at all. She looked like a snapshot of herself, frozen in the middle of a step.

He said, "I wanted to talk to you about something. I just came from the Chero-Strip, because Brad is involved too, but—"

She came to life and said politely, "Let me come in and sit down." There was still no expression on her face as she paused in the hallway to look at herself in the mirror. She smoothed some blemish on her cheek, fluffed her hair, went into the living room and sat down without taking off her hat. "It's awfully warm out today, isn't it?" she observed.

Roger sat down too, trying to collect his thoughts. It was important not to frighten her. Once he had watched a television program about how to break bad news, some shrink with a need for more patients and a fear of being labeled unethical keeping him from hiring a man with a sandwich board, going on the talk shows in the hope of catching a few live ones for his waiting room. Never be blunt, he said. Give the person a chance to prepare himself. Tell it a little at a time. At that period Roger had thought it was comic; he remembered telling Dorrie about it— *Honey, have you got your charge card? . . . Well, you'll need it for the black dress . . . The black dress for the funeral . . . The funeral we have to go to, and you'll want to look nice because of who it is . . . Well, after all, she was a pretty old lady. And you know she didn't drive very well. The policemen said she didn't suffer after she creamed the truck. Your father's bearing up very well.* They had both laughed about it.

"Please go ahead," Dorrie said invitingly, taking a cigarette out of the box on the coffee table. As she lit it, Roger saw the butane flame quiver and realized with astonishment that her hand was shaking. He was both surprised and a little pleased; evidently she was bracing herself for some kind of bad news. She had always been very perceptive, he thought admiringly, and now that she was ready, he plunged in.

"It's Willy Hartnett, dear," he said kindly. "Something went wrong this morning and—"

He paused, waiting for her to catch up to him. She did not look concerned as much as puzzled.

"He's dead," said Torraway shortly, and stopped to let it sink in.

She nodded thoughtfully. It wasn't penetrating, Roger thought regretfully. She didn't understand. She had liked Willy, but she was not crying or screaming or showing any emotion at all.

He finished the thought, giving up on tact: "And of course that means that I'm next in line," he said, trying to speak slowly.

"The others are out of it; you remember, I told you. So I'm the one they'll want to, uh, prepare for the Mars mission."

The look on her face perplexed him. It was fragile and apprehensive, almost as though she had been expecting something worse and still was not sure it was not coming. He said impatiently, "Don't you understand what I'm saying, dear?"

"Why, yes. That's—well, it's a little hard to take in." He nodded, satisfied, and she went on, "But I'm confused. Didn't you start by saying something about Brad and the Chero-Strip?"

"Oh, I'm sorry, I know I threw a lot at you at once. Yes. I said I had just been at the motel, looking for Brad. You see, it looks like it's the perceptual systems that went wrong and killed Willy. Well, that's Brad's baby. And today of all days he took a long lunch to—well, I don't have to tell you about Brad. He's probably shacked up somewhere with one of the nurses. But it's going to look bad if he isn't there for the meeting—" He stopped to look at his watch. "Wow, I've got to get back myself. But I did want to break this to you in person."

"Thank you, honey," she said absently, pursuing a thought. "Wouldn't it have been better to phone him?"

"Who?"

"Brad, of course."

"Oh. Oh, sure, except it was sort of private. I didn't want anyone listening in. And besides, I didn't think he'd be answering the phone. In fact, the desk clerk wouldn't admit he was ever there. And I had to go to Security to get a lead on where he might be." He had a sudden thought; he knew Dorrie liked Brad, and he wondered for a half second if she was upset at Brad's immorality. The thought dismissed itself, and he burst out admiringly, "Honey, I have to say you're taking this beautifully. Most women would be in hysterics by now."

She shrugged and said, "Well, what's the use of making a fuss? We both knew this could happen."

He ventured, "I won't look very good, Dorrie. And, you know, I think the physical part of our marriage will be down the drain for a while—even not counting the fact I'll be away on the mission for better than a year and a half."

She looked thoughtful, then resigned; then she looked directly at him and smiled. She got up to come over beside him and put her arms around him. "I'll be proud of you," she said. "And we'll have long, long lives after you get back." She ducked back as he reached to kiss her and said playfully, "None of that, you've got to get back. What are you going to do about Brad?"

"Well, I could go back to the motel—"

She said decisively, "Don't do it, Roger. Let him look out for himself. If he's up to something he shouldn't be, that's his problem. I want you to get back to the meeting, and— Oh, say, that's right! I'm going out again. I'll be passing quite near the motel. If I see Brad's car in the lot I'll put a note on it."

"That didn't even occur to me," he said admiringly.

"So don't worry. I don't want you thinking about Brad. With all that's coming up, we have to be thinking of you!"

Jonathan Freeling, M.D., F.A.C.S., A.A.S.M.

Jonny Freeling had been in aerospace medicine long enough to have lost the habit of dealing with cadavers. Particularly he was unused to cutting up the bodies of friends. Astronauts didn't usually leave their bodies behind when they died, anyway. If they died in line of duty it was unlikely there would be any p.m.; the ones that were lost in space stayed there, the ones that died nearer home were usually boiled to gas in the flame of hydrogen and oxygen. In neither case was there anything to put on a table.

It was hard to realize that this object he was dissecting was Willy Hartnett. It wasn't as much like an autopsy as like, say, field-stripping a carbine. He had helped put these parts together—these platinum electrodes here, these microminiaturized chips in their black box there; now it was time to take them apart again. Except that there was blood. In spite of everything, Willy had died with a lot of wet, seeping human blood still in him.

"Freeze and section," he said, serving up a gobbet on a glass slide to his general-duty nurse, who accepted it with a nod. That was Clara Bly. Her pretty black face reflected sadness, although one could not tell, Freeling reflected, lifting out a dripping metal strand that was part of the vision circuits, how much of the sadness was over the death of the cyborg and how much over her interrupted going-away party. She was leaving to get married the next day; the recovery room just behind that door was still festooned with crepe and paper flowers for her party. They had asked Freeling if they should clear it away for the autopsy, but of course there was no need to; no one would be recovering in that recovery room.

He looked up at his surgical assistant, standing where the anesthesiologist would have been in a normal operation, and barked, "Any word from Brad?"

"He's in the building," she said.

Then why doesn't he get his ass down here? is what Freeling thought, but he didn't say it, only nodded. At least he was back. Whatever grief was coming because of this, Freeling wouldn't have to carry it alone.

But the more he probed and fished, the more he found himself baffled. Where was the grief? What had killed Hartnett?

The electronic components didn't seem to be wrong; every time he removed one it was rushed off to the instrumentation people, who work-benched in on the spot. No problems. Nor did the gross physical structure of the brain give any immediate explanation . . .

Was it possible that the cyborg had died of nothing at all?

Freeling leaned back, conscious of sweat under the hot lights, instinctively waiting for his scrub nurse to wipe it off. She wasn't there, and he remembered and wiped his forehead on his sleeve. He went in again, carefully separating and removing the optical nerve system—what there was of it; the major sections had gone with the eyes themselves, replaced by electronics.

Then he saw it.

First blood seeping under the corpus callosum. Then, as he gently lifted and probed, the gray-white slippery sheath of an artery, with a bulge that had burst. Blown. A cardiovascular accident. A stroke.

Freeling left it there. The rest could be done later or not at all. Maybe it would be as well to leave what was left of Willy Hartnett as close to intact as it was. And it was time for the meeting.

The conference room doubled as the hospital library, which meant that when a meeting was going on, look-up research stopped. There were cushioned seats for fourteen people at the long table, and they were all filled, with the overflow on folding chairs, squeezed in where they could. Two seats were empty; they were for Brad and Jon Freeling, off on a last-minute run to the lab for final results on some slides, they said; actually so that Freeling could brief his boss on what had happened while he was "out to lunch." Everybody else was there, Don Kayman and Vic Samuelson (now promoted to Roger's back-up man, and not looking as though he liked it), Telly Ramez, the chief shrink, all of the cardiovascular people muttering among themselves, the top brass from the administrative sectors—and the two stars. One of the stars was Roger Torraway, uneasily sitting near the head of the table and listening with a fixed smile to other people's conversations. The other was Jed Griffin, the President's main man for breaking logjams. His title was only Chief Administrative Assistant to the President, but even the deputy director treated him like the Pope. "We can start any time, Mr. Griffin," urged the deputy director. Griffin's face spasmed a smile and he shook his head.

"Not until those other fellows get here," he said.

When Brad and Freeling arrived, all conversation stopped as though a plug had been pulled. "*Now* we can begin," snapped Jed Griffin, and the worry to his tone was evident to everyone in the room, every person of whom shared it. We were worried too, of course. Griffin did not want to carry his worry alone and promptly shared it with everyone in the room: "You don't know," he said, "how close this whole project is to being terminated, not next year or next month, not phased out, not cut down. *Through.*"

Roger Torraway took his eyes off Brad, and fixed them on Griffin.

"Through," repeated Griffin. "Washed out."

He seemed to take satisfaction in saying it, Torraway thought.

"And the only thing that saved it," said Griffin, "was these." He tapped the oval table with a folded wad of green-tinted computer printouts. "The American public wants the project to continue."

Torraway felt a clutching touch at his heart, and it was only in that moment that he realized how swift and urgent the feeling of hope that had preceded it had been. For a moment it had sounded like a reprieve.

The deputy director cleared his throat. "I had understood," he said, "that the polls showed a considerable, ah, apathy about what we were doing."

"Preliminary results, yes." Griffin nodded. "But when you add them all up and put them through the computer it comes out to a strong, nationwide support. It's real enough. Significant to two sigmas, as I believe you people say. The people want an American to live on Mars.

"However," he added, "that was before this latest fiasco. God knows what that would do if it got out. The administration doesn't need a dead end, something to apologize for. It needs a success. I can't tell you how much depends on it."

The deputy director turned to Freeling. "Dr. Freeling?" he said.

Freeling stood up. "Willy Hartnett died of a stroke," he said. "The full p.m. report is being typed up, but that's what it comes to. There's no evidence of systemic deterioration; at his age and condition, I wouldn't have expected it. So it was trauma. Too much strain for the blood vessels in his brain to stand." He gazed at his fingertips reflectively. "What comes next is conjecture," he said, "but it's the best I can do. I'm going to ask for consultations from Ripplinger at the Yale Medical School and Anford—"

"The hell you are," snapped Griffin.

"I beg your pardon?" Freeling was caught off balance.

"No consultations. Not without full-scale security clearance first. This is urgent-top, Dr. Freeling."

"Oh. Well—then I'll have to take the responsibility myself. The cause of the trauma was too many inputs. He was overloaded. He couldn't handle it."

"I never heard of anything like that causing a stroke," Griffin complained.

"It takes a good deal of stress. But it happens. And here we're into new kinds of stress, Mr. Griffin. It's like—well, here's an analogy. If you had a child who was born with congenital cataracts, you would take him to a doctor, and the doctor would remove them. Only you would have to do it before he reached the age of puberty—before he stopped growing, internally as well as externally, you see. If you don't do it by then, it's better if you leave him blind. Kids who have such cataracts removed after the age of thirteen or fourteen have, as a matter of historical record, an interesting phenomenon in common. They commit suicide before they're twenty."

Torraway was trying to follow the conversation, but not quite succeeding. He was relieved when the deputy director intervened. "I don't think I see what that has to do with Will Hartnett, Jon."

"There, too, it is a matter of too many inputs. In the case of kids after the cataract operation, what appears to happen is disorientation. They get new inputs that they have not grown a system to handle. If there is sight from birth onward, the visual cortex develops systems to handle, mediate and interpret it. If not, there are no developed systems, and it is too late to grow them.

"I think Willy's trouble was that we gave him inputs that he had no mechanism available to handle. It was too late for him to grow one. All the incoming data swamped him; the strain broke a blood vessel. And," he went on, "I think that will happen to Roger here, too, if we do the same thing with him."

Griffin turned a brief, assessing look at Roger Torraway. Torraway cleared his throat, but said nothing. There did not seem to be anything for him to say. Griffin said, "What are you telling me, Freeling?"

The doctor shook his head. "Only what I've said. I tell you what's wrong, it's up to somebody else to tell you how to fix it. I don't think you *can* fix it. I mean, not medically. You've got a brain—Willy's or Roger's. It has grown up as a radio receiver. Now you're putting TV pictures into it. It doesn't know how to deal with them."

All this time Brad had been scribbling, looking up from time to time with an expression of interest. He looked down again at his note pad, wrote something, regarded it thoughtfully, wrote again, while the attention of everyone in the room turned to him.

At last the deputy director said, "Brad? It sounds as though the ball's in your court."

Brad looked up and smiled. "That's what I'm working on," he said.

"Do you agree with Dr. Freeling?"

"No question about it. He's right. We can't feed raw inputs into a nervous system that hasn't got equipment to mediate and translate them. Those mechanisms don't exist in the brain, not in anybody's brain, unless we want to take a child at birth and rebuild him then so that the brain can develop what it needs."

"Are you proposing that we wait for a new generation of astronauts?" Griffin demanded.

"No. I'm proposing we build mediating circuits into Roger. Not just sensory inputs. Filters, translators—ways of interpreting the inputs, the sight from different wavelengths of the spectrum, the kinesthetic sense from the new muscles—everything. Look," he said, "let me go back a little bit. Do any of you know about McCulloch and Lettvin and the frog's eye?" He glanced around the room. "Sure, Jonny, you do, and one or two of the others. I'd better review a little of it. The frog's perceptual system—not just the eye, all of the vision parts of it—filters out what isn't important. If a bug passes in front of the frog's eye, the eye perceives it, the nerves transmit the information, the brain responds to it, and the frog eats the bug. If, say, a little leaf drops in front of the frog he doesn't eat it. He doesn't *decide* not to eat it. He doesn't *see* it. The image forms in the eye, all right, but the information is dropped out before it reaches the brain. The brain never becomes aware of what the eye has seen, because it doesn't need to. It simply is not relevant to a frog to know whether or not a leaf is in front of it."

Roger was following the conversation with great interest, but somewhat less comprehension. "Wait a minute," he said. "I'm more complicated—I mean, a man is a lot more complicated than a frog. How can you tell what I 'need' to see?"

"Survival things, Rog. We've got a lot of data from Willy. I think we can do it."

"Thanks. I wish you were a little more sure."

"Oh, I'm sure enough," said Brad, grinning. "This didn't catch me entirely by surprise."

Torraway said, his throat half-closed and his voice thin, "You mean you let Willy go ahead and—"

"No, Roger! Come on. Willy was my friend, too. I thought there was enough of a safety factor to at least keep him alive. I was wrong, and I'm at least as sorry as you are, Roger. But we all knew there was a risk that the systems wouldn't work right, that we'd have to do more."

"That," said Griffin heavily, "was not made very clear in your progress reports." The deputy director started to speak but Griffin shook his head. "We'll come to that another time. What are you saying now, Bradley? You're going to filter out some of the information?"

"Not just filter it out. Mediate it. Translate it into a form Roger can handle."

"What about Torraway's point that a man is more complicated than a frog? Have you ever done this with human beings?"

Surprisingly, Brad grinned; he was ready for that one. "As a matter of fact, yes. About six years ago, before I came here—I was still a graduate student. We took four volunteers and we conditioned them to a Pavlovian response. We flashed a bright light in their eyes, and simultaneously rang an electric doorbell that pulsed at thirty beats a second. Well, of course, when you get a bright light in your eyes, your pupils contract. It isn't under conscious control. You can't fake it. It is a response to light, nothing else, just an evolutionary capacity to protect the eye from direct sunlight.

"That sort of response, involving the autonomic nervous system, is hard to condition into human beings. But we managed it. When it takes, it sets pretty firmly. After—I think it was after three hundred trials apiece, we had the response fixed. All you had to do was ring the bell, and the subjects' pupils would shrink down to dots. You follow me so far?"

"I remember enough from college to know about Pavlovian reflexes. Standard stuff," said Griffin.

"Well, the next part wasn't standard. We tapped into the auditory nerve, and we could measure the actual signal going to the brain: ding-a-ling, thirty beats per second, we could read it on the oscilloscope.

"So then we changed the bell. We got one that rang at twenty-four beats a second. Care to guess what happened?" There was no response. Brad smiled. "The oscilloscope still showed *thirty beats a second*. The brain was hearing something that wasn't really happening.

"So, you see, it isn't just frogs that do this sort of mediation.

Human beings *perceive* the world in predigested ways. The sensory inputs themselves edit and rearrange the information.

"So what I want to do with you, Roger," he said genially, "is give you a little help in interpretation. We can't do much with your brain. Good or bad, we're stuck with it. It's a mass of gray jelly with a capacity-limiting structure and we can't keep pouring sensory information into it. The only place we have to work is at the interface—*before* it hits the brain."

Griffin slapped his open palm on the table. "Can we make the window date?" he growled.

"I can but try, sir," said Brad genially.

"You can but get your ass in a crack if we buy this and it doesn't work, boy!"

The geniality faded from Brad's face. "What do you want me to say?"

"I want you to tell me the odds!" Griffin barked.

Brad hesitated. "No worse than even money," he said at last.

"Then," said Griffin, smiling at last, "let it be so."

Even money, thought Roger on the way back to his own office, is not a bad bet. Of course, it depends on the stakes.

He slowed down to let Brad catch up with him. "Brad," he said, "you're pretty sure of what you were saying?"

Brad slapped him gently on the back. "More sure than I said, to tell you the truth. I just didn't want to stick my neck out for old Griffin. And listen, Roger, thanks."

"For what?"

"For trying to warn me today. I appreciate it."

"You're welcome," said Roger. He stood there for a moment, watching Brad retreating back, and wondering how Brad knew about something he had told only to his wife.

We could have told him—as in fact we could have told him many, many things, including why the polls showed what they showed. But no one really needed to tell him. He could have told himself—if he had allowed himself to know.

7

Mortal Becoming Monster

Don Kayman was a complex man who never let go of a problem. It was why we wanted him on the project as areologist, but it extended to the religious part of his life too. A religious problem was bothering him, in the corner of his mind.

It did not keep him from whistling to himself as he shaved carefully around his Dizzy Gillespie beard and brushed his hair into a neat pageboy in front of his mirror. It bothered him, though. He stared into the mirror, trying to isolate what it was that was troubling him. After a moment he realized that one thing, at least, was his T-shirt. It was wrong. He took it off and replaced it with a double-knit four-colored turtleneck that had enough of the look of a clerical collar to appeal to his sense of humor.

The interhouse phone buzzed. "Donnie? Are you nearly ready?"

"Coming in a minute," he said, looking around. What else? His sports jacket was over a chair by the door. His shoes were shined. His fly was zipped. "I'm getting absent-minded," he told himself. What was bothering him was something about Roger Torraway, for whom, at that moment, he felt very sorry.

He shrugged, picked up his jacket, swung it over his shoulder, went down the hall and knocked on the door of Sister Clotilda's nunnery.

"Morning, Father," said the novice who let him in. "Take a seat. I'll get her for you."

"Thanks, Jess." As she disappeared down the hall Kayman watched her appreciatively. The tight-fitting pants-suit habit did a lot for her figure, and Kayman let himself enjoy the faint, antique feeling of wickedness it gave him. It was a gentle enough vice, like eating roast beef on Friday. He remembered his parents doggedly chewing the frozen deep-fried scallops every Friday night, even after the dispensation had become general. It was not that they felt it was sinful to eat meat, it was simply that their digestive systems had become so geared to fish on Friday that they didn't know how to change. Kayman's feelings about sex were closely related to that. When the celibacy rule had been lifted, it had not taken away the genetic recollection of two thousand years of a priesthood that had pretended it didn't know what its sexual equipment was for.

Sister Clotilda came briskly into the room, kissed his freshly shaved cheek and took his arm. "You smell good," she said.

"Want to get a cup of coffee somewhere?" he asked, guiding her out the door.

"I don't think so, Donnie. Let's get it over with."

The autumn sun was a blast, hot air up out of Texas. "Shall we put the top down?"

She shook her head. "Your hair will blow all over. Anyway, it's too hot." She twisted in the seat belt to look at him. "What's the matter?"

He shrugged, starting the car and guiding it into the automatic lanes. "I—I'm not sure. I feel as if I have something I forgot to confess."

Clotilda nodded appraisingly. "Me?"

"Oh, no, Tillie! It's—I'm not sure what." He took her hand absent-mindedly, staring out the side window. As they passed over a throughway he could see the great white cube of the project building off on the horizon.

It wasn't his interest in Sister Clotilda that was bothering him, he was pretty sure of that. Although he liked the little tingle of mild wickedness, he was not in any sense willing to flout the laws of his Church and his God. Maybe, he thought, he might hire a good lawyer and fight, but not break a law. He considered his pursuit of Sister Clotilda daring enough, and what came of that would depend on what her order allowed when and if he ever got around to asking her to apply for a dispensation. He had no interest in the wilder splinter groups like the clerical communes or the revived Catharists.

"Roger Torraway?" she guessed.

"I wouldn't be surprised," he said. "There's something about tampering with his senses that bothers me. His perceptions of the world."

Sister Clotilda squeezed his hand. As a psychiatric social worker, she was cleared to know what was happening at the project, and she knew Don Kayman. "The senses are liars, Donnie. That's Scripture."

"Oh, sure. But does Brad have any right to say how Roger's senses lie?"

Clotilda lit a cigarette and let him think it out. It wasn't until they were near the shopping mall that she said, "Next turnoff, isn't it?"

"Right," he said, taking the wheel and turning the car back to manual. He slid into a parking space, still preoccupied with Roger Torraway. There was the immediate problem of Roger's wife. That was trouble enough. But beyond that there was the bigger problem: How could Roger deal with the greatest of personal questions—what is Right, and what is Wrong?—if the information he had to base a decision on was filtered through Brad's mediation circuits?

The sign over the shop window said PRETTY FANCIES. It was a small shop by the standard of the mall, which had a Two Guys with a quarter of a million feet of floor space and a supermarket almost as big. But it was big enough to be expensive. With rent, utilities, insurance, payroll for three salespeople, two of them part-time, and a generous managerial salary for Dorrie, it meant a net loss every month of nearly two thousand dollars. Roger paid it gladly, although some of our accountancy functions had pointed out to him that it would have been cheaper to give Dorrie the two thousand a month as an allowance.

Dorrie was stacking chinaware on a counter marked "Clearance Sale—Half Price." She nodded to the visitors politely enough. "Hello, Don. Nice to see you, Sister Clotilda. Want to buy some red teacups cheap?"

"They look nice," said Clotilda.

"Oh, they are. But don't buy them for the nunnery. The FDA just ordered them off the market. The glaze is supposed to be poison—provided you drink at least forty cups of tea out of one of them every day of your life for twenty years."

"Oh, that's too bad. But—you're selling them?"

"The order isn't effective for thirty days," Dorrie explained, and flashed a grin. "I guess I shouldn't have told that to a priest and a nun, right? But honestly, we've been selling this glaze for years and I never heard of anyone dying."

"Would you like to have a cup of coffee with us?" Kayman asked. "In other cups, of course."

Dorrie sighed, straightened a cup into line and said, "No, we might as well just talk. Come on back to my office." She led the way, and said over her shoulder, "I know why you're here, anyway."

"Oh?" said Kayman.

"You want me to go visit Roger. Right?"

Kayman sat down in a wide armchair, facing her desk. "Why don't you, Dorrie?"

"Cripes, Don, what's the use? He's out cold. He wouldn't know whether I was there or not."

"He's heavily sedated, yes. But he has periods of consciousness."

"Did he ask for me?"

"He asked *after* you. What do you want him to do, beg?"

Dorrie shrugged, fiddling with a ceramic chess piece. "Did you ever think of minding your own business, Don?" she asked.

He did not take offense. "That's what I'm doing. Roger's our one indispensable man right now. Do you know what's happening to him? He's been on the table twenty-eight times already. Thirteen days! He doesn't have any eyes any more. Or lungs, heart, ears, nose—he doesn't even have any skin, it's all gone, a few square inches at a time, replaced with synthetics. Flaying alive—men have become saints for that, and now we've got a man who can't even have his own wife—"

"Oh, shit, Don!" Dorrie flared. "You don't know what you're talking about. Roger *asked* me not to come and see him after the surgery started. He thought I wouldn't be able to— He just didn't want me to see him like that!"

"My impression of you," the priest said thinly, "is that you're made of pretty durable stuff, Dorrie. Would you be able to stand it?"

Dorrie grimaced. For a moment her pretty face did not look pretty at all. "It isn't a question of what I can stand," she said. "Don, look. Do you know what it's like being married to a man like Roger?"

"Why, pretty fine, I would guess," said Kayman, startled. "He's a good man!"

"He is, yes. I know that at least as well as you do, Don Kayman. And he's head over heels in love with me."

There was a pause. "I don't think I understand what you're saying," Sister Clotilda ventured. "Are you displeased by that?"

Dorrie looked at the nun consideringly. "Displeased. That's one way to put it." She set down the chess piece and leaned across the desk. "That's every girl's dream, right? To find a genuine hero, handsome and smart and famous and pretty nearly rich—and have him so crazily in love with her that he can't see anything wrong. That's why I married Roger. I couldn't believe I was that lucky." Her voice went up a half tone in pitch. "I don't think you know what it's like to have someone head over heels in love with you. What's the good of a man who's upside down? Sometimes when we're in bed together I'm trying to get to sleep and I can *hear* him being awake next to me, not moving, not getting up to go to the bathroom, just so fucking *considerate*. . . . Do you know that when we're traveling together Roger never goes to the bathroom until he thinks I'm asleep, or when I'm somewhere else? He shaves the minute he gets up—he doesn't want me to see him with his hair messed up. He shaves his armpits, uses deodorants three times a day. He—he treats me like I was the Virgin Mary, Don! He's *fatuous*. And it's been that way for *nine years*."

She looked beseechingly at the priest and the nun, who were silent, a little ill-at-ease. "And then," Dorrie said, "you come along and tell me I ought to go see him when they're turning him into something ghastly and ludicrous. You and everybody else. Kathleen Doughty dropped in last night. She had a skin full; she'd been drinking and brooding and she decided to come over and tell me, out of her bourbon wisdom, that I was making

Roger unhappy. Well, she's right. You're all right. I'm making him unhappy. Where you're wrong is thinking that my going to see him would make him happy. . . . Oh, hell."

The phone rang. Dorrie picked it up, then glanced at Kayman and Sister Clotilda. The expression on her face, which had been almost pleading, condensed into something like the porcelain figures on the table beside her desk. "Excuse me," she said, folding up the soft plastic petals around the mouthpiece that converted it into a hushphone and turning away from them in her chair. She talked inaudibly for a moment, then hung up and turned back to them.

Kayman said, "You've given me something to think about, Dorrie. But still—"

She smiled a porcelain smile. "But still you want to tell me how to run my life. Well, you can't. You've said your piece, both of you. I thank you for coming. I'll thank you, now, to go. There's nothing more to be said."

Inside the great white cube of the project building Roger lay, spread-eagled on a fluidized bed. He had been thirteen days like that, most of the time either unconscious or unable to tell whether he was conscious or not. He dreamed. We could tell when he was dreaming from the rapid eye movements at first, later from the twitches of the muscle endings after the eyes were gone. Some of his dreams were reality, but he could not distinguish between them.

We kept very close tabs on Roger Torraway every second of that time. There was hardly a flexure of a muscle or a flash of a synapse that did not kick over some monitor, and faithfully we integrated the data and kept continuous surveillance of his vital functions.

It was only the beginning. What had been done to Roger in the first thirteen days of surgery was not much more than had been done to Willy Hartnett. And that was not enough.

When all that was done, the prosthetic and surgical teams began doing things that had never been done to any human being before. His entire nervous system was revised and all the major pathways connected with coupling devices that led to the big computer downstairs. That was an all-purpose IBM 3070. It took up half a room and still did not have enough capacity to do all the jobs demanded of it. It was only an interim hookup. Two thousand miles away, in upstate New York, the IBM factory was putting together a special-purpose computer that would fit into a backpack. Designing that was the most difficult part of the project; we kept revising the circuits even while they were being fitted together on the workbenches. It could not weigh more than eighty pounds, Earth weight. Its greatest dimension could not be more than nineteen inches. And it had to work from DC batteries which were kept continually recharged by solar panels.

The solar panels were a problem at first, but we solved that one rather elegantly. They required an absolute minimum surface area of nearly thirty square feet. The surface area of Roger's body, even after it had been revised with various attachments, wasn't large enough, wouldn't have been even if all of it could have been accepting Mars's fairly feeble sunlight at once. The way we solved the problem was to design two great gossamer fairy wings. "He's going to look like Oberon," Brad said gleefully when he saw the drawings. "Or like a bat," grumbled Kathleen Doughty.

They did resemble bat wings, especially as they were jet-black. They would be no good for flying, even in a decently thick atmosphere if Mars had had one. They were thin film, with little structural strength. But they weren't meant for flying or for any kind of load-bearing. They were only meant to preen themselves out automatically, oriented to accept as much radiation as the sun could provide. As an afterthought, the design was changed to include a certain amount of control on Roger's part so he could use the wings as a tightrope walker uses his pole, to balance. All in all, they were an immense improvement over the "ears" we had put on Willy Hartnett.

The solar wings were designed and fabricated in eight days; by the time Roger's shoulders were ready to accept them, they were ready to attach. The skin was almost a stock item by now. So much had been used on Willy Hartnett, both as original equipment and as replacements for damage or for design changes as the project went along, that new grafts were loomed to Roger's shape as rapidly as the surgeons flayed away the integument he was born with.

From time to time he would rouse himself and look at his surroundings with what seemed recognition and intelligence. It was hard to be sure. His visitors—he had a constant stream of them—sometimes spoke to him, sometimes came to regard him as a laboratory specimen to be discussed and manipulated with no more person-to-person concern than they would give a titration flask. Vern Scanyon was in almost every day, staring at the developing creation with growing repugnance. "He looks like hell," he grumbled. "The taxpayers would love this!"

"Watch it, General," snarled Kathleen Doughty, interposing her huge body between the director and the subject. "How do you know he can't hear you?"

Scanyon shrugged and left to report to the President's office. Don Kayman came in as he was going. "Thanks, mother to all the world," he said gravely. "I appreciate your concern for my friend Roger."

"Yeah," she said irritably. "It's not sentiment. The poor sod's got to have some self-confidence; he's going to need it. You know how many amputees and paraplegics I've worked with? And do you know how many of them were certified basket cases that would never walk or move any muscle or even go to the toilet by themselves? It's will power that does it, Don, and for that you need to believe in yourself."

Kayman frowned; Roger's state of mind was still very much in his thoughts. "Are you arguing with me?" Kathleen said sharply, misreading the frown.

"Not in the least! I mean—be reasonable, Kathleen; am I the man to question the transcendence of the spiritual over the physical? I'm just grateful. You're a good person, Kathleen."

"Oh, crap," she grumbled around the cigarette in her mouth. "That's what they pay me for. And besides," she said, "I take it you haven't been in your office yet today? There's a buck-up note for all of us from His Starship the General, so we won't forget how important what we're doing is . . . and a little hint that if we blow our launch date we're for the concentration camps."

"As if we needed reminding," sighed Father Kayman, looking at Roger's grotesque and unmoving figure. "Scanyon's a good man, but he tends to think whatever he does is at the very center of the universe. Only this time he might be right. . . ."

It was at least a colorable claim. To us, there was not much question about it: the most important link in all the complex interrelationships of mind and matter that an earlier generation of scientists had called Gaia was right there, floating on its fluidized bed, looking like the star of a Japanese horror flick. Without Roger Torraway, the Mars launch could not take off on time. Billions of people might question the importance of that. We did not.

There was Roger at the hub of everything. Around him, in the bulk of the project building, there were all the ancillary and associated efforts that were going into making him what he had to be. In the surgery room next door Freeling, Weidner and Bradley tinkered new parts into him. Down in the Mars-normal tank where Willy Hartnett had died, those parts were bench-tested in the Martian environment to failure. Sometimes failure time was appallingly short; then they were redesigned if possible, or backed up—or sometimes used anyway, with crossed fingers and prayers.

The universe expanded away from Roger, like the shells of an onion. Still farther in the building was the giant 3070, clicking and whirring as it accreted new segments of programming to match the mediation facilities being built into Roger hour by hour. Outside the building was the community of Tonka, which lived or died by the health of the project, its principal employer and major reason for being. All around Tonka was the rest of Oklahoma, and spreading out in all directions the other fifty-four states, and around them the troubled, angry world that was busy snapping arrogant notes from one of its capitals to another on the policy level, and clawing for subsistence in each of its myriad personal lives.

The project people had come to close themselves off from most of that world. They didn't watch the television news when they could avoid it, preferred not to read anything but the sports sections of the newspapers. In high gear, they did not have a great deal of time, but that wasn't the reason. The reason was that they simply did not want to know. The world was going mad, and the isolated strangeness in the great white cube of the project building seemed sane and real to them, while the rioting in New York, the tac-nuke fighting around the Arabian Gulf and the mass starvation in what used to be called the "emerging nations" seemed irrelevant fantasy.

They were fantasy. At least, they did not matter to the future of our race.

And so Roger continued to change and survive. Kayman spent more and more time with him, every minute he could spare from supervising the Mars-normal tank. He watched with affection as Kathleen Doughty stumped around the room, dropping cigarette ashes on everything but Roger. But he was still troubled.

He had to accept Roger's need for mediation circuits to interpret the excess of inputs, but he had no answer for the great question: If Roger could not know what he was seeing, how could he see Truth?

8

Through Deceitful Eyes

The weather had changed quickly and for good. We had seen the shift coming as a wedge of polar air pushed down out of Alberta as far as the Texas Panhandle. Wind warnings had grounded the hovercars. Those of the project personnel who didn't have wheeled vehicles were forced to come by public transportation, and the parking lots were almost bare except for great ungainly knots of tumbleweed bouncing before the wind.

Not everyone had heeded the warnings, and there were the colds and flu bugs of the year's first real cold snap. Brad was laid up. Weidner was ambulatory, but not allowed near Roger for fear of infecting him with a trivial little illness that he was in no shape to handle. Most of the work of doing Roger was left to Jonathan Freeling, whose health was then guarded almost as jealousy as Roger's own. Kathleen Doughty, indestructibly tough old lady, was in Roger's room every hour, dropping cigarette ash and advice on the nurses. "Treat him like a *person*," she ordered. "And put some clothes on before you go home. You can show off your beautiful little butt any time—what you have to do now is keep from catching cold until we can spare you." The nurses did not resist her. They did their best, even Clara Bly, recalled from her honeymoon to fill in for the nurses on the sick list. They cared as much as Kathleen Doughty did, although it was hard to remember, looking down at the grotesque creature that was still named Roger Torraway, that he was in fact a human being, as capable of yearning and depression as themselves.

Roger was beginning to be more clearly conscious from time to time. Twenty hours and more each day he was out cold, or in a half-dreaming analgesic daze; but sometimes he recognized the people in the room with him, and sometimes even spoke coherently to them. Then we would put him out again.

"I wish I knew what he was feeling," said Clara Bly to her relief nurse.

The other girl looked down at the mask that was all there was left of his face, with the great wide eyes that had been fabricated for him. "Maybe you're better off if you don't," she said. "Go home, Clara."

Roger heard that; the oscilloscope traces showed that he had. By studying the telemetry we could form some notion of what was inside his mind. Often he was in pain, that was evident. But the pain was not a warning of something that needed attention, or a spur to action. It was simply a fact of his life. He learned to expect it and to accept it when it happened. He was not conscious of very much else that pertained to his own body. His body-knowledge senses had not yet come to deal with the reality of his new body. He did not know when his eyes, lungs, heart, ears, nose and skin were replaced or supplemented. He didn't know how to recognize the clues that might have given him information. The taste of blood and vomit at the back of his throat: how was he to know that that meant his lungs were gone? The blackness, the suppressed pain in the skull that was so unlike any other headache he had ever had: how could he tell what it meant, how could he distinguish between the removal of his entire optic system and the turning off of a light switch?

He realized dimly at one point that somewhen he had stopped smelling the familiar hospital aroma, scented odor killer and disinfectant. When? He didn't know. All he knew was that there were no smells in his environment any more.

He could hear. With a sharpness of discrimination and a level of perception he had never experienced before, he could hear every word that was said in the room, in however low a whisper, and most of what happened in the adjoining rooms as well. He heard what people said, when he was conscious enough to hear at all. He understood the words. He could feel the good will of Kathleen Doughty and Jon Freeling, and understood the worry and anger that underlay the voices of the deputy director and the general.

And above all, he could feel pain.

There were so many different kinds of pain! There were all the aches of all the parts of his body. There was the healing of surgery, and there was the angry pulsing of tissues that had been bruised as major work was done. There were the endless little twinges as Freeling or the nurses jacked instrumentation into a thousand hurtful places on the surface of his body so that they could study the readings they gave.

And there was the deeper, internal pain that sometimes seemed physical, that came when he thought of Dorrie. Sometimes, when he was awake, he remembered to ask if she had been there or had called. He could not remember ever getting an answer.

And then one day he felt a searing new pain inside his head . . . and realized it was light.

He was seeing again.

When the nurses realized that he could see them they reported to Jon Freeling at once, who picked up the phone and called Brad. "Be right over," Brad said. "Keep him in the dark till I get there."

It took more than an hour for Brad to make the trip, and when he turned up he was clearly wobbly. He submitted to an antiseptic shower, an oral spray and the fitting of a surgical mask, and then, cautiously, he opened the door and entered Roger's room.

The voice from the bed said, "Who's there?" It was weak and quavering, but it was Roger's voice.

"Me. Brad." He fumbled along the side of the door until he found the light knob. "I'm going to turn the lights on a little bit, Roger. Tell me when you can see me."

"I can see you now," sighed the voice. "At least I guess it's you."

Brad arrested his hand. "The hell you can—" he began, and then he paused. "What do you mean, you see me? What do you see?"

"Well," whispered the voice, "I'm not sure about the face. That's just a sort of glow. But I can see your hands, and your head. They're bright. And I can make out your body and arms pretty well. A lot fainter, though—yeah, I can see your legs, too. But your face is funny. The middle of it is just a splotch."

Brad touched the surgical mask, comprehending. "Infrared. You're seeing the heat. What else can you see, Roger?"

Silence from the bed for a moment. Then, "Well, there's a sort of square of light; I guess it's the door frame. I mostly just see the outline of it. And something pretty bright over against the wall, where I hear something too—the telemetry monitors? And I can see my own body, or at least I can see the sheet over me, with a sort of outline of my body on it."

Brad stared around the room. Even with time for dark adaptation he could see almost nothing: a polka-dot pattern of illuminated dials from the monitors, and a very faint seepage of light around the door behind him.

"That's pretty good, Rog. Anything else?"

"Yeah, but I don't know what they are. Some lights low down, over near you. Very dim."

"I think those are the heating ducts. You're doing fine, boy. All right, now hold on. I'm going to turn up the room lights a little bit. Maybe you can get along without them, but I can't and neither can the nurses. Tell me what you feel."

Slowly he inched the dimmer dial around, an eighth of a turn, a bit more. The surround lights behind the moldings under the ceiling came alive—weakly at first, then a trifle stronger. Brad could see the shape on the bed now, first the glitter of the spread wings that had revolved forward, over the body of Roger Torraway, then the body itself, with a sheet draped over it waist-high.

"I see you now," sighed Roger in his reedy voice. "It's a little different—I'm seeing color now, and you're not so bright."

Brad took his hand off the knob. "That's good enough for now." He leaned back against the wall giddily. "Sorry," he said. "I've got a cold or something. . . . How about you, do you feel anything? I mean, any pain, anything like that?"

"Christ, Brad!"

"No, I mean connected with vision. Does the light hurt your—your eyes?"

"They're about the only thing that doesn't hurt," sighed Roger.

"Fine. I'm going to give you a little more light—about that much, okay? No trouble?"

"No."

Brad walked delicately over to the bed. "All right, I want you to try something. Can you—well, close your eyes? I mean, can you turn off the vision receptors?"

Pause. "I—don't think so."

"Well, you can, Rog. The capacity is built in, you'll just have to find it. Willy had a little trouble at first, but he got it. He said he just sort of fooled around, and then it happened."

". . . Nothing's happening."

Brad pondered for a second. His head was muzzy from the infection, and he could feel his stamina ebbing away. "How about this? Did you ever have sinus trouble?"

"No—well, maybe. A little bit."

"Can you remember where it hurt?"

The shape moved uncomfortably on the bed, the great eyes staring into Brad's. "I—think so."

"Feel around near there," Brad ordered. "See if you can find muscles to move. The muscles aren't there, but the nerve endings that controlled them are."

". . . Nothing. What muscle am I looking for?"

"Oh, hell, Roger! It's called the *rectus laetralis*, and what good does that do you? Just fool around."

". . . Nothing."

"All right." Brad sighed. "Never mind for now. Keep on trying as often as you can, all right? You'll find how to do it."

"That's a comfort," whispered the resentful voice from the bed. "Hey, Brad? You're looking brighter."

"What do you mean, brighter?" Brad snapped.

"More bright. More light from your face."

"Yeah," said Brad, realizing he was beginning to feel giddy again. "I think I may be running a temperature. I'd better get out of here. This gauze, it's supposed to keep me from infecting you, but it's only reliable for fifteen minutes or so—"

"Before you go," whispered the voice insistently. "Do something for me. Turn off the lights again for a minute."

Brad shrugged and complied. "Yeah?"

He could hear the ungainly body shifting in the bed. "I'm just turning to get a better look," Roger reported. "Listen, Brad what I wanted to ask you is, how are things working out? Am I going to make it?"

Brad paused for reflection. "I think so," he said honestly. "Everything's all right so far. I wouldn't crap you, Roger. This is all frontier stuff, and something could go wrong. But so far it doesn't look that way."

"Thanks. One other thing, Brad. Have you seen Dorrie lately?"

Pause. "No, Roger. Not for a week or so. I've been pretty sick, and when I wasn't sick I was damn busy."

"Yeah. Say, I guess you might as well leave the lights the way you had them so the nurses can find their way around."

Brad turned up the switch again. "I'll be in when I can. Practice trying to close your eyes, will you? And you've got a phone— call me any time you want to. I don't mean if anything goes wrong—I'll know about that if it happens, don't worry; I don't go to the toilet without leaving the number where I can be reached. I mean if you just want to talk."

"Thanks, Brad. So long."

At least the surgery was over—or the worst of it, anyway. When Roger came to realize that, he felt a kind of relief that was very precious to him, although there were still more unrelieved stresses in his mind than he wanted to handle.

Clara Bly cleaned him up and against direct orders brought him flowers to boost his morale. "You're a good kid," whispered Roger, turning his head to look at them.

"What do they look like to you?"

He tried to describe it. "Well, they're roses, but they're not red. Pale yellow? About the same color as your bracelet."

"That's orange." She finished whipping the new sheet over his legs. It billowed gently in the upthrust from the fluidized bed. "Want the bedpan?"

"For what?" he grumbled. He was into his third week of a low-residue diet, and his tenth day of controlled liquid intake. His excretory system had become, as Clara put it, mostly ornamental. "I'm allowed to get up anyway," he said, "so if anything does happen I can take care of it."

"Big man," Clara grinned, bundling up the dirty linen and leaving. Roger sat up and began again his investigation of the world around him. He studied the roses appraisingly. The great faceted eyes took in nearly an extra octave of radiation, which meant half a dozen colors Roger had never seen before from IR to UV; but he had no names for them, and the rainbow spectrum he had seen all his life had extended itself to cover them all. What seemed to him dark red was, he knew, low-level heat. But it was not quite true even to say that it seemed to be red; it was only a different quality of light that had associations of warmth and well-being.

Still, there was something very strange about the roses, and it was not the color.

He threw off the sheet and looked down at himself. The new skin was poreless, hairless and wrinkle-free. It looked more like a wetsuit than the flesh he had known all his life. Under it, he knew, was a whole new musculature, power-driven, but there was no visible trace of that.

Soon he would get up and walk, all by himself. He was not quite ready for that. He clicked on the TV set. The screen lit up with a dazzling array of dots in magenta and cyan and green. It took an effort of will for Roger to look at them and see three girls singing and weaving; his new eyes wanted to analyze the pattern into its components. He clicked stations and got a newscast. New People's Asia had sent three more nuclear subs on a "courtesy visit" to Australia. President Deshantine's press secretary said sternly that our allies in the Free World could count on us. All the Oklahoma football teams had lost. Roger clicked it off; he found himself getting a headache. Every time he shifted position the lines seemed to slope off at an angle, and there was a baffling bright glow from the back of the set. After the current was off he watched for some time the cathode tube's light failing, and the glow from the back darkening and dimming. It was heat, he realized.

Now, what was it Brad had said? "Feel around, near where your sinuses are."

It was a strange feeling, being in the first place in an unfamiliar body and then trying to locate inside it a control that no one could quite define. Just in order to close the eyes! But Brad had assured him he could do it. Roger's feelings toward Brad were complex, and one component of them was pride; if Brad said it could be done by anyone, then it was going to be done by Roger.

Only it wasn't *being* done. He tried every combination of muscle squeezes and will power he could think of, and nothing happened.

A sudden recollection hit him: years old, a memory from the days when he and Dorrie had first been married. No, not married, not yet; living together, he remembered, and trying to decide if they wanted to publicly join their lives. That was their massage-and-transcendental-meditation period, when they were exploring each other in all the ways that had ever occurred to either of them, and he remembered the smell of baby oil with a dash of musk added, and the way they had laughed over the directions for the second chakra: "Take the air into your spleen and hold it, then breathe out as your hands glide up on either side of your partner's spine." But they had never been able to figure out where the spleen was, and Dorrie had been very funny, searching the private recesses of their bodies: "Is it there? There? Oh, Rog, look, you're not serious about this . . ."

He felt a sudden interior pain swell giddyingly inside him, and leaned back in desolation, *Dorrie!*

The door burst open.

Clara Bly flew in, bright eyes wide in her dark, pretty face. "Roger! What are you doing?"

He took a deep, slow breath before he spoke. "What's the matter?" He could hear the flatness in his own voice; it had little tone left, after what they had done to it.

"All your taps are jumping! I thought—I don't know what I thought, Roger. But whatever was happening, it was giving you trouble."

"Sorry, Clara." He watched as she hurried over to the monitors on the wall, studying them swiftly.

"They look a little better," she said grudgingly. "I guess it's all right. But what the hell were you doing to yourself?"

"Worrying," he said.

"About what?"

"Where my spleen is. Do you know?"

She stared at him thoughtfully for a moment before she

replied. "It's under your lower ribs, on your left side. About where you think your heart is. A little lower down. Are you putting me on, Roger?"

"Well, kind of. I guess I was reminiscing about something I shouldn't have, Clara."

"Please don't do it any more!"

"I'll try." But the thought of Dorrie and Brad was still lurking there, right under the conscious of his mind. He offered, "One thing—I've been trying to close my eyes, and I can't."

She approached and touched his shoulder in friendly sympathy. "You'll do it, hon."

"Yeah."

"No, really. I was with Willy around this time, and he got pretty discouraged. But he made it. Anyway," she said, turning, "I'll take care of it for you for now. Lights-out-time. You've got to be fresh as a daisy in the morning."

He said suspiciously, "What for?"

"Oh, not more cutting. That's over for a while. Didn't Brad tell you? Tomorrow they're going to hook you into the computer for all that mediation stuff. You're going to be a busy boy, Rog, so get some sleep." She turned off the light, and Brad watched as her dark face changed into a gentle glow that he thought of as peach.

Something occurred to him. "Clara? Do me a favor?"

She stopped with her hand on the door. "What's that, honey?"

"I want to ask you a question."

"So ask."

He hesitated, wondering how to do what he wanted to do. "What I want to know," he said, working it out in his head as he went along, "is, let's see—oh, yes. What I want to know, Clara, is, when your husband and you are in bed making love, what different ways do you use?"

"Roger!" The brightenss of her face suddenly went up half a decibel; he could see the tracing of veins under the skin as hot blood flooded through her veins.

He said, "I'm sorry, Clara. I guess—I guess lying here I get kind of horny. Forget I asked you, will you?"

She was silent for a moment. When she spoke her voice was a professional's, no longer a friend's: "Sure, Roger. It's okay. You just kind of caught me off-guard. It's . . . well, it's all right, it's just that you never said anything like that to me before."

"I know. Sorry."

But he wasn't sorry, or not exactly.

He watched the door close behind her and studied the rectangular tracing of light bleeding through from the hall outside. He was careful to keep his mind as calm as he could. He didn't want to start the monitors ringing alarm bells again.

But he wanted to think about something that was right on the borderline of the danger zone, and that was how come the flush he had tricked onto Clara Bly's face looked so much like the sudden brightness that had come onto Brad's when he asked if Brad had been with Dorrie.

We were fully mobilized next morning, checking the circuits, cutting in the stand-bys, insuring that the automatic switch-over relays were tuned to intervene at the faintest flicker of a malfunction. Brad came in at 6:00 A.M., weak but clear-headed and ready to work. Weidner and Jon Freeling were only minutes after him, although the primary job for the day was all Brad's. They could not stay away. Kathleen Doughty was there of course, as she had been at every step, not because her duty required it but because her heart did. "Don't give my boy a bad time," she growled over her cigarette. "He's going to need all the help he can get when I start on him next week."

Sounding every syllable, Brad said, "Kathleen. I will do the goddamned best I can."

"Yeah. I know you will, Brad." She stubbed out the cigarette and immediately lit another. "I never had any children, and I guess Roger and Willy sort of filled in."

"Yeah," grunted Brad, no longer listening. He was not qualified or allowed to touch the 3070 or any of the ancillary units. All he could do was watch while the technicians and the programmers did their job. When the third recheck had gone almost to completion without a glitch he finally left the computer room and took the elevator up three flights to Roger's room.

At the door he paused to breathe for a moment, then opened the door with a smile. "You're about ready to plug in, boy," he said. "Feel up to it?"

The insect eyes turned toward him. Roger's flat voice said, "I don't know what I'm supposed to feel. What I feel is mostly scared."

"Oh, there's nothing to be scared of. Today," Brad amended hastily, "all we're going to do is test out the mediation."

The bat wings shuddered and changed position. "Will that kill me?" asked the maddeningly monotone voice.

"Oh, come *on*, Roger!" Brad was suddenly angry.

"It's only a question," ticked the voice.

"It's a crappy question! Look, I know how you feel—"

"I doubt that."

Brad stopped, and studied Roger's uncommunicative face. After a moment he said, "Let me go over it again. What I'm going to do is not kill you, it's keep you alive. Sure, you're thinking of what happened to Willy. It isn't going to happen to you. You're going to be able to handle what happens—here, and on Mars, where it's important."

"It's important to me here," said Roger.

"Oh, for Christ's sake. When the system is all go you'll only see or hear what you need, understand? Or what you want. You'll have a good deal of volitional control. You'll be able—"

"I can't even close my eyes yet, Brad."

"You will. You'll be able to use all of it. But you won't unless we get started on it. Then all this stuff will filter out the unnecessary signals, so you won't be confused. That's what killed Willy: confusion."

Pause, while the brain behind the grotesque face ruminated. What Roger finally said was, "You look lousy, Brad."

"Sorry about that. I actually don't feel too good."

"Are you sure you're up to this?"

"I'm sure. Hey, Roger. What are you telling me? Do you want to put this off?"

"No."

"Well, what do you want?"

"I wish I knew, Brad. Get on with it."

We were all ready by then; the "go" lights had been flashing green for several minutes. Brad shrugged and said morosely to the duty nurse, "Let 'er rip."

There were ten hours, then, of phasing in the mediation circuits one by one, testing, adjusting, letting Roger try his new senses on projected Rorschach blots and Maxwell color wheels. For Roger the day raced by. His sense of time was unreliable. It was no longer regulated by everyman's built-in biological clocks but by his machine components; they slowed his perception of time down when there was no stress situation, speeded it up when needed. "Slow down," he begged, watching the nurses whiz past him like bullets. And then, when Brad, beginning to shake with fatigue, knocked over a tray of inks and crayons, to Roger the pieces seemed actually to float to the ground. He had no difficulty in catching two bottles of ink and the tray itself before they touched the floor.

When he came to think of it after, he realized that they were the pieces that might have spilled or broken. He had let the wax crayons fall free. In that fraction of a second of choice, he had chosen to catch the objects that needed catching and let the others go, without being aware of what he did.

Brad was highly pleased. "You're doing great, boy," he said, holding to the foot of the bed. "I'm going to take off now and get some sleep, but I'll be in to see you tomorrow after the surgery."

"Surgery? What surgery?"

"Oh," said Brad, "just a little touch-up. Nothing compared to what you've already had, believe me! From now on," he said, turning to leave, "you're just about through being born; now all you have to do is grow up. Practice. Learn to use what you've got. The hard parts are all behind you. How are you doing with cutting off vision when you want to?"

"Brad," rang out the flat voice, louder in amplitude but tonally gray, "what the hell do you want of me? I'm trying!"

"I know," Brad said, conciliating. "See you tomorrow."

For the first time that day Roger was left alone. He experimented with his new senses. He could see that they might be very useful to him in survival situations. But they were also very confusing. All the tiny noises of everyday life were magnified. From the hall he could hear Brad talking to Jonny Freeling and the nurses going off duty. He knew that with the ears his mother had cultured for him in her womb he would not have been able to perceive even a whisper; now he could make out the words at will: "—local anesthetic, but I don't want to. I want him out. He's got enough trauma to deal with." That was Freeling talking to Brad.

The lights were more brilliant than before. He tried to diminish the sensitivity of his vision, but nothing happened. What he really wanted, he thought, was a single Christmas-tree bulb. That was plenty of light; these floods of luminosity were disconcerting. Also, he observed, the lights were maddeningly rhythmical; he could perceive each pulse of the sixty-Hertz current. Inside the fluorescent tubes he observed the writhing of a glowing snake of gas. Incandescent bulbs, on the other hand, were almost dark, except for the bright filaments at the center, which he could examine in detail. There was no sense of eyestrain, even when looking at the brightest of lights.

He heard a new voice in the corridor, and sharpened his hearing to listen: Clara Bly, just coming on duty for the evening shift. "How's the patient, Dr. Freeling?"

"Just fine. He seems rested. You didn't have to give him a sleeping pill last night?"

"No. He was fine. Kind of"—she giggled—"kind of randy, though. He made a sort of a pass, which I never expected from Roger."

"Huh." There was a puzzled pause. "Well, that won't be a problem any more. I've got to check the readouts. Take care."

Roger thought he would have to be extra nice to Clara; it would not be hard to do, for she was his favorite among the nurses. He lay back, listening to the rustle of his own black wings and the rhythmic sounds from the telemetry panels. He was very tired. It would be nice to sleep—

He sprang up. The lights had stopped! Then they were on again, as soon as he became aware of it.

He had learned to close his eyes!

Satisfied, Roger let himself sink back onto the gently flowing bed. It was true enough; he was learning.

They woke him to feed him, and then to put him to sleep again for his last operation.

There was no anesthesia. "We're just going to turn you off," said Jon Freeling. "You won't feel a thing." And indeed he didn't. First he was wheeled into the surgery next door, intensive-care bottles, pipes, drains and all. He could not smell the smell of disinfectant, but he knew it was there; he could perceive the brightness gathered at the cusp of every metallic object, the heat from the sterilizer, like a sunburst against the wall.

And then Dr. Freeling ordered him out, and we compiled. We depressed his sensory inputs one by one; to him it was as though the sounds grew fainter, the lights dimmer, the body touches more gentle. We dampened the pain inputs throughout all his new skin, extinguished them completely where Freeling's knife would cut and needle would pierce. There was a complex problem there. Many of the pain inputs were to be maintained after he recovered. He would have to have some warning system when he was free on the surface of Mars, something to tell him if he was being burned or torn or damaged; pain was the sharpest alarm we could give him. But for much of his body, pain was over. Once we extinguished the inputs we programmed them out of his sensorium entirely.

Roger, of course, knew nothing of this. Roger just went to sleep and woke up again.

When he looked up he screamed.

Freeling, leaning back and flexing his fingers, jumped and dropped his mask. "What's the matter?"

Roger said, "Jesus! For a minute there I saw—I don't know. Could it have been a dream? But I saw you all around me, looking down, and you looked like a bunch of ghouls. Skulls. Skeletons. Grinning at me! And then you were you again."

Freeling looked at Weidner and shrugged. "I think," he said, "that that's just your mediation circuits at work. You know? Translating what you see into something you can grasp immediately."

"I don't like it," Roger flared.

"Well, we'll have to talk to Brad about it. But honestly, Roger, I think that's the way it's supposed to be. I think it's like the computer took your sensations of fear and pain—you know, what everyone feels when he has an operation—and put them together with the visual stimulus: our faces, the masks, all that stuff. Interesting. I wonder how much of it was in the mediation, and how much was plain postoperative delusion?"

"I'm glad you find it interesting," Roger sulked.

But truthfully, he found it interesting too. When he was back in his own room he let his mind roam. He could not summon the fantasy pictures at will. They came when they wanted to come, but they were not as fearsome as that first terrified glimpse of bare mandibles and hollow eye sockets. When Clara came in with a bedpan and left again after he waved it away, he watched her through the closing door; and the shadow of the door became a cave entrance, and Clara Bly, a cave bear growling irritably at him. She was still a little annoyed, he realized; some subsonic cue in her face was registering in his senses, and being analyzed by the buzzing 3070 downstairs and displayed as a warning.

But when she came back she was wearing Dorrie's face. It melted away and reclothed itself in her familiar dark skin and bright eyes, not like Dorrie at all; but Roger took it as a sign that things were all right between them again . . .

Between Clara and himself.

Not, he thought, between Dorrie and himself. He gazed at the phone by his bed. The vision circuits were permanently off at his request; he didn't want to call someone and forget what they might see. But he had not used it to call Dorrie at all. Often enough he reached out his hand for the phone, but every time he drew his hand back.

He didn't know what to say to her.

How do you ask your wife if she is sleeping with your best friend? You come right out and ask her, that's how, his gut feelings told Roger; but he could not quite make himself do it. He was not sure enough. He could not risk that accusation; he might be wrong.

The thing was, he couldn't discuss it with his friends, not any of them. Don Kayman would have been a natural for that; it was a priest's function. But Don was so clearly, so sweetly and tenderly in love with his pretty little nun that Roger could not put himself in the pain of discussing pain with him.

And for most of his friends, the trouble was that they honestly would not have seen what the trouble was. Open marriage was so common in Tonka—in most of the Western world, indeed—that it was the rare closed couple that caused gossip. To admit to jealousy was very difficult.

And anyway, Torraway told himself stoutly, it was not jealousy that troubled him. Not exactly jealousy. It was something else. It was not Sicilian machismo or the outrage of the property owner who finds someone trespassing in his own fertile gardens. It was that Dorrie should *want* to love only him. Since he only wanted to love her. . . .

He became aware that he was slipping into a state of mind that would surely ring the alarm bells on the telemetry readouts. He didn't want that. He resolutely took his mind away from his wife.

He practiced "closing his eyes" for a time; it was reassuring to be able to summon up this new skill when he wanted it. He could not have described, any better than Willy Hartnett had, what it was he did; but somehow he was able to reach the decision to stop receiving visual inputs, and somehow the circuitry inside his head and down in the 3070 room were able to convert that decision into blackness. He could even dim the light selectively. He could brighten it. He could, he discovered, filter out all but one band of wavelengths or suppress one or cause one or more of the rainbow colors to be brighter than the rest.

It was quite satisfying, really, although in time it cloyed. He wished he had lunch to look forward to, but there would be no lunch that day, partly because he had had an operation, partly because they were gradually deaccustoming him to eating. Over the next few weeks he would eat and drink less and less; by the time he was on Mars, he would really need to eat only about one square meal a month.

He flung back the sheet and gazed idly down at the artifact that his body had become.

A second later he shouted a great raw scream of fear and pain. The telemetry monitors all flashed blinding red. In the corridor outside Clara Bly turned in mid-step and dashed for his door. Back in Brad's bachelor apartment the warning bells went off a split-second later, telling him of something urgent and serious that woke him out of an unsound, fatigued sleep.

When Clara opened the door she saw Roger, curled fetally on the bed, groaning in misery. One hand was cupping his groin, between his closed legs. "Roger! What's the matter?"

The head lifted, and the insect eyes looked at her blindly. Roger did not stop the animal sounds that were coming from him, did not speak. He only lifted his hand.

There, between his legs, was nothing. Nothing at all of penis, testicles, scrotum; nothing but the gleaming artificial flesh, with a transparent bandage over it, concealing the surgery lines. It was as if nothing had ever been there. Of the diagnostic signs of manhood . . . nothing. The tiny little operation was over, and what was left was nothing at all.

9

Dash Visits a Bedside

Don Kayman didn't like the timing, but he had no choice; he had to visit his tailor. Unfortunately, his tailor was in Merritt Island, Florida, at the Atlantic Test Center.

He flew there worried, and arrived worried. Not only at what had happened to Roger Torraway. That seemed to be under control, praise be to Divine Mercy, although Kayman couldn't help feeling that they had almost lost him and somebody had blundered badly in not preparing him for that last little bit of "minor cosmetic surgery." Probably, he thought charitably, it was because Brad had been ill. But surely they had come close to blowing the whole project.

The other thing he was fretting about was that he could not avoid the secret feeling of sin that seemed to be a realization that internally, in his heart of hearts, he wished the project *would* be blown. He had had a tearful hour with Sister Clotilda when the probability that he would go to Mars had firmed up into the cutting of orders. Should they marry first? No. No on pragmatic, practical reasons: although there was not much doubt that both could ask for and receive the dispensation from Rome, there was also not much hope that it would come through in less than six months.

If only they had applied earlier . . .

But they hadn't, and both of them knew that they were not willing to marry without it, or even to go to bed together without the sacrament. "At least," said Clotilda toward the end, attempting to smile, "you won't have to worry about my being unfaithful to you. If I wouldn't break my vows for you, I doubt I'd do it for any man."

"I wasn't worried," he said; but now, under the gleaming blue skies of Florida, staring up at the gantries that rose to reach for the fluffy white clouds, he was worrying. The Army colonel who had volunteered to show him around was aware that something was troubling Kayman, but he had no way of diagnosing the trouble.

"It's safe enough," he said, probing at random. "I wouldn't give a thought to the low-injection rendezvous orbit."

Kayman tore his attention away from his interior and said, "I promise you I wasn't. I don't even know what you mean."

"Oh. Well, it's just that we're putting your bird and the two support launches into a lower orbit than usual: two twenty kilometers instead of four hundred. It's political, of course. I hate it when the bureaucrats tell us what we have to do, but this time it doesn't really make a difference."

Kayman glanced at his watch. He still had an hour to kill before returning for his last fitting of Mars-suit and spacesuit, and he was not anxious to spend it fretting. He judged accurately that the colonel was one of those happy folk who like to talk about nothing as much as their work, and that all he need give would be an occasional grunt to keep the colonel explaining everything that could be explained. He gave the grunt.

"Well, Father Kayman," said the colonel expansively, "we're

giving you a big ship, you know. Too big to launch in one piece. So we're putting up three birds, and you'll meet in orbit—two twenty by two thirty-five, optimal, and I expect we'll be right on the money—and—"

Kayman nodded without really listening. He already knew the flight plan by heart; it was in the orders he had been given. The only open questions were who the remaining two occupants of the Mars bird would be, but it would only be a matter of days before that was decided. One would have to be a pilot to stay in orbit while the other three crowded into the Mars-lander and went down to the surface of the planet. The fourth man should, ideally, be someone who could function as back-up to pilot, areologist and cyborg; but of course no such person existed. It was time to make the decision, though. The three human beings—the three *unaltered* human beings, he corrected himself—would not have Roger's capacity for surviving naked on the surface of Mars. They would have to have the same fittings he was going through now, and then the final brush-up training in procedures that all of them would need, even Roger.

And launch time was only thirty-three days away.

The colonel had finished with the docking and reassembly maneuvers and was getting ready to outline the day-by-day calendar of events on all the long months to Mars. Kayman said, "Wait a minute, Colonel. I didn't quite get that about political considerations. What does that have to do with how we take off?"

The colonel grumbled resentfully, "Damn ecology freaks, they get everybody upset. These Texas Twin launch vehicles, they're big. About twenty times the thrust of a Saturn. So they make a lot of exhaust. It comes to something like twenty-five metric tons of water vapor a second, times three birds—a lot of water vapor. And admittedly there's some risk that the water vapor—well, no, let's be fair; we know damn well—excuse me, Father—that what all that water vapor would do at normal orbit-injection altitudes would be to knock out the free electrons in a big patch of sky. They found that way back in, let's see, I think it was '73 or '74, when they put the first Spacelab up. Knocked the free electrons out of a volume of atmosphere that stretched from Illinois to Labrador when it was measured. And of course that's what keeps you from getting sunburned. One of the things. They help filter out the solar UV. Skin cancer, sunburn, destruction of flora—well, they're all real; they *could* happen. But it's not our own people Dash is worried about! The NPA, that's what bugs him. They've given him an ultimatum that if your launch damages their sky they will consider it a 'hostile act.' Hostile act! What the hell do you call it when *they* parade five nuclear subs off Cape May, New Jersey? Claim it's oceanographic research, but you don't use cruiser-killer subs for oceanography, not in our Navy, anyway. . . .

"Anyway," the colonel said, bringing himself back to his guest and smiling, "it's okay. We'll just put you into rendezvous orbit a little lower down, out of the free-electron layer. Costs more fuel. Winds up making *more* pollution, the way I look at it. But it keeps their precious free electrons intact—not that there's any real chance they'd survive across the Atlantic into Africa even, much less Asia. . . ."

"You've been very interesting, Colonel," Kayman said courteously. "I think it's time for me to get back, though."

The fitters were ready for him. "Just slip into this for size." The physiotherapist member of the team grinned. "Slipping into" the spacesuit was twenty minutes of hard work, even if the whole team had been helping. Kayman insisted on doing it himself. In the spacecraft he wouldn't have any more help than the rest of the crew, who would be busy with their own affairs; and in an emergency he wouldn't have any help at all. He wanted to be ready for any emergency. It took an hour, and another ten minutes to get out of it after they'd checked all the parameters and pronounced everything fine; and then there were all the other garments to try.

It was dark outside, a warm Florida autumn night, before he was finished. He looked at the row of vestments laid out on the worktables and grinned. He pointed to the comm-antenna fabric that dangled from one wrist, the radiation cloak for use in solar-flare conditions, the body garment that went under the suits themselves. "You've got me all fixed up. That's the maniple, there's the chasuble, that's my alb. Couple more pieces and I'd be all ready to say Mass." Actually he had included a complete set of vestments in his weight allotment—it had seriously depleted the available reserve for books, music tapes and pictures of Sister Clotilda. But he was not prepared to discuss that with these worldly people. He stretched and sighed. "Where's a good place to eat around here?" he asked. "A steak, or maybe some of that red snapper you people talk about— and then bed—"

The Air Force MP who had been standing by for two hours, glancing at his watch, stepped forward and spoke up. "Sorry, Father," he said. "You're wanted elsewhere right now, and you're due in, let's see, about twenty minutes."

"Due where? I've got a long flight tomorrow—"

"I'm sorry, sir. My orders are to bring you to the Ad Building at Patrick Air Force Base. I expect they'll tell you what it's all about then."

The priest drew himself up. "Corporal," he said, "I'm not under your jurisdiction. I suggest you tell me what it is you want."

"No, sir," the MP agreed. "You're not. But my orders are to bring you, and with all due respect, sir, I will."

The physiotherapist touched Kayman's shoulder. "Go ahead, Don," he said. "I have a feeling you're in pretty high echelons right now."

Grumbling, Kayman allowed himself to be led out and put into a hoverjeep. The driver was in a hurry. He did not bother with the roads, but aimed the vehicle out toward the surf, judged his time and distance and skittered out onto the surface of the ocean between waves. Then he turned south and gunned it; in ten seconds they were doing at least a hundred and fifty kilometers an hour. Even on high-lift thrust, with three meters of air between them and the average height of the water, the rolling, twisting chop from the waves corkscrewing under them had Kayman swallowing saliva and looking for a throw-up bag against a rather possible need in no time at all. He tried to get the corporal to slow down. "Sorry, sir"; it was the MP's favorite expression, it seemed.

But they managed to reach the beach at Patrick before Kayman quite vomited, and back on land the driver slowed to reasonable speeds. Kayman tottered out and stood in the damp, lush night until two more MPs, radio-alerted to his coming, saluted and escorted him inside a white stucco building.

Before ten minutes had elapsed he was stripped to the skin and being searched, and he realized what high echelons he was indeed moving in.

The President's jet touched down at Patrick at 0400 hours. Kayman had been dozing on a beach chair with a throw rug over his legs; he was shaken courteously awake and led to the boarding steps while refueling tankers were topping off the wing tanks in peculiarly eerie silence. There was no conversation, no banging of bronze nozzles against aluminum filler caps, only the throbbing of the tank truck's pumps.

Somebody very important was asleep. Kayman wished with all his heart that he was too. He was conducted to a recliner chair, strapped in and left; and even before his WAC hostess had left his side the jet was picking its way to the takeoff strip.

He tried to doze, but while the jet was still climbing to cruise altitude the President's valet came back and said, "The President will see you now."

Sitting down and freshly shaved around his goatee, President Deshatine looked like a Gilbert Stuart painting of himself. He was at ease in a leather-backed chair, unfocused eyes peering out of the window of the presidential jet while he listened to some sort of tape through earphones. A full coffee cup was steaming next to his elbow, and an empty cup was waiting by the silver pot. Next to the cup was a slim box of purple leather embossed with a silver cross.

Dash didn't keep him waiting. He looked around, smiled, pulled off the earphones, and said, "Thank you for letting me kidnap you, Father Kayman. Sit down, please. Help yourself to coffee if you'd like it."

"Thanks." The valet sprang to pour and retired to stand behind Don Kayman. Kayman didn't look around; he knew that the valet would be watching every muscle tremor, and so he avoided sudden moves.

The President said, "I've been in so many time zones the last forty-eight hours that I've forgotten what the real world is like. Munich, Beirut, Rome. I picked up Vern Scanyon in

Rome when I heard about the trouble with Roger Torraway. Scared the shit out of me, Father. You almost lost him, didn't you?"

Kayman said, "I'm an areologist, Mr. President. It was not my responsibility."

"Cut it out, Father. I'm not assigning blame; there's plenty to go around, if it comes to that. I want to know what happened."

"I'm sure General Scanyon could tell you more than I can, Mr. President," Kayman said stiffly.

"If I wanted to settle for Vern's version," the President said patiently, "I wouldn't have stopped to pick you up. You were there. He wasn't. He was off in Rome at the Vatican Pacem in Excelsis Conference."

Kayman took a hasty sip from his coffee cup. "Well, it was close. I think he wasn't properly briefed for what was going to happen, because there was a flu epidemic, really. We were short of staff. Brad wasn't there."

"That has happened before," the President observed.

Kayman shrugged and did not pick up the lead. "They castrated him, Mr. President. What the sultans used to call a complete castration, penis and all. He doesn't need it, because there's so little consumable going into him now that it all gets excreted anally, so it was just a vulnerable spot. There's no question it had to come off, Mr. President."

"What about the—what do you call it—prostatectomy? Was that a vulnerable spot too?"

"You really should ask one of the doctors about this, Mr. President," Kayman said defensively.

"I'm asking you. Scanyon said something about 'priest's disease,' and you're a priest."

Kayman grinned. "That's an old expression, from the days when all priests were celibate. But, yes, I can tell you about it;

we talked about it a lot in the seminary. The prostate produces fluid—not much, a few drops a day. If a man doesn't have ejaculations, it mostly just passes out with the urine, but if he is sexually excited there's more and it doesn't all pass out. It backs up, and the congestion leads to trouble."

"So they cut out his prostate."

"And implanted a steroid capsule, Mr. President. He won't become effeminate. Physically, he's now a complete self-contained eunuch, and— Oh. I mean unit."

The President nodded. "That's what they call a Freudian slip."

Kayman shrugged.

"And if you think that way," the President pressed, "what the hell do you think Torraway thinks?"

"I know it's not easy for him, Mr. President."

"As I understand it," Dash went on, "you aren't just an areologist, Don, you're a marriage counselor, too. And not doing too well, right? That trampy little wife of his is giving our boy a hard time."

"Dorrie has a lot of problems."

"No, Dorrie has *one* problem. Same problem we all have. She's screwing up our Mars project, and we can't afford to have that happen. Can you straighten her out?"

"No."

"Well, I don't mean make her a perfect person. Cut it out, Don! I mean, can you get her to put his mind at rest, at least enough so he doesn't go into shock any more? Give him a kiss and a promise, send him a Valentine when he's on Mars—God knows Torraway doesn't expect any more than that. But he has a right to that much."

"I can try," said Kayman helplessly.

"And I'm going to have a few words with Brad," the President said grimly. "I've told you, I've told you all, *this project has to work.* I don't care about somebody's cold in the head or somebody else's hot pants, I want Torraway on Mars and I want him happy there."

The plane banked to change course away from the traffic around New Orleans, and a glint of morning sun shone up from the greasy oil-slick surface of the Gulf. The President squinted down at it angrily. "Let me tell you, Father Kayman, what I've been thinking. I've been thinking that Roger would be happier mourning over the death of his wife in a car smash than worrying about what she's doing when he's not around. I don't like thinking that way. But I have just so many options, Kayman, and I have to pick the one that's least bad. And now," he said, suddenly smiling, "I've got something for you, from His Holiness. It's a present; take a look at it."

Wondering, Kayman opened the purple box. It held a rosary, coiled on purple velvet inside the leather case. The Ave Marias were ivory, carved into rosebuds; the big Paternoster beads were chased crystal. "It has an interesting history," the President went on. "It was sent back to Ignatius Loyola from one of his missions in Japan, and then it was in South America for two hundred years with the—what do you call them?—the Reductions of Paraguay? It's a museum piece, really, but His Holiness wanted you to have it."

"I—I don't know what to say," Kayman managed.

"And it has his blessing." The President leaned back and suddenly looked a great deal older. "Pray with it, Father," he said. "I'm not a Catholic. I don't know how you feel about these things. But I want you to pray for Dorrie Torraway's getting her head straightened out enough to last her husband a while. And if that doesn't work, you'd better pray real hard for all of us."

Back in the main cabin, Kayman strapped himself in his seat and willed himself asleep for the remaining hour or so of the flight to Tonka. Exhaustion triumphed over worry, and he drifted off. He was not the only one worried. We had not properly estimated the trauma Roger Torraway would receive from the loss of his genitals, and we had nearly lost him.

The malfunction was critical. It could not be risked again. We had already arranged for beefed-up psychiatric attendance on Roger, and in Rochester the backpack computer was being recircuited to monitor major psychic stress and react before Roger's slower human synapses could oscillate into convulsions.

The world situation was proceeding as predicted. New York City was of course in turmoil, the Near East was building up pressures past the safety valves, and New People's Asia was pouring out furious manifestos denouncing the squid kill in the Pacific. The planet was rapidly reaching critical mass. Our projections were that the future of the race was questionable on Earth past another two years. We could not allow that. The Mars landing had to succeed.

When Roger came out of the haze after his seizure he did not realize how close he had come to dying, he only realized that he had been wounded in all of his most sensitive parts. The feeling was desolation: wiped-out, hopeless desolation. He not only had lost Dorrie, he had lost his manhood. The pain was too extreme to be relieved by crying, even if he had been able to cry. It was the agony of the dentist's chair without anesthesia, so acute that it no longer felt like a warning but became merely a fact of the environment, something to be experienced and endured.

The door opened, and a new nurse came in. "Hi. I see you're awake."

She came over and laid warm fingers on his forehead. "I'm Sulie Carpenter," she said. "It's Susan Lee, really, but Sulie's what they call me." She withdrew her hand and smiled. "You'd think I'd know better than feeling for fever, wouldn't you? I already know what it is from the monitors, but I guess I'm an old-fashioned girl."

Torraway hardly heard her; he was preoccupied with seeing her. Was it a trick of his mediation circuits? Tall, green-eyed, dark-haired: she looked so very much like Dorrie that he tried changing the field of vision of his great insect eyes, zooming down on the pores in her slightly freckled skin, altering the color values, decreasing the sensitivity so that she seemed to fade into a twilight. No matter. She still looked like Dorrie.

She moved to scan the duplicate monitors at the side of the room. "You're doing real well, Colonel Torraway," she called over her shoulder. "I'm going to bring you your lunch in a little while. Anything you want now?"

He roused himself and sat up. "Nothing I can have," he said bitterly.

"Oh, no, Colonel!" Her eyes showed shock. "I mean—well, excuse me. I don't have any right to talk to you like that. But, dear Lord, Colonel, if there's anybody in this world who can have anything he wants, you're it!"

"I wish I felt that way," he grumbled; but he was watching her closely and curiously, he did feel something—something he could not identify, but something which was not the pain that had overwhelmed him only moments before.

Sulie Carpenter glanced at her watch and then pulled up a chair. "You sound low, Colonel," she said sympathetically. "I guess all this is pretty hard to take."

He looked away from her, up to where the great black wings

were rippling slowly over his head. He said, "It has its bad parts, believe me. But I knew what I was getting into."

Sulie nodded. She said, "I had a bad time when my—my boyfriend died. Of course, that's nothing like what you're doing. But in a way maybe it was worse—you know, it was so *pointless*. One day we were fine and talking about getting married. The next day he came back from the doctor's and those headaches he'd been having turned out to be—" She took a deep breath. "Brain tumor. Malignant. He was dead three months later, and I just couldn't handle it. I had to get away from Oakland. I applied to be transferred here. Never thought I'd get it, but I guess they're still shorthanded from the flu—"

"I'm sorry," Roger said quickly.

She smiled. "It's all right," she said. "It's just that there was a big empty place in my life, and I'm really grateful I've got something to fill it here." She glanced again at her watch and jumped up. "The floor nurse'll be on my back," she said. "Now, listen, really, is there anything I can get for you? Book? Music? You've got the world at your command, you know, including me."

"Not a thing," Roger said honestly. "Thanks anyway. How come you picked coming here?"

She looked at him thoughtfully, the corners of her lips curving very faintly. "Well," she said, "I knew something about the program here; I've been in aerospace medicine for ten years in California. And I knew who you were, Colonel Torraway. Knew! I used to have your picture on my wall when you were rescuing those Russians. You wouldn't believe the active role you played in some of my fantasies, Colonel Torraway, sir."

She grinned and turned away, stopping at the door. "Do me a favor, will you?"

Roger was surprised. "Sure. What?"

"Well, I'd like a more recent picture. You know what security is like here. If I sneak in a camera, can I take a quick snapshot of you now? Just so I can have something to show my grandchildren, if I ever have any."

Roger protested, "They'll kill you if they catch you, Sulie."

She winked. "I'll take my chances; it's worth it. Thanks."

After she had gone Roger made an effort to go back to thinking about his castration and his cuckolding, but for some reason they seemed less overwhelming. Nor did he have a great deal of time. Sulie came in with a low-residue lunch, a smile and a promise to be back the following morning. Clara Bly gave him an enema, and then he lay wondering while three identical fair-mustached men came in and went over every inch of floor, wall and furniture with metal detectors and electronic mops. They were total strangers, and they stayed in the room, on new-brought chairs, silent and watching, while Brad came in.

Brad was looking not merely ill but seriously worried. "Hi, Roger," he said. "Jesus, you scared us. It's my fault; I should have been on tap, but this damn flu bug—"

"I survived," Roger said, studying Brad's rather ordinary face and wondering just why he wasn't feeling outrage and resentment.

"We're going to have to keep you pretty busy now," Brad began, dragging up a chair. "We've phased out some of your mediation circuits for the moment. When they're full in again we're going to have to limit your sensory inputs—let you work up to handling a total environment a little at a time. And Kathleen's jumping to get you started on retraining—you know, learning how to use your muscles and all that." He glanced over at the three silent watchers. His expression, Roger thought, was suddenly full of fear.

"I guess I'm ready," Roger said.

"Oh, sure. I know you are," said Brad, surprised. "Haven't they been giving you updates on your readouts? You're functioning like a seventeen-jewel watch, Roger. All the surgery is over now. You've got everything you need." He sat back, studying Roger. "If I do say so"—he grinned—"you're a work of art, Roger, and I'm the artist. I just wish I could see you on Mars. That's where you belong, boy."

One of the watchers cleared his throat. "It's getting toward that time, Dr. Bradley," he said.

The worried look returned to Brad's face. "Coming right away. Take care, Rog. I'll be back to see you later."

He left, and the three government agents followed him, as Clara Bly came in and fussed around the room.

A mystery was suddenly clear. "Dash is coming to see me," Roger guessed.

"Smart!" sniffed Clara. "Well, I guess it's all right for you to know. It wasn't all right for me to know. They think it's a secret. But what kind of secret is it when they turn the whole hospital upside down? They've had those guys all over the place since before I came on duty."

"When will he get here?" Roger asked.

"That's the part that is a secret. From me, anyway."

But it did not stay a secret very long; within the hour, to an unheard but strongly felt "Hail to the Chief," the President of the United States came into the room. With him was the same valet he had had on the presidential jet, but this time he was obviously not a valet, only a bodyguard.

"Marvelous to see you again," said the President, holding out his hand. He had never seen the revised and edited version of the astronaut before, and certainly the dully gleaming flesh, the great faceted eyes, the hovering wings must have looked strange, but what showed in the President's well-disciplined face was only friendship and pleasure. "I stopped off a little while ago to say hello to your good wife, Dorrie. I hope she's forgiven me for messing up her fingernail polish last month; I forgot to ask. But how are you feeling?"

How Roger was feeling was once again amazed at the thoroughness of the President's briefing, but what he said was, "Fine, Mr. President."

The President inclined his head toward the bodyguard without looking at him. "John, have you got that little package for Colonel Torraway? It's something Dorrie asked me to bring over to you; you can open it when we've gone." The bodyguard placed a white-paper package on Roger's bedside table and slid a chair over for the President in almost the same motion, just as the President was preparing to sit down. "Roger," said the President, sharpening the creases in his Bermudas, "I know I can be honest with you. You're all we've got now, and we need you. The indices are looking worse every day. The Asians are spoiling for trouble, and I don't know how long I can keep from giving it to them. We have to get you to Mars, and you have to function when you get there. I can't overestimate the importance of it."

Roger said, "I think I understand that, sir."

"Well, in a way, I guess you do. But do you understand it in your gut? Do you really feel, deep down, that you're that one man, maybe two, in a generation who somehow or other gets himself in a position that's so important to the whole human race that even inside his own mind what happens to him doesn't measure up in importance? That's where you are, Roger. I know," the President went on sorrowfully, "that they've taken some mighty sacrificial liberties with your person. Didn't give you a chance to say yes, no or maybe. Didn't even tell you. It's a piss-poor way to treat any human being, let alone somebody who means as much as you do—and somebody who deserves as well as you do, too. I've kicked a bunch of asses around here about that. I'll be glad to kick a lot more. If you want it done, tell me. Any time. It's better if I do it than you—with those steel muscles they've given you, you might damage a few of those pretty behinds on the nurses past the point of repair. Do you mind if I smoke?"

"What? Oh, hell, no, Mr. President."

"Thanks." The valet had an open cigarette case in one hand and a glowing lighter in the other as soon as the President stretched out his hand. He took a deep draw and leaned back. "Roger," he said, "let me tell you my fantasy about what I think is in your mind. You're thinking, 'Here's old Dash, politician to the end, full of bullshit and promises, trying to trick me into pulling his chestnuts out of the fire. He'd say anything, he'd promise anything. All he wants is what he can get out of me.' Anywhere near right, so far?"

"Why—no, Mr. President! Well . . . a little bit."

The President nodded. "You'd be crazy if you didn't think a little bit of that," he said matter-of-factly. "It's all true, you know. Up to a point. It's true I'd promise you anything, tell you any lies I could think of to get you to Mars. But the other thing that's true is that you have us all by the genital organs, Roger. We *need* you. There's a war coming if we don't do something to stop it, and it's crazy but the trend projections say the only thing that can stop it is putting you on Mars. Don't ask me why. I just go by what the technical people tell me, and they claim that's what the computers print out."

Roger's wings were stirring restlessly, but the eyes were intent on the President.

"So you see," said the President heavily, "I'm appointing myself your hired hand, Roger. You tell me what you want. I'll make damn sure you get it. You pick up that phone any time, day or night. They'll put you through to me. If I'm asleep, you can wake me if you want to. If it can wait, you can leave a message. There's going to be no more fucking you around in this place, and if you even think it's happening you tell me and I'll stop it. Christ," he said, grinning as he started to stand up, "do you know what the history books are going to say about me? 'Fitz-James Deshatine, 1943–2026, forty-second President of the United States. During his administration the human race established its first self-sustaining colony on another planet.' That's what I'll get, Roger, if I get that much—and you're the only one who can give it to me.

"Well," he said, moving toward the door, "there's a governor's conference waiting for me in Palm Springs. They expected me six hours ago, but I figured you mattered a hell of a lot more than they did. Kiss Dorrie for me. And call me. If you don't have anything to complain about, call me to say hello. Any time."

And he left, with a dazzled astronaut staring after him.

Take it any way you liked, Roger reflected, it was really a pretty spectacular performance, and it left him feeling both awed and pleased. Subtracting 99 percent of it as bullshit, what was left was highly gratifying.

The door opened, and Sulie Carpenter came in, looking faintly scared. She was carrying a framed photograph. "I didn't know what kind of company you were moving in," she said. "Do you want this?"

It was a picture of the President, signed, "For Roger from his admirer, Dash."

"I guess I do," said Roger. "Can you hang it up?"

"When it's a picture of Dash, you can," she said. "It has a self-hanging gadget. Right up here?" She pressed it against the wall near the door and stepped back to admire it. Then she looked around, winked and pulled a flat black camera the size of a cigarette pack out of her apron. "Smile at the birdie," she said, and snapped away. "You won't rat on me? Okay. I've got to be going—I'm not on duty now, but I wanted to look in on you."

Roger leaned back and folded his hands on his chest. Things were turning out rather interestingly. He had not forgotten the internal pain of the discovery of his castration, and he had not put Dorrie out of his mind. But neither was perceived as pain any more. There were too many newer, more pleasant thoughts overlaying them.

Thinking of Dorrie reminded him of her gift. He opened it. It was a ceramic cup in harvest colors, ornamented with a cornucopia of fruits. The card said, "This is a way of telling you that I love you." And it was signed *Dorrie.*

All of Torraway's signs were stable now, and we were getting ready to phase in the mediation circuits.

This time Roger was well briefed. Brad was with him every hour—after taking a large share of the President's ass-kicking, he was chastened and diligent. We deployed one task force to oversee the phasing-in of the mediation circuits, another to buffer the readout-readin of data from the 3070 in Tonka to the new backpack computer in Rochester, New York. Texas and Oklahoma were going through one of their periodic brownouts just then, which complicated all machine data handling, and the aftereffects of the flu were still with the human beings on the staff. We were definitely short-handed.

Moreover, we needed still more. The backpack computer was rated at 99.999999999 percent reliable in every component, but there were something like 10^8 components. There was a lot of backup, and a full panoply of cross-input paths so that failure of even three or four major subsystems would leave enough capacity to keep Roger going. But that wasn't good enough. Analysis showed that there was one chance in ten of critical-path failure within half a Martian year.

So the decision was made to construct, launch and orbit around Mars a full-size 3070, replicating all the functions of the backpack computer in triplicate. It would not be as good as the backpack. If the backpack experienced total failure, Roger would have the use of the orbiter only 50 percent of the time—when it was above the horizon in its orbit and thus could interlink with him by radio. There would be a worst-case lag of a hundredth of a second, which was tolerable. Also he would have to stay in the open, or linked with an external antenna otherwise.

There was another reason for the back-up orbiter, and that was the high risk of glitches. Both the orbiting 3070 and the backpack were heavily shielded. Nevertheless they would pass through the Van Allen belts at launch, and the solar wind all through their flight. By the time they got to the vicinity of Mars the solar wind would be at a low enough level to be bearable—except in the case of flares. The charged particles of a flare could easily bug enough of the stored data in either computer to critically damage its function. The backpack computer would be helpless to defend itself. The 3070, on the other hand, had enough reserve capacity for continuous internal monitoring and repair. In idle moments—and it would have many idle moments, as much as 90 percent of its function time even when in use by Roger—it would compare data in each of its triplicate arrays. If any datum differed from the same datum in the other arrays it would check for compatibility with the surround data; if all data were compatible, it would examine all three arrays and make the one aberrant bit conform with the other two. If two did not conform, it would check against the backpack if possible.

That was all the redundancy we could afford, but it was quite a lot. On the whole, we were very pleased.

To be sure, the orbiting 3070 would require a good deal of

power. We calculated the probably maximum draw against the probable worst-case supply of any reasonable set of solar panels, and concluded that the margin was too thin. So Raytheon got a preempt order for one of its MHD generators, and crews went to work on Route 128 to modify it for space launch and automatic operation in orbit around Mars. When the 3070 and the MHD generator arrived in orbit they would lock to each other. The generator would supply all the power the computer needed, and have enough left over to microwave a useful surplus down to Roger on the surface of Mars, which he could use both to power his own machine parts as needed or for whatever power-using equipment he might like to install.

Once we had completed all the plans we could hardly see how we had thought we could get along without them in the first place. Those were happy days! We requested, and were promptly given, all the reinforcements we needed. Tulsa went without lights two nights a week so we could have the energy reserves we needed, and Jet Propulsion Laboratories lost their entire space-medicine staff to our project.

The read-in of data proceeded. Glitches chased themselves merrily around both new computers, the backpack in Rochester and the duplicate 3070 that had been rushed to Merritt Island. But we hunted them down, isolated them, corrected them and were keeping right on schedule.

The world outside, of course, was not as pleasant.

Using a home-made plutonium bomb made out of materials hijacked from the breeder reactor at Carmarthen, Welsh nationalists had blown up the Hyde Park Barracks and most of Knightsbridge. In California the Cascade Mountains were burning out of control, the fire-fighting helicopters grounded because of the fuel shortage. An exploding epidemic of smallpox had depopulated Poona and was already out of control in

Bombay; cases were being reported from Madras to Delhi as those who were able fled the plague. The Australians had declared Condition Red mobilization, the NPA had called for an emergency meeting of the U.N. Security Council, and Capetown was under siege.

All of this was as the graphs had predicted. We were aware of all of it. We continued with our work. When one of the nurses or technicians took time to worry, he had the President's orders to reassure him. On every bulletin board, and placarded in most of the workrooms, was a quote from Dash:

> *You take care of Roger Torraway, and I'll take*
> *care of the rest of the world.*
>
> *Fitz-James Deshatine*

We didn't need the reassurance, we knew how important the work was. The survival of our race depended on it. Compared to that, nothing else mattered.

Roger woke up in total blackness.

He had been dreaming, and for a moment the dream and the reality were queerly fused. The dream had been of a long time ago, when he and Dorrie and Brad had driven down to Lake Texoma with a few friends who owned a sailboat, and in the evening they had sung to Brad's guitar while the huge moon rose over the water. He thought he heard Brad's voice again . . . but he listened more closely, his brain clearing from sleep, and there was nothing.

There was nothing. *That* was strange. No sound at all, not even the purrs and clicks of the telemetry monitors along the wall, not even a whisper from the hall outside. However much he tried, with all the enhanced sensitivity of his new ears, there was no sound at all. Nor was there light. Not in any color, not anywhere, except for the dullest of dim red glows from his own body, and a glow equally dull from the baseboards of the room.

He moved restlessly, and discovered he was tethered to the bed.

For a moment terror flooded through his mind: trapped, helpless, alone. Had they turned him off? Were his senses deliberately blacked out? What was happening?

A small voice near his ear spoke again: "Roger? This is Brad. Your readouts say you're awake."

The relief was overpowering. "Yes," he managed. "What's going on?"

"We've got you in a sensory-deprivation environment. Apart from my voice, can you hear anything?"

"Not a sound," said Roger. "Not *anything*."

"How about light?"

Roger reported the dim heat glow. "That's all."

"Fine," said Brad. "Now, here's the thing, Roger. We're going to let you work in your new sensorium a little bit at a time. Simple sounds. Simple patterns. We've got a slide projector through the wall over the head of your bed, and a screen by the door—you can't see it, of course, but it's there. What we're going to do—wait a minute. Kathleen's determined to talk to you."

Faint friction sounds and scuffles, and then Kathleen Doughty's voice: "Roger, this shithead forgot one important thing. Sensory deprivation's dangerous, you know that."

"I've heard it," Roger admitted.

"According to the experts the worst part of it is feeling impotent to end it. So any time you begin to feel bad, just talk; one of us will always be here, and we'll answer. It'll be Brad, or me, or Sulie Carpenter, or Clara."

"Are you all there right now?"

"Christ, yes—plus Don Kayman and General Scanyon and, cripes, half the staff. You won't lack for company, Roger. I promise you that. Now. What about my voice, is that giving you any trouble?"

He thought. "Not that I notice. You do sound a little bit like a creaking door," he evaluated.

"That's bad."

"I don't think so. You sound kind of that way all the time, Kathleen."

She giggled. "Well, I'm going to stop talking in a minute anyway. What about Brad's voice?"

"I didn't notice anything. Or anyway, I'm not sure. I was sort of dreaming and for a minute I thought he was singing 'Aura Lee' along with his guitar."

Brad cut in. "That's *interesting*, Roger! What about now?"

"No. You sound like yourself."

"Well, your readouts look good. All right. We'll go into that later. Now, what we're going to do is give you pure, simple visual inputs to deal with. As Kathleen says, you can speak to us any time and we'll answer if you want us to. But we won't speak much for a while. Let the visual circuits work themselves in before we confuse things with simultaneous sight and sound, got it?"

"Go ahead," said Roger.

There was no answer, but in a moment a pale point of light appeared against the far wall.

It was not bright. With the eyes he had been born with, Roger suspected, he would not have been able to see it at all; as it was, he could make it out clearly, and even in the filtered air of his hospital room, he could see the faint path of light from projector to wall over his head.

Nothing else happened for a long time.

Roger waited as patiently as he could.

More time passed.

Finally he said, "All right, I see it. It's a dot. I've been watching it all along, and it's still just a dot. I do observe," he said, turning his head about, "that there's enough reflected light from it that I can see the rest of the room a little bit, but that's all."

When Brad's voice came, it sounded like thunder: "Okay, Roger, hold on and we'll give you something else."

"Wow!" Roger said. "Not so loud, okay?"

"I wasn't any louder than before," Brad objected. And in fact his voice had reduced itself to normal proportions.

"Okay, okay," Roger muttered. He was getting bored. After a moment another point of light appeared, a few inches from the first one. Both held for another long time, and then a line of light leaped into being between them.

"This is pretty dull," he complained.

"It's meant to be." It was Clara Bly's voice this time.

"Hi," Roger greeted her. "Listen. I can see pretty well now, in all this light you're giving me. What are all these wires sticking into me?"

Brad cut in: "They're your telemetry, Roger. That's why we had to tie you down, so you wouldn't roll over and mess up the leads. Everything's on remote now, you know. We had to take almost everything out of your room."

"So I noticed. All right, go ahead."

But it was tedious and remained tedious. These were not the kinds of things that were calculated to keep one's mind busy. They might be important, but they were also dull. After an interminable stretch of simple geometric figures of light, the intensity reduced so that there was less and less spill of reflection to illuminate the rest of the room, they began feeding him sounds: clicks, oscillator beeps, a chime, a hiss of white noise.

In the room outside the shifts kept changing. They stopped only when the telemetry indicated Roger needed sleep or food or a bedpan. None of those needs were frequent. Roger began to be able to tell who was on duty from the tiniest of signs: the faintly mocking note in Brad's voice that was only there when Kathleen Doughty was in the room, the slower, somehow more affectionate chirping of the sound tapes when Sulie Carpenter was monitoring the responses. He discovered that his time sense was not the same as that of those outside, or of "reality," whatever that was. "That's to be expected, Rog," said the weary voice of Brad when he reported it. "If you work at it, you'll find you can exercise volitional control over that. You can count out seconds like a metronome if you want to. Or move faster or slower, depending on what's needed."

"How do I do that?" Roger demanded.

"Hell, man!" Brad flared. "It's your body, learn to use it." Then, apologetically, "The same way you learned to block off vision. Experiment till you figure it out. Now pay attention; I'm going to play you a Bach partita."

Somehow the time passed.

But not easily and not quickly. There were long periods when Roger's altered time sense contrarily dragged his tedium out, times when, against his will, he found himself thinking again about Dorrie. The lift that Dash's visit had given him, the pleasant concern and affection from Sulie Carpenter—these were good things; but they did not last forever. Dorrie was a reality of his reverie, and when his mind was empty enough to wander it was to Dorrie that it wandered. Dorrie and their joyous early years together. Dorrie, and the terrible knowledge that he was

no longer enough of a man to gratify her sexual needs. Dorrie
and Brad . . .

Kathleen Doughty's voice snapped, "I don't know what the
hell you're doing, Roger, but it's screwing up your vital signs!
Cut it out."

"All right," he grumbled. He put Dorrie out of his mind. He
thought of Kathleen's rancorous, affectionate voice, of what the
President had said, of Sulie Carpenter. He made himself tranquil.

As a reward they showed him a slide of a bunch of violets, in
full color.

10

The Batman's Entrechats

Suddenly, amazingly, there were only nine days left.

Outside the clerical condominium Father Kayman shivered in the cold, waiting for his ride to the project. The fuel shortage had worsened a great deal in the past two weeks, with the fighting in the Middle East and the Scottish Freedom Fighters blowing up the North Sea pipelines. The project itself had overriding priorities for whatever it needed even though some of the missile silos had not enough fuel for topping off their birds; but all the staff had been urged to turn off lights, share rides, turn down their home thermostats, watch less TV. An early snowstorm had dusted the Oklahoma prairies, and outside the condominium a seminary student was sleepily pushing the snow off the walks. There was not much of it, and, Kayman thought, it was not particularly nice-looking. Was it his imagination, or was it tattletale gray? Could the ash from the blazing California and Oregon forests have soiled the snow fifteen hundred miles away?

Brad beeped his horn, and Kayman jumped. "Sorry," Kayman said, getting in and closing the door. "Say, shouldn't we take my car next time? Uses a lot less fuel than this thing of yours."

Brad shrugged morosely and peered into his rearview mirror. Another hovercar, this one a light, fast sports job, was swinging around the corner after them. "I drive for two anyway," he said. "That's the same one that was tailing me on Tuesday. They're getting sloppy. Or else they want to make sure I know I'm being followed."

Kayman looked over his shoulder. The following car was certainly taking no pains to be inconspicuous. "Do you know who it is, Brad?"

"Is there any doubt?"

Kayman didn't answer. Actually, there wasn't. The President had made clear to Brad that he was not under any circumstances to fool around with the monster's wife, in a half-hour interview of which Brad vividly recalled every painful second. The shadowing had begun immediately thereafter, to make sure Brad didn't forget.

But it was not a subject that Kayman wanted to discuss with Brad. He turned on the radio, tuned to a news broadcast. They listened for a few minutes of censored but still overpowering disaster until Brad wordlessly reached out and snapped it off. Then they rode in silence, under the leaden sky, until they reached the great white cube of the project, alone on the desolate prairie.

Inside there was nothing gray: the lights were strong and glaring; the faces were tired, sometimes concerned, but they were alive. In here at least, Kayman thought, there was a sense of accomplishment and purpose. The project was right on schedule.

And in nine days the Mars craft would be launched, and he himself would be on it.

Kayman was not afraid to go. He had shaped his life toward it, from the first days in the seminary when he had realized that he could serve his God in more places than a pulpit and was encouraged by his father superior to continue his interest in all heavens, whether astrophysical or theological. Nevertheless, it was a weighty thought.

He felt unready. He felt the world was unready for this venture. It all seemed so curiously impromptu, in spite of the eternities of work that they had put in, himself included. Even the crew was not finally decided. Roger would go; he was the raison d'être of the whole project, of course. Kayman would go, that had been decided firmly. But the two pilots were still only provisional. Kayman had met them both and liked them. They were among NASA's best, the one had flown with Roger in a shuttle mission eight years before. But there were fifteen others on the short list of eligibles—Kayman did not even know all the names, only that there were a lot of them. Vern Scanyon and the director general of NASA had flown to reason with the President in person, urging him to confirm their choices; but Dash, for Dash's own reasons, had reserved the right of final decision to himself, and was withholding his hand.

The one thing that seemed fully ready for the venture was the link in the chain that had once seemed most doubtful, Roger himself.

The training had gone beautifully. Roger was fully mobile now, all over the project building, commuting from the room he still kept as "home" to the Mars-normal tank, to the test facilities, to any place he cared to go. The whole project was used to seeing the tall black-winged creature loping down a hall, the huge, faceted eyes recognizing a face and the flat voice calling a cheery greeting. The last week and more had been all Kathleen Doughty's. His sensorium appeared under perfect control; now it was time to learn to exploit all the resources of his musculature. So she had brought in a blind man, a ballet dancer and a former paraplegic, and as Roger began to expand his horizons they took over his tutorial tasks. The ballet dancer was past stardom now, but he had known it, and as a child he had studied with Nureyev and Dolin. The blind man was no longer blind. He had no eyes, but his optic system had been replaced with sensors very like Roger's own, and the two of them compared notes over subtle hues and tricks of manipulating the parameters of their vision. The paraplegic, who now moved on motorized limbs that were precursors of Roger's, had had a year to learn to use them, and he and Roger took ballet classes together.

Not always physically together, not quite. The ex-paraplegic, whose name was Alfred, was still far more human than Roger Torraway, and among other human traits he possessed was a need for air. As Kayman and Brad came into the control chamber for the Mars-normal tank, Alfred was doing entrechats on one side of the great double glass pane and Roger, inside the almost airless tank, was duplicating his moves on the other. Kathleen Doughty was counting cadence, and the loud-speaker system was playing the A-major waltz from *Les Sylphides*. Vern Scanyon was sitting over by a wall on a reversed chair, hands clasped over the back of the chair and chin resting on his hands. Brad went over to him at once, and the two of them began to talk inaudibly.

Don Kayman found a place to sit near the door. Paraplegic and monster, they were doing incredibly rapid leaps, twiddling their feet in blurs of motion. It was not the right music for entrechats, Kayman thought, but neither of them seemed to care. The ballet dancer was staring at them with an unreadable expression. He probably wishes he were a cyborg, Kayman thought. With muscles like that he could take over any stage in the country.

It was a mildly amusing thought, but for some reason Kayman

felt ill-at-ease. Then he remembered: this was just where he had been sitting when Willy Hartnett had died before his eyes.

It seemed so long ago. It had only been a week since Brenda Hartnett had brought the kids around to say goodbye to him and Sister Clotilda, but she had almost dropped out of their minds already. The monster named Roger was the star of the show now. The death of another monster in that place, so short a time ago, was only history.

Kayman took up his rosary and began to count the fifteen decades of the Blessed Virgin. While one part of him was repeating the Aves, another was conscious of the pleasant, warm, heavy feel of the ivory beads and the crisp contrast of the crystal. He had made up his mind to take the Holy Father's gift to Mars with him. It would be a pity if it were lost—well, it would be a pity if *he* were lost too, he thought. He could not weigh risks like that, so he decided to do what His Holiness had evidently meant him to do and take this gift on the longest journey it had ever known.

He became conscious of someone standing behind him. "Good morning, Father Kayman."

"Hello, Sulie." He glanced at her curiously. What was strange about her? There seemed to be golden roots to her dark hair, but that was nothing particularly surprising; even a priest knew that women chose their hair color at will. For that matter, so did some priests.

"How's it going?" she asked.

"I'd say perfect. Look at them jump! Roger looks as ready as he'll ever be and, *Deo volente,* I think we'll make the launch date."

"I envy you," the nurse said, peering past him into the Mars-normal tank. He turned his face to her, startled. There had been more feeling in her voice than a casual remark seemed to justify. "I mean it, Don," she said. "The reason I got into the space program in the first place was that I wanted to go up myself. Might have made it if—"

She stopped and shrugged. "Well, I'm helping you and Roger, I guess," she said. "Isn't that what they used to say women were for? Helpmates. It isn't a bad thing, anyway, when it's as important a thing to help as this."

"You don't really sound convinced of that," Kayman offered.

She grinned and then turned back to the tank.

The music had stopped. Kathleen Doughty took the cigarette out of her lips, lit another and said, "Okay, Roger, Alfred. Take ten. You're doing great."

Inside the tank Roger allowed himself to sit cross-legged. He looked exactly like the Devil squatting on a hilltop in the classical old Disney tape, Kayman thought. *A Night on Bald Mountain?*

"What's the matter, Roger?" Kathleen Doughty called. "You're surely not tired."

"Tired of this, anyway," he groused. "I don't know why I need all this ballet-dancing. Willy didn't have it."

"Willy died," she snapped.

There was a silence. Roger turned his head toward her, peering through the glass with his great compound eyes. He snarled, "Not because of lack of entrechats."

"How do you know that? Oh," she admitted grudgingly, "I suppose you could survive without some of this. But you're better with it. It's not just a matter of learning how to get around. The other thing you have to learn to do is avoid destroying your environment. Do you have any idea how strong you are now?"

Inside the tank Roger hesitated, then shook his head. "I don't feel strong, particularly," his flat voice said.

"You can punch through a wall, Roger. Ask Alfred. What do you run the metric mile in, Alfred?"

The ex-paraplegic folded his hands over his fat belly and grinned. He was fifty-eight years old and had not been much of an athlete even before the myasthenia gravis destroyed his natural limbs. "A minute forty-seven," he said with pride.

"I expect you to do better than that, Roger," called Kathleen. "So you have to learn how to control it."

Roger made a noise that wasn't quite a word, then stood up. "Balance the locks," he said. "I'm coming out."

The technician touched a switch and the great pumps began to let air into the exit chamber with a sound like ripping linoleum. "Oh," moaned Sulie Carpenter, next to Don Kayman, "I don't have my contacts in!" And she fled before Roger could come into the room.

Kayman stared after her. One puzzle was solved: he knew what had looked strange about her. But why would Sulie wear contacts that changed her brown eyes to green?

He shrugged and gave up.

We knew the answer. We had gone to a lot of trouble to find Sulie Carpenter. The critical factors made a long list, and the least important of the items on that list were the color of hair and the color of eyes, since either could be so easily changed.

As the deadline approached, Roger's position began to change. For two weeks he had been meat on a butcher's block, slashed and rolled and chopped with no personal participation and no control over what happened to him. Then he had been a student, following the orders of his teachers, learning the control of his senses and the use of his limbs. It was a transition from laboratory preparation to demigod, and he was more than halfway there.

He felt it happening. For days now he had been questioning

everything he was told to do and sometimes refusing, Kathleen Doughty was no longer his boss, capable of ordering him to do a hundred chinups and an hour of pirouettes. She was his employee, retained by him to help in what he wanted to do. Brad, who had become far less offhandedly humorous and far more intense, was now asking Roger for favors: "Try these color discrimination tests for me, will you? It'll look good on my paper about you." Often Roger humored them, but sometimes not.

The one he humored most frequently and surely was Sulie Carpenter, because she was always there and always cared about him. He had almost forgotten how much she looked like Dorrie. He only was aware that she looked very good.

She met his moods. If he was edgy she was quietly cheerful. If he wanted to talk, she talked. They played board games sometimes; she was a highly competitive Scrabble player. Once, late at night, when Roger was experimenting with the length of wakefulness he could handle, she brought in a guitar and they sang, her pleasant, unobtrusive contralto ornamenting his flat and almost toneless whisper. Her face changed while he looked at it, but he had learned to handle that. The interpretation circuits in his sensorium reflected his feelings when he let them, and there were times when Sulie Carpenter looked more like Dorrie than Dorrie did herself.

After he had finished his day's run in the Mars-normal tank, Sulie raced him back to his room, laughing girl against thudding monster down the wide lab corridors; he won easily, of course. They chatted for a while and then he sent her away.

Nine days to liftoff.

It was less than that, really. He would be flown to Merritt Island three days before the launch, and his last day in Tonka would be devoted to fitting the backpack computer and retuning some of his sensorium for the special Martian conditions. So he had six—no, five—days.

And he had not seen Dorrie for weeks.

He looked at himself in the mirror he had demanded they install: insect eyes, bat wings, dully gleaming flesh. He amused himself by letting his visual interpretations flow, from bat to giant fly to demon . . . to himself, as he remembered himself, pleasant-faced and youthful.

If only Dorrie had a computer to mediate her sight! If only she could see him as he had been! He swore he would not call her; he could not force her to look at the comic-strip contraption that was her husband.

Having sworn, he picked up the phone and dialed her number.

It was an impulse that could not be denied. He waited. His accordion-pleated time sense prolonged the interval, so that it was an eternity before the raster blaze from the screen and the buzz from the speaker sounded the first ring.

Then time betrayed him again. It seemed forever until the second ring. Then it came, and lasted an eternity, and was over.

She did not answer.

Roger, who was the sort of person who counted things, knew that most persons did not respond until the third ring. Dorrie, however, was always eager to know who the phone was bringing into her life. From a sound sleep or out of the bathtub, she seldom let it ring past twice.

At length the third ring came, and still no reply.

Roger began to hurt.

He controlled it as best he could, unwilling to sound the alarms on the telemetry. He could not stop it entirely. She was out, he thought. Her husband had turned into a monster and she was not at home sympathizing or worrying; she was shopping or visiting a friend or seeing a flick.

Or with a man.

What man? Brad, he thought. It wouldn't be impossible; he had left Brad down at the tank twenty-five minutes ago by the clock. Time enough for them to rendezvous somewhere. Even time enough for Brad to get to the Torraway home. Perhaps she was not out at all. Perhaps—

Fourth ring—

Perhaps they were there, the two of them, naked and coupling on the floor in front of the phone. She would be saying, "Go in the other room, honey, I want to see who it is." And he would say, laughing, "No, let's answer this way." And she would say—

Fifth ring—and the raster blossomed into the colors of Dorrie's face. Her voice said, "Hello?"

Quick as sound Roger's fist shot out and covered the lens. "Dorrie," he said. His voice sounded flat and harsh again to him. "How are you?"

"Roger!" she cried. The pleasure in her voice sounded very real. "Oh, honey, I'm so glad to hear you! How are you feeling?"

His voice automatically said, "Fine." It went on, without the need of help from his conscious mind, to correct the statement, to say what had been happening to him, cataloging the tests and the exercises. At the same time he was staring into the screen with every sense on high gain.

She looked—what? Tired? Looking tired was confirmation of his fears. She was carousing with Brad every night, heedless of her husband in pain and clownish humiliation. Rested and cheerful? Looking rested and cheerful was confirmation, too. It meant she was relaxing, enjoying herself—heedless of her husband's torment.

There was really nothing wrong with Torraway's brain, in that it had a lifelong habit of analysis and logic. It did not fail to occur to him that the game he was playing with himself was called "You Lose." *Everything* was evidence of Dorrie's guilt. Yet no matter how carefully he scanned her image, with what multiplied senses, she didn't look hostile or cloyingly overaffectionate. She only looked like Dorrie.

When he thought that he felt a burst of tenderness that made his voice break. "I've missed you, honey," he said flatly. The only thing that spoke of feelings was that one syllable was retarded a fraction of a second: "Hon . . . ee."

"And I've missed you. I've kept myself busy, dear," she chattered. "I've been painting your den. It's a surprise, but of course it's going to be such a long time till you see it that— Well, it's going to be peach. With buttercup woodwork and I think maybe a pale-blue ceiling. You like? I was going to make it all ochre and brown, you know, fall colors, Mars colors, to celebrate. But I thought by the time you got back you'd be pretty sick of Mars colors!" And quickly, without pause: "When am I going to see you?" The change in her voice caught him by surprise.

"Well, I look pretty awful," he said.

"I know what you look like. Dear God, Roger, do you think Midge and Brenda and Callie and I haven't talked this over for the last two years? Ever since the program started. We've seen the sketches. We've seen the photos of the mockups. And we've seen the pictures of Willy."

"I'm not exactly like Willy any more. They've changed things—"

"And I know about that too, Roger. Brad told me all about it. I'd like to see you."

At that moment his wife's face changed without warning to a witch's. The crochet hook she held became a peasant twig broom. "You've been seeing Brad?"

Was there a microsecond pause before she answered? "I suppose he shouldn't have told me," she said, "because of security and all. But I wanted him to. It's not that bad, honey. I'm a big girl. I can handle it."

For a moment Roger wanted to snatch his hand away from the lens and let himself be seen, but he was becoming confused, feeling strange. He could not interpret his feelings. Was it vertigo? Emotion? Some malfunction in his machine half? He knew it would be only moments until Sulie or Don Kayman or someone came in, warned by the telltale telemetry outside. He tried to control himself.

"Maybe later," he said without conviction. "I—I think I'd better hang up now, Dorrie."

Behind her their familiar living room was changing too. The depth of field of the phone lens was not very good; even to his machine senses the rest of the room was blurred. Was that a man standing in the shadows? Was it wearing a Marine officer's shirt? Would Brad be doing that?

"I have to hang up now," he said, and did.

Clara Bly came in, full of questions and concern. He shook his head at her without speaking.

There were no lachrymeal ducts in his new eyes, so of course he could not cry. Even that relief was denied him.

11

Dorothy Louise Mintz Torraway as Penelope

Our trendline projections had shown that the time was right to let the world know about Roger Torraway, warts and all. So it had all gone out, and every TV screen in the world had seen Roger on point in a dozen perfect fouettés, in between the close-ups of the starved dead in Pakistan and the fires in Chicago.

It had the effect of making Dorrie a celebrity. Roger's call had upset her. Not as much as the note from Brad saying that he wouldn't be able to see her again, not nearly as much as the forty-five minutes the President had spent with her impressing on her what would happen if she messed up his pet astronaut. Certainly not as much as the knowledge that she was being followed, her telephone tapped, her home certainly bugged. But she hadn't known how to deal with Roger. She suspected she never would, and did not mind at all that in a few days he would be launched into space, where there would be little necessity for her to worry about their relationship for at least a year and a half.

She also did not mind the sudden glare of publicity.

Now that the newspapers had it all the TV reporters had been to see her, and she had seen her own courageous face on the six o'clock report. *Fem* was sending someone around. The someone phoned first. She was a woman of about sixty, veteran of the lib years, who sniffed, "We never do this, interviewing somebody just because she's somebody's wife. But they wanted it. I couldn't turn down the assignment, but I want to be honest with you and let you know that it's distasteful to me."

"I'm sorry," Dorrie apologized. "Do you want me to cancel out?"

"Oh, no," said the woman, speaking as though it were Dorrie's fault, "it's not your fault, but I think it's a betrayal of everything *Fem* stands for. Never mind. I want to come up to your home. We'll do a fifteen-minute spread for the cassette edition, and I'll write it up for the print. If you can—"

"I—" Dorrie began.

"—try to talk about you, rather than him. Your background. Your interests. Your—"

"I'm sorry, but I'd really prefer—"

"—feelings about the space program and so on. Dash says it's an essential American objective and the future of the world depends on it. What do you think? I don't mean answer the question now, I mean—"

"I don't want to have it in my home," Dorrie inserted into the conversation, without waiting for a place for it.

"—think about it, and answer on camera. Not at your home? No, that's not possible. We'll be over in an hour."

Dorrie was left with a dwindling spot of light to talk to, and then even that was gone. "Bitch," she said, almost absent-mindedly. She didn't really mind having the interview in her home. She minded not being given a choice. That she minded a lot. But there was no choice available to her, except to go out before the *Fem* person showed up.

Dorrie Torraway, Dee Mintz as was, felt strongly about having choices. One of the things that had attracted her to Roger in the first place, apart from the glamour of the space program and the security and money that went with it—and apart from Roger's rather nice-looking, studly self—was that he was willing to listen to what she wanted. Other men had been mostly interested in what they wanted, which was not the same from man to man but very consistent within the range of relationships of any one man. Harold always wanted to dance and party, Jim always wanted sex, Everett wanted sex *and* parties, Tommy wanted political dedication, Joe wanted mothering. What Roger wanted was to explore the world with her along and he seemed perfectly willing to explore the parts of it that she wanted as much as the parts that were important to him.

She had never regretted marrying him.

There were a lot of lonely times. Fifty-four days when he was in Space Station Three. Any number of shorter missions. Two years on tour duty all over the world, working with the whole system of ground monitoring stations from Aachen to Zaire, with no proper home anywhere. Dorrie had given that up, after a while, and gone back to the apartment in Tonka. But she hadn't minded. Perhaps Roger had; the question had never crossed her mind. Anyway, they had seen each other quite often enough. He had been home every month or two, and she kept her time full. There was her shop—she had opened it while Roger was in Iceland, with a five-thousand-dollar check he sent her for her birthday. There were her friends. There were, from time to time, men.

None of these filled her life, but she didn't expect it to be filled. She rather expected to be lonely. She had been an only child, with a mother who could not stand her neighbors, and so she had not had very many friends. The neighbors couldn't stand her mother very well, either, because her mother was a speed freak on a small scale, likely to be burned right out of her mind most afternoons, which made things complicated for Dorrie. But she didn't mind that; she didn't know there was any other way to live.

At thirty-one Dorrie was as healthy, as pretty and as competent to deal with the world as she ever had been or would be again. She described herself as happy. This diagnosis did not come from any welling up of joy inside herself. It came from the observed fact, looking at herself objectively, that whenever she decided she wanted something she always got it, and what other definition of happiness could there be?

She used the time until Ms. Hagar Hengstrom and her crew from *Fem* arrived to assemble a selection of ceramic ware from her shop on the coffee table before the couch she intended to sit in. What time was left she devoted to the less important task of brushing her hair, checking her make-up and changing into her newest laced-pants suit.

When the door bell rang she was quite ready.

Ms. Hagar Hengstrom pumped her hand and walked in, brilliant blue hair and a curly black cigar. She was followed by her lightperson, her soundperson, her cameraperson and her prop boys. "Room's small," she muttered, appraising the furnishings with contempt. "Torraway will sit over there. Move it."

The prop boys jumped to manhandle an easy chair from its place by the window to the corner now occupied by a breakfront, which they tugged into the center of the room. "Wait a minute," said Dorrie. "I thought I'd just sit on the couch here—"

"Don't you have the light reading yet?" Hengstrom demanded. "Sally, start the camera. You never know what we might use for rollunder."

"I mean it," Dorrie said.

Hengstrom looked at her. The voice had not been loud, but

the tone was dangerous. She shrugged. "Let's set it up," she proposed, "and if you don't like it we'll talk it over. Run through for me, will you?"

"Run through what?" The pale young girl with the hand-held camera was pointing it at her, Dorrie noticed; it distracted her. The lightperson had found a wall socket and was holding a crucifix of floods in each hand, moving them gently to erase shadows as fast as they formed each time Dorrie moved.

"Well, for openers, what are your plans for the next two years? You're surely not just going to hang around waiting for Roger Torraway to come home."

Dorrie tried to make her way to the couch, but the lightperson frowned and waved her in the other direction, and two of the prop boys shoved the coffee table out of reach. She said, "I've got my shop. I thought you might like to have some of the pieces from it on camera while you interviewed me—"

"That's fine, sure. I meant personally. You're a healthy woman. You have sexual needs. Back up a little, please—Sandra's getting a buzz from something on the sound system."

Dorrie found herself standing in front of the chair, and there seemed nothing to do but to sit in it. "Of course—" she began.

"You have a responsibility," Hengstrom said. "What sort of an example are you going to set young womanhood? Turning yourself into a dried-up old maid? Or living a naturally full life?"

"I don't know if I want to discuss—"

"I've checked you out pretty carefully, Torraway. I like what I've found out. You're your own person—as much as any person can be, anyway, who accepts the ridiculous farce of marriage. Why'd you do it?"

Dorrie hesitated. "Roger's really a very nice person," she offered.

"What about it?"

"Well, I mean, he offered me a great deal of comfort and support—"

Hagar Hengstrom sighed. "Same old slave psychology. Never mind. The other thing that puzzles me is your getting involved in the space program. Don't you feel it's a sexist shuffle?"

"Why, no. The President told me himself," Dorrie said, aware that she was trying to score points in case of another visit from Dash, "that putting a man on Mars was absolutely indispensable to the future of the human race. I believe him. We owe a—"

"Play that back," Hengstrom commended.

"What?"

"Play back what you just said. Putting a what on Mars?"

"A man. Oh. I see what you mean."

Hengstrom nodded sadly. "You see what I mean, but you don't change the way you think. Why a man? Why not a person?" She looked commiseratingly at the soundperson, who shook her head in sympathy. "Well, let's get to something more important: do you know that the whole crew of the Mars voyage is supposed to be male? What do you think of that?"

It was quite a morning for Dorrie. She never did get her ceramic pieces on camera.

When Sulie Carpenter came on duty that afternoon she brought Roger two surprises: a cassette of the interview, borrowed from the project public-relations (read: censorship) office, and a guitar. She gave him the cassette first, and let him watch the interview while she remade his bed and changed the water for his flowers.

When it was over she said brightly, "Your wife handled herself very well, I thought. I met Hagar Hengstrom once. She's a very difficult woman."

"Dorrie looked fine," said Roger. You could not read any

expression in the remade face or hear it in the flat tones, but the bat wings were fluttering restlessly. "I always liked those pants."

Sulie nodded and made a note to herself: the open lacing up both sides of each leg showed a great deal of flesh. Evidently the steroids implanted in Roger were doing their job. "Now I've got something else," she said, and opened the guitar case.

"You're going to play for me?"

"No, Roger. *You're* going to play."

"I can't play the guitar, Sulie," he protested.

She laughed. "I've been talking to Brad," she said, "and I think you're going to be surprised. You're not just different, you know, Roger. You're better. For instance, your fingers."

"What about them?"

"Well, I've been playing the guitar since I was nine, and if I stop for a couple of weeks my calluses go and I have to start all over again. Your fingers don't need calluses; they're hard enough and firm enough to fret the strings first time perfectly."

"Fine," said Roger, "only I don't even know what you're talking about. What's 'fret'?"

"Press them down. Like this." She strummed a G chord, then a D and a C.

"Now you do it," she said. "The only thing to watch out for, don't use too much strength. It's breakable." She handed him the guitar.

He swept his thumb over the open strings, as he had seen her do.

"That's fine." She applauded. "Now make a G. Ring finger on the third fret of the high E string—there. First finger on the second fret of the A. Middle finger on the third fret of the low E." She guided his hands. "Now hit it."

He strummed and looked up at her. "Hey," he said. "Nice."

She grinned and corrected him. "Not nice. Perfect. Now, this is a C. First finger on the second fret of the B string, middle finger there, ring finger there. . . . Right. And this is a D chord: first and middle finger on the G and E strings, there, ring finger one fret lower on the B. . . . Perfect again. Now give me a G."

To his surprise, Roger strummed a perfect G.

She smiled. "See? Brad was right. Once you know a chord, you know it; the 3070 remembers it for you. All you have to do is think 'G chord,' and your fingers do it. You are now," she said in mock sorrow, "about three months ahead of where I was the first time I tried to play the guitar."

"That's pretty nice," Roger said, trying all three chords, one after another.

"That's only the beginning. Now strum a four-beat, you know, dum, dum, dum, dum. With a G chord—" She listened, then nodded. "Fine. Now do it like this: G, G, G, G, G, G, G, G, C, C, G, G, G, G, G, G, G. . . . Fine. Now again, only this time, after the C, C do D, D, D, D, D, D. . . . Fine again. Now do them both, one after the other—"

He played, and she sang with him: "'Kumbaya, my lord. Kumbaya! Kumbaya, my lord. Kumbaya . . .'"

"Hey!" Roger cried, delighted,

She shook her head in mock dismay. "Three minutes from the time you pick up the guitar, and you're already an accompanist. Here, I brought you a chord book and some simple pieces. By the time I get back, you should be playing all of them, and I'll start you on finger-plucking, sliding and hammering."

She showed him how to read the tabulature for each chord and left him happily puzzling out the first six modulations of the F.

Outside his room she paused to take out her contacts, rubbed her eyes and marched to the office of the director. Scanyon's secretary waved her in.

"He's happy with his guitar, General," she reported. "Less happy about his wife."

Vern Scanyon nodded, and turned up a knob on the comm set on his desk: the sound of the chords for "Kentucky Babe" came from the tap in Roger's room. He turned it down again "I know about the guitar, Major Carpenter. What about his wife?"

"I'm afraid he loves her," she said slowly. "He's all right up to a point. Past that point I think we're in trouble. I can bolster him up as long as he's here at the project, but he'll be a long time away and—I'm not sure."

Scanyon said sharply, "Get the marbles out of your mouth, Major!"

"I think he'll miss her more than he can handle. It's bad enough now. I watched him while he was looking at that tape. He didn't move a muscle, rigid concentration, didn't want to miss a thing. When he's forty million miles away from her— Well. I've got everything taped, General. I'll run a computer simulation, and then maybe I can be more specific. But I'm concerned."

"*You're* concerned!" Scanyon snapped. "Dash will have my ass if we get him up there and he blows!"

"What can I tell you, General? Let me run the simulation. Then maybe I can tell you how to handle it."

She sat down without waiting to be asked and ran her hands over her forehead. "Leading a double life takes a lot out of you, General," she offered. "Eight hours as a nurse and eight hours as a shrink isn't any fun."

"Ten years on staff duty in Antarctica is even less fun than that," Vern Scanyon said simply.

———

The presidential jet had reached its cruising altitude of 31,000 meters and slid into high gear—Mach 3 and a bit, grotesquely faster than even a presidential CB-5 was supposed to go. The President was in a hurry.

The Midway Summit Conference had just ended in disarray. Stretched out on his chaise longue with his eyes closed, pretending to be asleep to keep the Senators who had accompanied him out of his hair, Dash bleakly considered his options. They were few.

He had not hoped for a great deal from the conference, but it had begun well enough. The Australians indicated they would accept limited cooperation with the NPA in developing the Outback, subject to appropriate guarantees, et cetera, et cetera. The NPA delegation murmured among themselves and announced that they would be happy to provide guarantees, since their real objectives were only to provide a maximum of the necessities of life for all the world's people, considered as a single unit regardless of antiquated national boundaries, et cetera. Dash himself shook off his whispering advisers and stated that America's interest in this conference was only to provide good-offices assistance to its two dearly beloved neighbors and sought nothing for itself, et cetera, and for a time there, all of two hours, it had seemed that there might be a substantive, useful product of the conference.

Then they began getting into the fine detail. The Asians offered a million-man Soil Army plus a stream of tankers carrying three million gallons a week of concentrated sludge from the sewers of Shanghai. The Australians accepted the fertilizer but spoke of a maximum of 50,000 Asians to till the land. Also, they pointed out politely, that as it was Australian land and

Australian sunshine that was being used, it would be Australian wheat that would be grown. The man from the State Department reminded Dash of American commitments to Peru, and with a heavy heart Dash rose to insist on at least a 15 percent allocation to good neighbors on the South American continent. And tempers began to rise. The precipitating incident was an NPA shuttle plane that ran into a flock of black-footed albatrosses as it took off from the Sand Island runway, crashed and burned on an islet in the lagoon, in full view of the conference members on the rootfop of the Holiday Inn. Then there were harsh words. The Japanese member of the NPA delegation allowed himself to say what he had previously only thought: that America's insistence on holding the conference at the site of one of the most famous battles of World War II was a calculated insult to Asians. The Australians commented that they had controlled their own gooney-bird populations without much trouble, and were astonished that the Americans had not succeeded in doing the same. And the maximum gain of three weeks of preparation and two days of hope was a tightly worded announcement that all three powers had agreed to further discussions. Sometime. Somewhere. Not very soon.

But what it all meant, Dash admitted to himself as he tossed restlessly on the chaise longue, was that the confrontation was eyeball to eyeball. Somebody would have to give, and nobody would.

He got up and called for coffee. When it came there was a scribbled note on Airborne White House stationery from one of the Senators: "Mr. President, we must settle the disaster-area proclamation before we land."

Dash crumpled it up. That was Senator Talltree, full of complaints: Lake Altus had shrunk to 20 percent of its normal size, tourism in the Arbuckle Mountains was dead because there was no water coming over Turner Falls, the Sooner State Fair had had to be canceled because of blowing dust. Oklahoma should be declared a disaster area. He had fifty-four states, Dash reflected, and if he listened to all the Senators and governors he would be declaring fifty-four disaster areas. There really was only one disaster area. It merely happened to be world-wide.

And I *ran* for this job, he marveled.

Thinking of Oklahoma made him think of Roger Torraway. For a moment he considered calling the pilot and diverting the flight to Tonka. But the meeting with the Combined Chiefs of Staff would not wait. He would have to content himself with the telephone.

It was not really himself who was playing the guitar, Roger knew, it was the 3070 that remembered all the subroutines involved and commanded his fingers to do whatever his brain decreed. It had taken him less than an hour to learn every chord in the book, and to use them in effortless succession. A few minutes more to record in the downstairs data banks the meaning of time signals on a musical staff; then his inner clocks took over the tempi and he never had to think about the beat again. For melody, he learned which fret on which string corresponded to each note on the staff; once imprinted on the magnetic cores, the correspondence between printed music and plucked string was established forever. Sulie took ten minutes to show him which notes to sharp and which to flat when called for, and from then on the galaxy of sharps and flats sprinkled over the bars at the key signature held no further terrors for him. Finger-plucking: for human nervous systems, it is a matter of two minutes to learn the principle and a hundred hours of practice before it becomes automatic: thumb on the D string, ring finger on the high E, middle finger on the B, thumb on the A, ring on the E, middle on the B and so on. The two minutes of learning sufficed for Roger. From then on the subroutines commanded the fingers, and the only limit to his tempo was the speed at which the strings themselves could produce a tone without breaking.

He was playing a Segovia recital from memory, from a single hearing of the tape, when the President's phone call came in.

There was a time when Roger would have been awed and delighted by a call from the President of the United States. Now it was an annoyance; it meant taking time away from his guitar. He hardly listened to what the President had to say. He was struck by the care on Dash's face, the deep lines that had not been there a few days before, the sunken eyes. Then he realized that his interpretation circuits were exaggerating what they saw to call his attention to the changes; he overrode the mediation circuits and saw Dash plain.

But he was still careworn. His voice was all warmth and good fellowship as he asked Roger how things were going. Was there anything Roger needed? Could he think of an ass to kick to get things goin' right? "Everything's fine, Mr. President," Roger said, amusing himself by letting his trick eyes deck the President's face out in Santa Claus beard and red tasseled cap, with a bundle of intangible gifts over his shoulder.

"Sure now, Roger?" Dash pressed. "You're not forgetting what I told you: whatever you want, you just yell."

"I'll yell," Roger promised. "But I'm doing fine. Waiting for the launch." And waiting for you to get off the phone, he thought, bored with the conversation.

The President frowned. Roger's interpreters immediately changed the image: Dash was still Santa Claus, but ebony black and with enormous fangs. "You're not overconfident, are you?" he asked.

"Well, how would I know if I was?" Roger asked reasonably. "I don't think so. Ask the staff here; they can tell you more about me than I can."

He managed to terminate the conversation a few exchanges later, knowing that the President was unsatisfied and vaguely troubled, but not caring much. There was less and less that Roger really cared about, he thought to himself. And he had been truthful: he really was looking forward to the launch. He would miss Sulie and Clara. He was, in the back of his mind, faintly worried about the danger and the duration of the trip. But he was also buoyed up with anticipation of what he would find when he got there: the planet he was made to inhabit.

He picked up the guitar and started again on the Segovia, but it did not go as well as he would like. After a time he realized that the gift of absolute pitch was also a handicap: Segovia's guitar had not been tuned to a perfect 440 A, it was a few Hertz flat, and his D string was almost a quarter-tone relatively flatter still. He shrugged—the bat wings flailed with the gesture—and put the guitar down.

For a moment, he sat upright on his guitar chair, straight-backed and armless, inviting his thoughts.

Something *was* troubling him, The name of the something was Dorrie. Playing the guitar was pleasant and relaxing, but behind the pleasure was a day-dream: a fantasy of sitting on the deck of a sailboat with Dorrie and Brad, and casually borrowing Brad's guitar and astonishing them all.

In some arcane way all the processes of his life terminated in Dorrie. The purpose of playing the guitar was to please Dorrie. The horror of his appearance was that it would offend Dorrie.

The tragedy of castration was that he would fail Dorrie. Most of the pain had lifted from these things, and he could look at them in a way that had been impossible a few weeks before; but they were still there buried inside him.

He reached for the phone, and then drew back his hand.

Calling Dorrie was not satisfactory. He had tried that.

What he really wanted was to see her.

That, of course, was impossible. He was not allowed to leave the project. Vern Scanyon would be furious. The guards would stop him at the door. The telemetry would reveal at once what he was doing; the closed-circuit electronic surveillance would locate him at every step; all the resources of the project would be mobilized to prevent his leaving.

And there would be no point in asking permission. Not even in asking Dash; the most that would happen would be that the President would give an order and Dorrie would be delivered, coerced and furious, in his room. Roger did not want Dorrie to be forced to come to him, and he was sure he would not be allowed to go to her.

On the other hand . . .

On the other hand, he reflected, why did he need permission?

He thought for a minute, sitting perfectly still in his straight-backed chair.

Then he put the guitar carefully away in its case and moved.

The first thing he did was bend down to the wall, pull a baseboard plug out of its moorings and stick his finger into it. The copper nail on his finger was as good as a penny any day. The fuses blew. The lights in the room went out. The whicka-whicka and gentle whisper of the reels of the recording machines slowed and stopped. The room went dark.

There was still heat, and that was light enough for Roger's

eyes. He could see quite well enough to pull the telemetry leads out of his body. He was out of the door before Clara Bly, pouring cream into a cup on her coffee break, looked around at the buzzing readout board.

He had done better than he planned with the fuses; the hall lights were out as well. There were people in the corridor, but in the dark they could not see. Roger was past them and taking the fire stairs four at a time before they knew he was gone. He settled into the workings of his body with ease and grace. All of Kathleen Doughty's ballet training was paying off; he danced down the stairs, plié-ed through a door, leaped along a corridor and was out into the cold night air before the security man at the door looked around from his TV set.

He was in the open, racing down the freeway toward the city of Tonka at forty miles an hour.

The night was bright with kinds of light he had never seen before. Overhead there was a solid layer of clouds, stratocumulus scudding along from the north and thick middle-level clouds above them; even so, he could see dim glows where the brightest stars filtered some of their radiation through. The Oklahoma prairie on either side was somberly glowing with the tiny residual heat retained from the day, punctuated with splotches of brilliance where there was a home or a farm building. The cars on the freeway were tailed by great plumes of light, bright where they left the exhaust pipe, reddening and darkening as the clouds of hot gas expanded into the chilling air. As he entered the city itself he saw and avoided an occasional pedestrian, each a luminous Halloween figure, dully glowing in his own body heat. The buildings around him had trapped a little heat from the end of the day and were spilling more from their own central heating; they glowed like fireflies.

He stopped at the corner of his own home street. There was

a car with two men inside it parked across from the door. Warning signals flashed in his brain, and the car became a tank, howitzer pointed at his head. They were no problem. He changed course and ran through the backyards, scaling fences and slipping through gates, and at his own home he extruded the copper nails in his fingers for purchase and climbed right up the outside wall.

It was what he wanted to do. Not just to avoid the men in the car outside, but to act out a fantasy: the moment when he would burst in on Dorrie through the window, to catch her at—what?

In the event itself, what he caught her at was watching a late movie on television. Her hair was sticky with coloring compound, and she was propped up in bed eating a solitary dish of ice cream.

As he slid the unlocked window open and crawled through, she turned toward him.

She screamed.

It was not just a cry, it was instant hysterics. Dorrie spilled her ice cream and leaped out of bed. The TV set toppled and crunched to the floor. Sobbing, Dorrie pressed herself against the far wall, eyes squeezed tight and fists pressed against them.

"I'm sorry," Roger said inadequately. He wanted to approach her, but reason prevented. She looked very helpless and appealing, in her see-through butcher-boy smock and tiny bikini-ribbon panties.

"*Sorry,*" she gasped, looked at him, averted her eyes and fumbled her way into the bathroom, slamming the door behind her.

Well, thought Roger, she was not to be blamed; he had a clear notion of what a grotesque sight he had been, coming through a window without warning. "You did say you knew what I looked like," he called.

There was no answer from the bathroom; only, a moment later, the running of water. He glanced around the room. It looked exactly as it had always looked. The closets were as full of her clothes and his as they had always been. The spaces behind the couches were as empty of lovers as ever. He was not proud of himself for searching the apartment like any medieval cuckold, but he did not stop until he was certain she had been alone.

The phone rang.

Roger's instant reflexes had him grabbing the earpiece out of its cradle almost before the first *brrr* sounded, so quickly and brutally that it was deformed into scrap in his hand. The vision screen flickered and then went dark again, its circuitry linked with the sound. "Hello?" Roger said. But there was no answer; he had made sure that nobody would ever speak on that instrument again.

"Christ," he said. He had had no clear idea of how this meeting would go, but it was apparent that it had begun badly.

When Dorrie came out of the bathroom she wasn't crying, but she wasn't speaking either. She went into the kitchen without looking at him. "I want a cup of tea," she said over her shoulder.

"Wouldn't you rather I made you a drink?" Roger offered hopefully.

"No."

Roger could hear the sounds of the electric kettle being filled, the faint susurrus as it began to simmer and, several times, a cough. He listened harder and heard his wife's breathing, which became slower and steadier.

He sat down in the chair that had always been his chair and

waited. His wings were in the way. Even though they elevated themselves automatically over his head he could not lean back. Restlessly he roamed into the living room. His wife's voice called through the swinging doors: "Do you want some tea?"

"No." Then he added, "No, thank you." Actually he would have liked it very much, not because of any need for fluids or nutrients but for the feeling of participating in some normal, precedented event with Dorrie. But he did not want to spill and slobber in front of her, and he had not practiced much with cups and saucers and liquids.

"Where are you?" She hesitated at the swinging doors, the cup in her hands, and then saw him. "Oh. Why don't you turn a light on?"

"I don't want to. Honey, sit down and close your eyes for a minute." He had an idea.

"Why?" But she did as he requested, seating herself in the wing chair on one side of the fake fireplace. He picked up the chair, with her in it, and turned it away, so that she was facing into the wall. He looked around for something to sit in himself—there was nothing, or nothing that comported with his new geometry: floor pillows and couches, all awkward for his body or his wings—but on the other hand, he knew, he had no particular need to sit. His artificial musculature did not need that sort of relaxation very much.

So he stood behind her and said, "I'd feel better if you weren't looking at me."

"I understand that, Roger. You frightened me, is all. I wish you hadn't burst in the window like that! On the other hand, I shouldn't have been so positive I could see you, I mean like *that*, without— Without going into hysterics, I guess is what I want to say."

"I know what I look like," he said.

"It's still you, though, isn't it?" Dorrie said to the wall. "Although I don't remember you ever climbing the outside of a building to get into my bed before."

"It's easy," he said, taking a chance on what was almost an attempt at lightness.

"Well"—she paused for a sip of tea—"tell me. What's this about?"

"I wanted to see you, Dorrie."

"You did see me. On the phone."

"I didn't want it to be on the phone. I wanted to be in the same room with you." He wanted even more than that to touch her, to reach out to the nape of her neck and press and caress the tendons into relaxing, but he did not quite dare that. Instead he reached down and ignited the gas flame in the fireplace, not so much for warmth as for a little light to help Dorrie. And for cheerfulness.

"We aren't supposed to do that, Roger. There's a thousand-dollar fine—"

He laughed. "Not for you and me, Dorrie. Anybody gives you any trouble, you call up Dash and say I said it was all right."

His wife took a cigarette from the box on the end table and lit it. "Roger, dear," she said slowly, "I'm not used to all this. I don't just mean the way you look. I understand about that. It's hard, but at least I knew what it was going to be before it happened. Even if I didn't think it would be *you*. But I'm not used to your being so—I don't know, important."

"I'm not used to it either, Dorrie." He thought back to the TV reporters and the cheering crowds when he returned to Earth after rescuing the Russians. "It's different now. I feel as if I'm carrying something on my back—the world, maybe."

"Dash says that's exactly what you're doing. Half of what he says is crap, but I don't think that part is. You're a pretty significant man, Roger. You were always a famous one. Maybe that's why I married you. But that was like being a rock star, you know? It was exciting, but you could always walk away from it if you got tired of it. This I don't think you can walk away from."

She stubbed out her cigarette. "Anyway," she said, "you're here, and they're probably going crazy at the project."

"I can handle that."

"Yes," she said thoughtfully, "I guess you can. What shall we talk about?"

"Brad," he said. He had not intended it. The word came out of his artificial larynx, shaped by his restructured lips, with no intervention by his conscious mind.

He could feel her stiffening up. "What about Brad?" she asked.

"Your sleeping with him, that's what about Brad," he said. The back of her neck was glowing dully now, and he knew that if he could see her face it would display the revealing tracery of veins. The dancing gas flames from the fireplace made an attractive spectrum of colors on her dark hair; he watched the play appreciatively, as though it did not matter what he was saying to his wife, or she to him.

She said, "Roger, I really don't know how to deal with you. Are you angry with me?"

He watched the dancing colors silently.

"After all, Roger, we talked this out years ago. You have had affairs, and so have I. We agreed they didn't mean anything."

"They mean something when they hurt." He willed his vision to stop, and welcomed the darkness as an aid to thought. "The others were different," he said.

"Different how?" She was angry now.

"Different because we talked them over," he said doggedly. "When I was in Algiers and you couldn't stand the climate, that was one thing. What you did back here in Tonka and what I did in Algiers didn't affect you and me. When I was in orbit—"

"I never slept with anybody else while you were in orbit!"

"I know that, Dorrie. I thought that was kind of you. I really did, because it wouldn't have been fair, would it? I mean, my own opportunities were pretty limited. Old Yuli Bronin wasn't my type. But now it's different. It's like I was in orbit again, only worse. I don't even have Yuli! I not only don't have a girl friend, I don't have the equipment to do anything about it if I did."

She said wretchedly, "I know all that. What can I tell you?"

"You can tell me you'll be a good wife to me!" he roared.

That frightened her; he had forgotten what his voice could sound like. She began to cry.

He reached out to touch her and then let his hand fall. What was the use?

Oh, Christ, he thought. What a mess! He took consolation only in that this interview had been here, in the privacy of their own home, quite unplanned and secret. It would have been unbearable in the presence of anyone else; but naturally we had monitored every word.

12

Two Simulations and a Reality

Copper-fingered Roger had blown more than a fuse. He had shorted a whole box of circuit breakers. It took twenty minutes to get the lights on again.

Fortunately the 3070 had stand-by power for its memory, so the cores were not wiped. The computations that were in process were compromised. All of them would have to be done over again. The automatic surveillance was out of service until long after Roger was gone.

One of the first ones to know what had happened was Sulie Carpenter, catching a cat nap in the office next to the computer room, waiting for Roger's simulation to finish. It didn't finish. The alarm bells signifying interruption of the information being processed woke her. The bright fluorescent rod-lights were out, and only the red incandescents gave a dim, despairing glow.

Her first thought was her precious simulation. She spent twenty minutes with the programmers, studying the partial printout, hoping that it would be all right, before she gave up and charged out to Vern Scanyon's office. That was when she found out that Roger had run off.

Power was back by then; it had come on while she was taking the fire stairs two at a time. Scanyon was already on the phone, ordering the people he wanted to blame in for an emergency conference. Clara Bly was the one who told Sulie about Roger; one by one, as the others entered the room, they were brought up to date. Don Kayman was the only major figure who was out of the project; they located him watching television in his clerical condominium. Kathleen Doughty came up from the physiotherapy room in the basement, dragging Brad with her, all pink-skinned and damp; he had been trying to substitute an hour in the sauna for a night's sleep. Freeling was at Merritt Island, but not needed particularly; half a dozen others came in and slumped, dispiritedly or worriedly, into the leather chairs around the conference table.

Scanyon had already ordered an Air Force spotter-copter into the air, in a search pattern all around the project. Its TV cameras were sweeping the freeway, the access roads, the parking lots, the fields and prairie, and displaying what they saw on the wall TV at the end of the room. The Tonka police force had been alerted to watch for a strange devil-like creature running around at seventy kilometers an hour, which had led to trouble for the Tonka desk sergeant. He made a bad mistake. He asked the project security officer if he had been drinking. Ten seconds later, with his head filled with visions of pounding a beat in Kiska, the sergeant was on the police radio to all vehicles and foot patrolmen. The orders for the police were not to arrest Roger, not even to approach him. They were only to find him.

What Scanyon wanted was someone to blame. "I hold you responsible, Dr. Ramez," he barked at the staff shrink. "You and Major Carpenter. How could you let Torraway get into this sort of action without advance warning?"

Ramez said placatingly, "General, I told you Roger was unstable with regard to his wife. That's why I asked for someone like Sulie. He needed another object to fixate on, someone directly connected with the project—"

"Didn't work very well, did it?"

Sulie stopped listening. She knew very well that her turn was next, but she was trying to think. Over Scanyon's desk she saw the moving view from the copter. It was expressed as a schematic, the roads as lines of green, the vehicles, a point of blue, buildings yellow. The few pedestrians were bright red. Now, if one of those red dots should suddenly start to move at the speed of a blue vehicle, that would be Roger. But he had had plenty of time to get farther away than the area the copter was covering.

"Tell them to scan the town, General," she said suddenly.

He frowned, but he picked up the phone and gave the order. He didn't get a chance to put it down again; there was an incoming call he could not refuse.

Telly Ramez got up from his chair next to the director and came around to Sulie Carpenter. She didn't look up from the folded transcript of the simulation. He waited patiently.

The director's call was from the President of the United States. They would have known that from the sweat that rolled down beneath Scanyon's temples, even if they had not seen Dash's tiny face in the screen on the director's desk. Faintly the voice leaked through to them: ". . . spoke to Roger he seemed—I don't know, disinterested. I thought it over, Vern, and then I decided to call you. Is everything going all right?"

Scanyon swallowed. He glanced around the table and abruptly folded up the privacy petals on the phone; the image dwindled to postage-stamp size. The voice faded to nothingness as the sound was transferred to a parabolic speaker aimed directly at Scanyon's head, and Scanyon's own words were swallowed by the petal-like shields. The rest of the room had no difficulty in following the conversation anyway; it was written very clearly on Scanyon's face.

Sulie looked up from the transcript at Telly Ramez. "Get him off the phone," she said impatiently. "I know where Roger is."

Ramez said, "At his wife's house."

She rubbed her eyes wearily. "I guess we didn't need a simulation for that, did we? I'm sorry, Telly. I guess I wasn't keeping him on the hook as firmly as I thought I was."

They were right; of course; we had known that for some time. As soon as Scanyon got off the phone with the President the security office called to say that the bugs in Dorrie's bedroom had picked up the sound of Roger coming in through the window.

Scanyon's lemony small eyes seemed almost at the point of tears. "Put the sound on the horn," he ordered. "Display the house." And then he switched his phone to an outside line and dialed Dorrie's number.

From the loudspeaker came the sound of one ring, then a metallic noise and Roger's flat cyborg voice rasping, "Hello?" And a moment later, softer but equally toneless, "Christ."

Scanyon jerked the earpiece away and rubbed his ear. "What the hell happened?" he demanded. There was no answer from anyone to the rhetorical question, and gingerly he put the phone back. "I'm getting some kind of trouble signal," he announced.

"We can send a man in, General," the assistant security chief suggested. "There are two of our men in that car out in front of the house there." The helicopter pickup had slid across the screen and settled at 1,800 feet over the Courthouse Square in the city of Tonka. The camera was set for infrared, and in the upper corner of the screen the broad dark band of the Ship

Canal identified the edge of the town. A rectangle of darkness surrounded by the moving lights of cars just below the screen's center point was the Courthouse Square, and Roger's home was marked with a tracer star in red. The assistant reached up and touched the blob of light nearby to show the car. "We're in voice contact with them, General," he went on. "They didn't see Colonel Torraway go in."

Sulie stood up. "I don't recommend it," she said.

"Your recommendations aren't too popular with me right now, Major Carpenter," Scanyon snarled.

"All the same, General—" She stopped as Scanyon raised his hand.

From the speaker Dorrie's voice came faintly: *I want a cup of tea.* And then Roger's: *Wouldn't you rather I made you a drink?* And her almost inaudible *No.*

"All the same," Sulie spoke up, "he's stable enough now. Don't screw it up."

"I can't let him just sit out there! Who the hell knows what he'll do next? *You?*"

"You've got him spotted. I don't think he'll move, anyway, not for a while. Don Kayman's not far from there and he's a friend. Tell him to go get Roger."

"Kayman's not much of a combat specialist."

"Is that what you want? If Roger doesn't come back peacefully, exactly what are you going to do about it?"

Do you want some tea?

No. . . . No, thank you.

"And turn that off," Sulie added. "Leave the poor bastard a little privacy."

Scanyon sat slowly back in his chair, patting the top of his desk with both hands at once, very gently. Then he picked up the phone and gave orders. "We'll do it your way one more time,

Major," he said. "Not because I have much confidence. I just
don't have much choice, either. I can't threaten you with anything. If this goes wrong again, I doubt I'll be in a position to
punish anybody. But I'm pretty sure *somebody* will."

Telesforo Ramez said, "Sir, I understand your position, but
I think this isn't fair to Sulie. The simulation shows that he has
to have a confrontation with his wife."

"The point of a simulation, Dr. Ramez, is that it should tell
you what's going to happen *before* it happens."

"Well, it also shows that Torraway is basically pretty stable in
every other respect. He'll handle this, General."

Scanyon went back to patting his desk.

Ramez said, "He's a complicated person. You've seen his The-
matic Apperception Test patterns, General. He's high in all the
fundamental drives: achievement, affiliation—not quite so high
in power, but still healthy. He's not a manipulator. He's introspective. He needs to work things out in his head. Those are
the qualities you want, General. He'll need all that. You can't
ask him to be one person here in Oklahoma and another person
on Mars."

"If I'm not mistaken," the general said, "that's what you promised me, with your behavior modification."

"No, General," the psychiatrist said patiently. "I only promised that if you gave him a reward like Sulie Carpenter he'd find
it easier to reconcile himself to his problems with his wife. He
has."

"B-mod has its own dynamics, General," Sulie put in. "You
called me in pretty late."

"What are you telling me?" Scanyon asked dangerously. "Is
he going to crack up on Mars?"

"I hope not. The odds are as good as we know how to make
them, General. He's cleaned up a lot of old shit; you can see it

in his latest TATs. But six days from now he'll be gone, and I won't be in his life any more. And that's wrong. B-mod should *never* be cut off cold turkey. It should be phased out—a little less of me being around and then a little less than that until he's had a chance to build up his defenses."

The gentle patting on the desk was slower now, and Scanyon said, "It's a little late to tell me that."

Sulie shrugged, and did not speak.

Scanyon looked thoughtfully around the table. "All right. We've done all we can here tonight. You're all dismissed until eight—no, make that ten in the morning. By then I expect every one of you to have a report, no more than three minutes long, on where your own area of responsibilities stands, and what we should do."

Don Kayman got the message from a Tonka police patrol car. It swooshed up behind him, lights flashing and siren screaming, and pulled him over to order him to turn around and go back to Roger's apartment.

He knocked on the door with some trepidation, unsure of what he would find. And when the door opened, with Roger's gleaming eyes peering out from behind it, Kayman whispered a quick Hail Mary as he tried to look past Roger into the apartment—for what? For the dismembered body of Dorrie Torraway? For a shambles of destruction? But all he saw was Dorrie herself, huddled in a wing chair and obviously weeping. The sight almost pleased him, since he had been prepared for so much worse.

Roger came along with no argument. "Goodbye, Dorrie," he said, and did not wait for an answer. He had trouble fitting himself into Don Kayman's little car, but his wings folded down.

By pushing the reclining seat back as far as it would go he was able to manage, in a cramped and precarious position that would have been hopelessly uncomfortable for any normal human being. Roger, of course, was not a normal human being. His muscular system was content with prolonged overloads in almost any configuration it could bend into at all.

They were silent until they were almost at the project. Then Don Kayman cleared his throat. "You had us worried."

"I thought I would," said the flat cyborg voice. The wings stirred restlessly, writhing against each other like a rubbing of hands. "I wanted to see her, Don. It was important to me."

"I can understand that." Kayman turned into the broad, empty parking lot. "Well?" he probed. "Are things all right?"

The cyborg mask turned toward him. The great compound eyes gleamed like faceted ebony, without expression, as Roger said: "You're a jerk, Father Kayman, sir. How all right can they be?"

Sulie Carpenter thought wistfully of sleep, as she might think of a vacation on the French Riviera. They were equally out of the question at that moment. She took two caps of amphetamines and a B-12 injection, self-administered into the places in her arm she had learned to locate long ago.

The simulation of Roger's reactions had been compromised by the power failure, so she did it over again from punch-in to readout. We were content that this should be so. It gave us a chance to make a few corrections.

While she was waiting she took a long, hot soak in a hydrotherapy tub, and when the simulation had run she studied it carefully. She had taught herself to read the cryptic capital letters and integers, to guard against programming errors, but this time she spared the hardware no time and went at once to the plain-language readout at the end. She was very good at her job.

That job did not happen to be ward nurse. Sulie Carpenter had been one of the first of the aerospace female doctors. She had her degree in medicine, had specialized in psychotherapy, all the myriad eclectic disciplines of it, and had gone into the space program because nothing on Earth seemed really worth doing to her. After completing astronaut training she had come to wonder if there was anything in space that was worth doing either. Research had seemed at least abstractly worth while, so she had applied for work with the California study teams and got it. There had been a fair number of men in her life, one or two of them important to it. None of them had worked out. That much of what she had told Roger had been true; and after the most recent bruising failure she had contracted her area of interest until, she told herself, she grew up enough to know what she wanted from a man. And there she stayed, sidetracked in a loop off the main current of human affairs, until we turned up her card out of all the hundreds of thousands of punched cards, to fill Roger's need.

When her orders came, wholly without warning, they were directly from the President himself. There was no way she could have refused the assignment. Actually she had no desire to. She welcomed the change. Motherhenning a hurting human being stroked the feelgood centers of her personality; the importance of the job was clear to her, because if there was any faith in her it was in the Mars project; and she was aware of her competence. Of competence she had a great deal. We rated her very high; a major piece in the game we were playing for the survival of the race.

When she had finished with Roger's simulation it was nearly four in the morning.

She slept a couple of hours in a borrowed bed in the nurses' quarters. Then she showered, dressed and put her green contact lenses in. She was not happy with that particular aspect of her job, she reflected on the way to Roger's room. The dyed hair and the change of eye color were deceptions; she did not like to deceive. One day she would like to leave out the contacts and let her hair go back to its muddy blond—oh, maybe helped out a little with a rinse, to be sure; she did not object to artifice, only to pretending to be something she wasn't.

But when she entered Roger's room she was smiling. "Lovely to see you back. We missed you. How was it, running around on your own?"

"Not bad at all," said the flat voice. Roger was standing by the window, staring out at the blobs of tumbleweed lumping and bouncing across the parking lot. He turned to her. "You know, it's all true, what you said. What I've got now isn't just different, it's better."

She resisted the desire to reinforce what he had said, and only smiled as she began to strip his bed. "I was worried about sex," he went on. "But you know what, Sulie? It's like being told I can't have any caviar for the next couple of years. I don't like caviar. And when you come right down to it, I don't want sex right now. I suppose you punched that into the computer? 'Cut down sex drive, increase euphoria'? Anyway, it finally penetrated my little brain that I was just making trouble for myself, worrying about whether I could get along without something I really didn't want. It's a reflection of what I think other people think I should want."

"Acculturation," she supplied.

"No doubt," he said. "Listen, I want to do something for you."

He picked up the guitar, propped himself against the window frame with one heel against the sill, and settled the instrument across his knee. His wings quietly rearranged themselves over his head as he began to play.

Sulie was startled. He was not merely playing; he was singing. Singing? No, it was a sound more like a man whistling through his teeth, faint but pure. His fingers on the guitar strummed and plucked an accompaniment while the keening whistle from his lips flowed through the melody of a tune she had never heard before.

When he had finished she demanded, "What was *that?*"

"It's a Paganini sonata for guitar and violin," he said proudly. "Clara gave me the record."

"I didn't know you could do that. Humming, I mean—or whatever it was."

"I didn't either until I tried. I can't keep enough volume for the violin part, of course. And I can't keep the guitar sound low enough to balance it, but it didn't sound bad, did it?"

"Roger," she said, meaning it, "I'm impressed."

He looked up at her and impressed her again by managing a smile. He said, "I bet you didn't know I could do *that*, either. I didn't know it myself till I tried."

At the meeting Sulie said flatly, "He's ready, General."

Scanyon had managed enough sleep to look rested, and enough of something else, some inner resource or whatever, to look less harried. "You're sure, Major Carpenter?"

She nodded her head. "He'll never be readier." She hesitated. Vern Scanyon, reading her expression, waited for the amendment. "The problem, as I see it, is that he's right to go *now*. All his systems are up to operating level. He's worked through his thing with his wife. He's ready. The longer he stays around here, the more chance that she'll do something to upset his balance."

"I doubt that very much," said Scanyon, frowning.

"Well, she knows what trouble she'll be in. But I don't want to take that chance, I want him to move."

"You mean take him down to Merritt Island?"

"No. I want to put him on hold."

Brad spilled coffee from the cup he had been raising to his lips. "No way, sweetie!" he cried, genuinely shocked. "I have seventy-two more hours testing on his systems! If you slow him down I can't get readings—"

"Testing for what, Dr. Bradley? For his operating efficiency, or for the sake of the papers you're going to write on him?"

"Well—Christ, certainly I'm going to write him up. But I want to check him as thoroughly as possible, every minute I can, for his sake. And for the mission's."

She shrugged. "That's still my recommendation. There's nothing for him to do here but wait. He's had enough of that."

"What if something goes wrong on Mars?" Brad demanded.

She said, "You wanted my recommendation. That's it."

Scanyon put in, "Please make sure we all know what you're talking about. Especially me."

Sulie looked toward Brad, who said, "We've planned to do that for the voyage, General, as you know. We have the capacity to override his internal clocks by external computer mediation. There are—let's see—five days and some hours to launch; we can slow him down so that his subjective time is maybe thirty minutes over that period. It makes sense—but what I said makes sense, too, and I can't take the responsibility for letting him out of my hands until I've made every test I want to make."

Scanyon scowled. "I understand what you're saying; it's a good point, and I've got a point of my own, too. What happened to what you were saying last night, Major Carpenter? About not cutting off his behavior modification too abruptly."

Sulie said, "He's at a plateau stage, General. If I could have another six months with him I'd take it. Five days, no; there's more risk than there is benefit. He's found a real interest in his guitar—you should hear him. He's built up really structurally good defenses in regard to his lack of sexual organs. He has even taken things into his own hands by running out last night— that's a major step, General; his profile was much too passive to be good, when you consider the demands of this mission. I say put him on hold now."

"And I say I need more time with him," flared Brad. "Maybe Sulie's right. But I'm right too, and I'll take it to the President if I have to!"

Scanyon looked thoughtfully at Brad, then around the room. "Any other comments?"

Don Kayman put in, "For what it's worth, I agree with Sulie. He's not happy about his wife, but he's not shaken up either. This is as good a place as any for him to go."

"Yeah," said Scanyon, gently patting the desk top again. He looked into space, and then said, "There's something none of you know. Your simulation isn't the only one of Roger that has been done lately." He looked at each face and emphasized, "This is not to be discussed with *anyone* outside this room. The Asians are doing one of their own. They've tapped into our 3070 circuits somewhere between here and the two other computers and stolen all the data, and they've used it to make their own simulation."

"Why?" Don Kayman demanded, only a beat before the others at the table.

"That's what I wish I knew," said Scanyon heavily. "They're not interfering. We wouldn't have known about it if it wasn't for a routine line check that uncovered their tap—and then some cloak and dagger stuff in Peking that I don't know about and don't want to. All they did was read everything out and make their own program. We don't know what use they are going to make out of it, but there's a surprise in it. Right after that they dropped their protest against the launch. In fact, they offered the use of their Mars orbiter to expedite telemetry for the mission."

"I wouldn't trust them as far as I could throw them!" Brad flared.

"Well, we're not going to put much reliance on their bird, you can bet on that. But there it is: they say they want the mission to work. Well," he said, "that's just one more complication, but it all comes down to a single decision right now, correct? I have to make up my mind whether or not to put Roger on hold. Okay. I'll do it. I accept your recommendation, Major Carpenter. Tell Roger what we're going to do, and tell him whatever you and Dr. Ramez think you should about why. As for you, Brad"—he raised his hand to ward off Brad's protests—"I know what you're going to say. I agree. Roger needs more time with you. Well, he'll get it. I'm ordering you along on the mission." He slid a sheet of paper closer to him on his desk, crossed out one name on a list, wrote in another. "I'm going to drop one of the pilots to make room for you. I already checked. There's plenty of back-up, with the machine guidance systems and the fact that you all have had some pilot training anyhow. That's the final crew roster for the Mars launch: Torraway, Kayman, General Hesburgh as pilot—and you."

Brad protested. It was only a reflex. Once the idea had settled in he accepted it. What Scanyon had said was true enough, and besides, Brad perceived instantly that the career he had programmed for himself could not help but be enhanced by actual physical participation in the mission itself. It would be a pity to leave Dorrie, and all the Dorries, but there would be so *many* Dorries when he got back . . .

And everything else followed as the night the day. That was the last decision. Everything else was only implementation. On Merritt Island the crews began fueling the launch vehicle. The rescue ships were deployed across the Atlantic in case of failure. Brad was flown to the island for his fitting, with six ex-astronauts detailed to cram in all the touch-up teaching he needed and could get in the time available. Hesburgh was one of them, short, sure and smiling, his demeanor a constant reassurance. Don Kayman took a precious twelve-hour relief to say good-by to his nun.

With all of this we were quite content. We were content with the decision to send Brad along. We were content with the trendline extrapolations that every day showed more positive results from the effect of the launch on world opinion and events. We were content with Roger's state of mind. And with the NPA simulation of Roger we were most content of all; in fact, that was an essential to our plans for the salvation of the race.

13

When We Pass the Point of No Return

The long Hohmann-orbit trip to Mars takes seven months. All previous astronauts, cosmonauts and sinonauts had found them very wearing months indeed. Each day had 86,400 seconds to fill, and there was very little to fill them with.

Roger was different from all the others in two ways. First, he was the most precious passenger any spaceship had yet carried. In and around his body were the fruits of seven billion Man Plus dollars. To the maximum extent possible, he had to be spared.

The other way was that, uniquely, he *could* be spared.

His body clocks had been disconnected. His perception of time was what the computer told him it should be.

They slowed him down gradually, at first. People began to seem to move a little more briskly. Mealtime came sooner than he was ready for it. Voices grew shriller.

When that phased in nicely, they increased the retardation in his systems. Voices passed into high-pitched gibberish, and then out of his perception entirely. He hardly saw people at all, except as flickers of motion. They sealed off his room from the day—it was not to keep him from escaping, it was to protect him from the quick transition from day to night. Platters of room-temperature, picnic-style food appeared before him. When he had begun to push them away to signal he was done or didn't want them, they whisked out of sight.

Roger knew what was being done to him. He didn't mind. He accepted Sulie's promise that it was good, and needful, and all right. He thought he was going to miss Sulie and looked for a way to tell her so. There was a way, but it all went so rapidly; messages were chalked as if by magic on a board in front of him. When he responded, he found his answers snatched away and erased before he was quite sure he was through:

HOW ARE YOU FEELING?

Pick up the chalk, write one word.

FINE.

and then the board is gone, brought back with another message—

WE'RE TAKING YOU TO MERRITT ISLAND.

And his reply:

I'M READY.

snatched away before he could add the rest, which he scrawled rapidly on his bedside table—

GIVE MY LOVE TO DORRIE

He had intended to add "and Sulie," but there was no time;

suddenly the table was gone. He was gone from the room. There was a sudden dizzying lurch of movement. He caught a quick glimpse of the ambulance entrance to the project, and a quick phantom glimpse of a nurse—was it Sulie?—with her back to him, adjusting her panty hose. His whole bed seemed to leap into the air, into a brutal blaze of winter sunlight, then into—what? A car? Before he could even question, it sprang into the air, and he realized that it was a helicopter, and then that he was very close to being sick. He felt his gorge rising in his throat.

The telemetry faithfully reported, and the controls were adequate to the problem. He still felt he would like to vomit, feeling himself thrown around as though in the most violent sort of cross-chop sea, but he did not.

Then they stopped.

Out of the helicopter.

Bright sunlight again.

Into something else—which he recognized, after it had begun to move, as the interior of a CB-5, fitted up as a hospital ship. Safety webbing spun magically around him.

It was not comfortable—there was still the hammering and the twisting vertigo, though not as unbearable—but it did not last long. A minute or two, it seemed to Roger. Then pressure smote his ears and they were taking him out of the plane, into blinding heat and light—Florida, of course, he realized tardily; but by then he was in an ambulance, then out of it . . .

Then, for a time that seemed to Roger ten or fifteen minutes and was actually the better part of a day, nothing happened except that he was in a bed, and was fed, and his wastes were removed by catheter, and then a note appeared before him:

GOOD LUCK, ROGER, WE'RE ON OUR WAY.

and then a steam hammer smote him from underneath and he lost consciousness. It is all very well, he thought, to spare me the inconvenience of boredom, but you may be killing me to do it. But before he could think of a way to communicate this to anyone he was out.

Time passed. A time of dreams.

He realized groggily that they had been keeping him sedated, not only slowed down but asleep; and in realizing his, he was awake.

There was no feeling of pressure. In fact, he was floating. Only a spiderweb of retaining straps kept him in place.

He was in space.

A voice spoke next to his ear: "Good morning Roger. This is a tape recording."

He turned his head and found a tiny speaker grille next to his ear.

"We've slowed it down so that you can understand it. If you want to speak to us, you just tape what you want to say, in a minute. Then we'll speed it up so *we* can understand it. Ain't science grand?

"Anyway, we're into day thirty-one as I tape this. In case you don't remember me any more, I'm Don Kayman. You had a little trouble. Your muscle system fought against the takeoff acceleration, and you pulled some ligaments. We had to do a little surgery. You're mending nicely. Brad rebuilt part of the cybernetics, and you probably can handle the deltas when we land in good shape. Let's see. There's nothing else important to say, and probably you have some questions, but before you take your turn there's a message for you."

And the tape whispered scratchily for a moment, and then Dorrie's voice came on, bent and attenuated. Over a background hiss of static she said: "Hi, honey. Everything's fine back home, and I'm keeping the home fires burning for you. I think of you. Take care of yourself."

And then Kayman's voice again: "Now here's what you do. First off, if there's anything important—if you hurt, or anything like that—tell us that right away. There's a lot of real-time loss in this, so say the important stuff first, and when you're through just hold up your hand while we change tapes, and then you can go on to the chitchat. Now go."

And the tape stopped, and a small red light that had said "Play" next to the speaker grille went out, and a green one came on to say "Record." He picked up the microphone and was getting ready to say that no, there wasn't any particular problem, when he happened to look down and notice that his right leg was missing.

We were, of course, monitoring every moment in the spacecraft.

The communication link had stretched pretty thin even after the first month. The geometry was troublesome. While the spacecraft was climbing out toward Mars's orbit, Mars was moving. So was the Earth, and a good deal faster. It would go around the sun almost twice before Mars completed a single one of its orbits. The telemetry from the spacecraft now took something like three minutes to reach Goldstone. We were passive listeners. It would get worse. Any command from Earth would come half an hour late by the time the spacecraft was circling Mars, round-trip time at the speed of light. We had surrendered instant control; the ship and its passengers were effectively on their own.

Later still the Earth and Mars would be on opposite sides of the sun. The weak signals from the spacecraft would be so compromised by solar interference that we would not even receive reliably. But by then the 3070 would be in orbit, and shortly thereafter the MHD generator would join it. Then there would be plenty of power for everything. It was all planned out, where each would go, how they would interlink with each other, with the orbiting ship, with the ground station and with Roger, wherever he might roam.

We launched the 3070, powered down into stand-by mode. It was a robot run. The ionization risk turned out, on analysis, to be unacceptable in a spacecraft of normal configuration, so the Cape engineers stripped away all the life support, all the telemetry, the demolition system and half of the maneuver capability. The weight went into shielding. Once it was launched it was silent and lifeless, and would stay that way for seven months. Then General Hesburgh would capture control and play both ends of the docking maneuver. It would be difficult, but that was what he was paid for.

We launched the MHD generator a month later, with a crew of two volunteers and a maximum of publicity. Everyone was interested now. And no one objected, not even the NPA. They disdained the first launch. They acknowledged tracking the launch of the 3070 and offered their data to the NASA net. When the generator went up, their ambassador sent a polite note of congratulations.

Clearly something was happening.

It was not all psychological. New York City had two straight weeks without rioting, and garbage was collected from some of the main streets. Winter rains put out the last of the great fires in the Northwest, and the governors of Washington, Oregon, Idaho and California sent out a joint call for volunteers. More than a hundred thousand young people signed up to replant the mountain slopes.

The President of the United States was the last to notice the change; he was too busy with the internal disasters of a nation that had overbred and overspent itself into tragedy. But the time came when he realized there had been a change, not only within the United States but world-wide, not only in a change in mood but in a change in tactics. The Asians withdrew their nuclear subs to the waters of the Western Pacific and the Indian Ocean, and when Dash got confirmation of that he picked up the phone and called Vern Scanyon.

"I think—" He paused, and reached out to touch the smooth wood of his desk top. "I think it's working. Pat your staff on the back for me. Now, what else do you need?"

But there was nothing.

We were fully committed now. We had gone as far as we could go, and the rest was up to the expedition itself.

14

Missionary to Mars

Not more than six times a day Don Kayman allowed himself to pray. He prayed for various things—sometimes for relief from the sound of Titus Hesburgh sucking his teeth, sometimes to be spared the smell of stale farts that smogged the interior of the spacecraft—but there were always three petitions in each prayer: the success of the mission, the fulfillment of God's plan for Man and, most particularly, the health and well-being of his friend Roger Torraway.

Roger had the distinction of a private stateroom of his own. It was not much of a room, and the privacy was only an elastic curtain, gossamer thin and not wholly opaque; but it was all his. The other three shared the crew cabin. Sometimes Roger shared it, too, or at least parts of Roger did. He was all over the place, Roger was.

Kayman looked in on him often. The trip was a long, dull time for him. His own specialty, which was of course not operative until they actually set foot on the surface of Mars, needed no touch-up or practice. Areology was a static science, and would remain so until he himself, hopefully, added something to it after landing. So he had let Titus Hesburgh teach him the instrument board, and a little later had let Brad teach him something about fieldstripping a cyborg. The grotesque form that slowly writhed and postured in its foam cocoon was no longer unfamiliar. Kayman knew every inch of it, inside and out. As the weeks wore on he lost the abhorrence that had deterred him from wrenching an eye from its socket or opening a panel into a plastic-lined gut.

It was not all he had to do. He had his music tapes to listen to, an occasional microfiche to read, games to play. At chess he and Titus Hesburgh were pretty evenly matched. They played interminable tournaments, best 38 games out of 75, and used their personal comm allotments to have chess texts radioed up to them from Earth. It would have been relaxing for Father Kayman to pray more, but after the first week it had occurred to him that even prayer could be carried to excess. He rationed it out: on awakening, before meals, in midevening and before retiring. That was all. That was not, of course, to count the quick lift from a Paternoster or from telling His Holiness's rosary. And then he would go back to the endless refurbishing of Roger. He had always had a queasy stomach, but obviously Roger was oblivious to these invasions of his person and took no harm from them. Kayman gradually began to appreciate the inner beauty of Roger's anatomy, both that part which was Man's handiwork and that part which was God's; he gave thanks for both.

He could not quite give thanks for what God and man had done to the interior of Roger's mind. It troubled him that seven months were being stolen out of his friend's life. It drew forth compassion that Roger's love went to a woman who held it cheap.

But, everything considered, Kayman was happy.

He had never been on a Mars mission before, but this was where he belonged. Twice he had been in space: a shuttle run to an orbiter, when he was still a graduate student seeking his doctorate in planetology; then a ninety-day tour in Space Station Betty. Both were acknowledged to be mere practice for the mission that would complete his study of Mars.

All that he knew of Mars he had learned telescopically or deductively or from the observations of others. He knew a lot of that. He had played and replayed the synoptic tapes of all the Orbiters and Mariners and Surveyors. He had analyzed returned bits of soil and rock. He had interviewed every one of the Americans, French and British who had landed in their various Mars expeditions, and most of the Russians, Japanese and Chinese as well.

He knew all about Mars. He always had.

As a child he had grown up on the Edgar Rice Burroughs Mars, the colorful Barsoom of the ocher dead sea bottoms and hurtling tiny moons. As he grew older he distinguished fact from fiction. There was no reality in the four-armed green warriors and the red-skinned, egg-laying, beautiful Martian princesses, to the extent that science was in touch with "reality." But he knew that scientists' estimates of "reality" changed from year to year. Burroughs had not invented Barsoom out of airy imaginings. He had taken it almost verbatim from the most authoritative scientific "reality" of his day. It was Percival Lowell's Mars, not Burroughs's, that was finally denied by bigger telescopes and by space probes. In the "reality" of scientific opinion, life on Mars had been born and died a dozen times.

But even that had never been settled, really. It depended on a philosophical question. What was "life"? Did it have to mean a creature that resembled an ape or an oak tree? Did it necessarily mean a creature which dissolved its nutrients in a water-based biology, took part in an oxidation-reduction cycle of energy transfer, reproduced itself and grew thereby from the environment? Don Kayman did not think so. He considered it arrogance to limit "life" so parochially, and he was humble in the face of his Creator's all-potentiating majesty.

In any case, the case for life genetically related to Earth life was still open. Well, ajar. True, no ape or oak tree had been found. Not even a lichen. Not even a growing cell. Not even (he had to confess with rue, because Dejah Thoris died hard in his bosom) such prerequisites as free oxygen or water.

But Kayman did not accept that the fact that because no one had slipped on a bed of Martian moss, there was none anywhere on Mars to slip on. Less than a hundred human beings had ever set foot on Mars. The combined area of their explorations was only a matter of a few hundred square miles. On Mars! Where there were no oceans, so the land surface to explore was greater than the Earth's! It was almost like pretending to know the Earth by making four quick trips to the Sahara, the top of the Himalayas, Antarctica and the Greenland icecap . . .

Well, no, Kayman conceded to himself. That wasn't strictly fair. There had been innumerable fly-bys and orbiters, surveyors that landed and snatched up samples of soil.

Nevertheless, the principle was sound. There was too much of Mars. No one could pretend that it did not possess secrets still. Water might yet be found. Some of the rifts looked hopeful. Some of the valleys had shapes that could hardly be understood unless you assumed they were carved out by streams. Even if they were dry there still might be water, vast oceans of water even, locked under the surface. Oxygen one knew was present. Not a great deal on the average, but averages were not important. Locally there could be plenty. And so there might be . . .

Life.

Kayman sighed. It was one of his great regrets that he had not been able to deflect the decision on a landing place to one of his personal favorites for suspicion of life, the Solis Lacus area. The decision had gone against him. It had been taken on very high authority—in fact, it was Dash himself who said, "I don't give a leaping shit where something may be alive now. I want to put this bird down where our boy can expect to stay alive the easiest."

So they had picked a spot nearer the equator and in the northern hemisphere; the main features were called Isidius Regio and Nepenthes, and at their interface was a gentle crater that Don Kayman had privately christened *Home.*

Also privately, he regretted the loss of Solis Lacus and its seasonally changing shape (growing plants? Probably not—but one could hope!), the bright W-shaped cloud around the canals of Ulysses and Fortunae that had formed and reformed every afternoon through one long conjunction, the brilliant flash (reflected sunlight? a hydrogen-fusion blast?) that Saheki saw in Tithonius Lacus on the first of December 1951, as bright as a sixth-magnitude star. Somebody else would have to investigate these things. He would not.

But apart from such regrets, he was content enough. The northern hemisphere was a wise choice. Its seasons were better arranged because, just as on Earth, the northern hemisphere had its winter when it was closest to the sun and so kept marginally warmer all year around. Winter there was twenty days shorter than summer; in the south, of course, it was the other way around. And although Home had never been observed to change shape or emit flashes of light, it had in fact been identified with a fair number of recent cloud formations. Kayman had not given up hope that some of the clouds were of water ice, if not water itself! He fantasized afternoon thundershowers on the Martian plain, and more soberly thought about the large stretches of limonite that had been identified nearby. Limonite contained bound water in quantity; it would be a resource for Roger, even if no Martian plant or animal had evolved to exploit it.

On the whole, he was content about everything.

He was en route to Mars! That was a source of great joy to him, for which he rendered thanks six times each day. Also he had a hope.

Don Kayman was too good a scientist to confuse his hopes with observations. He would report what he found. But he knew what he *wanted* to find. He wanted to find life.

To the extent that the mission's purposes permitted, in the ninety-one Martian days he would be able to stay on the planet's surface, he would keep his eyes open. Everyone knew he would do this. It was in fact part of his contingent, time-permitting briefing instructions.

What not everyone knew was *why* Kayman was so interested.

Dejah Thoris was not quite dead for him. He still had hope that there would be life; not only life but intelligent life; not only intelligent life, but life with a soul to save and bring to his God.

Everything that happened on the spacecraft was under constant surveillance, and synoptic transmissions took place to Earth regularly. So we kept tabs on them. We watched the chess games and the arguments. We monitored Brad's currycombing of Roger's bodily functions, both meat and metal. We saw the night when Titus Hesburgh wept for five hours, gently and dreamily, rebuffing all of Kayman's offers to sympathize with a smile through tears. In some ways Hesburgh had the lousiest job aboard; seven months coming, seven months going and in between three months of nothing. He would be all alone in orbit while Kayman, Brad and Roger were disporting themselves on the surface. He would be lonely, and he would be bored.

He would be worse than that. Seventeen months in space was a practical guarantee that for the last few decades of his life he would be plagued by a hundred different muscle, bone and circulatory disorders. They exercised faithfully, wrestling each other and struggling against springs, flailing their arms and pumping their legs; that would not be enough. There was inevitably calcium resorption from the bone, and there was loss of muscle tone. For those who landed, the three months on Mars would make a great difference. In that time they would repair much of the damage and be in better shape for the return. For Hesburgh there was no such break. His seventeen months in zero-G would be uninterrupted, and the experience of previous spacefarers had made the consequences clear. It meant lowering his life expectancy by a decade or more. And if he wept once in a while, there was no one who had better reason.

Time passed, time passed. A month, two months, six months. Beyond them in the skies the capsule with the 3070 was climbing after them; behind it, the magnetohydrodynamic power plant with its crew of two. When they were two weeks out they ceremoniously switched watches, changing to new quartz-crystal timepieces set to the Martian day. From then on they lived by the Martian clock. It made little enough practical difference; the day for Mars is just a bit more than thirty-seven minutes longer than Earth's; but the difference was significant in their minds.

One week before arrival, they began to speed Roger up.

For Roger the seven months had felt like thirty hours, subjective time. It had been time enough. He had eaten a few meals, exchanged several dozen communications with the rest of the crew. He had received messages from Earth and returned a few of them. He had asked for his guitar, been refused it on the grounds that he couldn't play it, asked for it anyway out of curiosity and found that that was quite true: he could pluck a string, but he could not hear the note that resulted from it. In fact, apart from the specially slowed-down tapes, he could hear nothing at all most of the time, and only a sort of high-pitched scurrying sound ever. Air did not conduct the sort of vibrations he could perceive. When the tape recorder was out of contact with the metal frame to which he was bound, he could not hear even it, nor could his own voice be made to record.

They warned him they were beginning to accelerate his perceptions. They left the curtain to his cubicle open, and he began to notice flickers of motion. He caught a glimpse of Hesburgh dozing nearby, then saw figures actually moving; after a time he even recognized who they were. Then they put him to sleep, to make final adjustments on his backpack, and when he woke up he was alone, the curtain was drawn—and he heard voices.

He pushed the curtain aside and looked out, and there was the smiling face of his wife's lover greeting him. "Good morning, Roger! Nice to have you with us again."

. . . And eighteen minutes later, twelve travel time and the rest decoding and relaying, the President watched it happen from more than a hundred million miles away, on the screen in the Oval Office.

He was not the only one. The TV nets put the scene on the air, and the satellites rebroadcast it all over the world. They were watching in the Under Palace in Peking, and inside the Kremlin; on Downing Street and the Champs Élysées and Ginza.

"Son of a bitch," said Dash historically, "they've made it."

Vern Scanyon was with him. "Son of a bitch," he echoed. Then he said, "Well, almost made it. They've still got to land."

"Any problem about that?"

Cautiously: "Not as far as I know—"

"God," said the President positively, "would not be so unfair. I think you and I are going to taste some bourbon right now; it's about that time."

They stayed and watched for half an hour, and a quarter of a bottle. On and off over the next few days they watched more, they and the rest of the world. The whole world saw Hesburgh making final checks and preparing the Mars-lander for separation. Watched Don Kayman go through a dry run under the pilot's microscopic observation, since he would be at the controls for the trip down out of orbit. Watched Brad make a final, ultimate recheck on Roger's telemetry, find it all functioning in the green, and then do it over one more time. Watched Roger himself moving about the crew cabin and squeezing into the lander.

And watched the lander separate and Hesburgh look wistfully out at its minus-delta flare as it began to drop out of orbit.

We figured that three and a quarter billion people watched the landing. It was not much to watch; if you have seen one landing you have seen them all. But it was important.

It began at a quarter to four in the morning, Washington time, and the President had himself awakened to see it. "That priest," he said, frowning, "what kind of a pilot is he? If anything goes wrong—"

"He's checked out, sir," soothed his NASA aide. "Anyway, he's actually only about a third-place backup. The automatic sequencing is in primary control. If anything goes wrong, General Hesburgh is monitoring it from the orbiter and he can override. Father Kayman doesn't have anything to do unless everything goes wrong at once."

Dash shrugged, and the aide noticed that the President's fingers were crossed. "What about the follow-up flights?" he asked, staring at the screen.

"No sweat at all, sir. The computer will inject into Mars orbit in thirty-two days, and the generator twenty-seven days later. As soon as the lander is down General Hesburgh is going to perform a course correction and overtake the moon Deimos. We expect to land both the computer and the generator there, probably in the crater Voltaire; Hesburgh will make that determination for us."

"Um," said the President. "Has Roger been told who's on the generator spacecraft?"

"No, sir."

"Um." The President abandoned the television screen and got up. At the window, staring out at the pretty White House lawn, June-green and blossoming, he said, "There's a man coming over from the computer center in Alexandria. I'd like you to be here when he arrives."

"Yes, sir."

"Commander Chiaroso. Supposed to be pretty good. Used to be a professor at M.I.T. He says there's something strange about our projections about this whole project. Have you heard any gossip?"

"No, sir," said the NASA aide, alarmed. "Strange, sir?"

Dash shrugged. "That's all I need," he said, "getting this whole son-of-a-bitching thing going and then finding out— Hey! What the hell's happening?"

On the TV screen the image was jumping and breaking up; it

went out entirely, restored itself and disappeared again, leaving only the tracery of raster.

"That's all right sir," said the aide quickly. "It's reentry buffeting. When they hit the atmosphere they lose video contact. Even the telemetry's affected, but we've got ample margins all around; it'll be all right."

The President demanded, "Why the hell is that? I thought the whole point was that Mars didn't *have* any atmosphere?"

"Not a lot, sir. But it does have some, and because it's smaller it's got a shallower, flatter gravity well. In the upper atmosphere it's just about as dense as the Earth's is, at the same altitude, and that's where the buffeting happens."

"God damn it," snarled the President, "I don't like surprises! Why didn't somebody tell me this?"

"Well, sir—"

"Never mind! I'll take it up later. I hope surprising Torraway isn't going to be a mistake— Well, forget it. What's happening now?"

The aide looked not at the screen but at his watch. "Parachute deployment, sir. They've completed retrofire. Now it's just a matter of coming down. In a few seconds—" The aide pointed to the screen, which obediently built itself into a picture again. "There! They're in controlled descent mode now."

And they sat and waited while the lander slid down through the thin Martian air under its immense canopy, quintuple the size of a parachute built for air.

When it hit the sound came a hundred million miles, and then sounded like trash cans falling off a roof. But the lander had been built for it; and the crew were long since in their protective cocoons.

There was a hissing sound from the screen and the clicking of cooling metal.

And then Brad's voice. "We're on Mars," he said prayerfully, and Father Kayman began to whisper the words from the Ordinary of the Mass, *"Laudamas te, benedicimus te, adoramus te, glorificamus te. Gloria in excelsis Deo, et in terra pax hominibus bonae voluntatis."*

And to the familiar words he added, *"Et in Martis."*

15

How the Good News Went from Mars to Earth

When we first realized that there was a serious risk that a major war would destroy civilization and make the Earth uninhabitable—which is to say, shortly after we collectively began to realize anything at all—we decided to take steps to colonize Mars.

It wasn't easy for us.

The whole human race was in trouble. Energy was in short supply the world over, which meant fertilizer was expensive, which meant people were hungry, which meant explosively dangerous tensions. The world's resources were none too ample for the bare necessity of keeping billions of people alive. We had to find ways to divert capacities that were badly needed elsewhere to long-range planning. We set up three separate think tanks and gave them all the facilities we could steal from daily needs. One explored options for solving the growing tensions on Earth. One was charged with setting up refuges on Earth itself, so that even if a thermonuclear war did occur a small fraction of us could survive.

The third looked into extraterrestrial possibilities.

In the beginning it seemed as though we had a thousand options to choose from, and each of the three major tracks had branches that looked hopeful. One by one the tracks closed off. Our best estimates—not the ones we gave the President of the United States, but the private ones we showed to nobody but ourselves—were of point nine to ten nines probability of thermonuclear war within a decade; and we closed down the center for solving international tensions in the first year. Setting up refuges was a little more hopeful. It developed that worst-case analysis indicated a few places on the Earth that would be unlikely to experience direct attack—Antarctica, parts of the Sahara, even some of Australia and a number of islands. Ten sites were selected. Each one had only a point zero one or less probability of being destroyed; if all ten were considered, the probability that they would all be destroyed was relatively insignificant. But fine-grain analysis showed that there were two flaws. For one, we could not be sure how much long-life isotope would remain in the atmosphere after such a war, and the indications were that there would be excessive levels of ionizing radiation for as much as a thousand years. Over that time scale, the probability that even one of the refugees would survive became far less than point five. Worst of all, there was the necessity for capital investment. To build the refuges underground and fill them with the immense quantity needed of complex electronic equipment, generators, fuel reserves and so on was, as a practical matter, impossible. There was no way for us to get the money.

So we terminated that think tank and put all the resources we could manage into extraterrestrial colonization. At the beginning, that had looked like the least hopeful solution of all.

But—almost!—we had managed to make it work. When Roger Torraway landed, that completed the first and hardest step. By the time the ships that were following him reached their positons, in orbit or on the surface of the planet, we would be able, for the first time, to plan for a future, with the survival of the race assured.

So we watched with great satisfaction as Roger stepped out on the surface of the planet.

Roger's backpack computer was a triumph of design. It had three separate systems, cross-linked and sharing facilities, but with enough redundancy so that all systems had point nine reliability at least until the 3070 backup computer reached orbit. One system mediated his perceptions. Another controlled the subsystems of nerve and muscle that let him walk and move. The third telemetered all of his inputs. Whatever he saw, we saw on Earth.

We had gone to some trouble to arrange this. By Shannon's Law there was not enough band width to transmit everything, but we had included a random sampling feature. Approximately one bit per hundred was transmitted—first to the radio in the landing craft, where we had assigned one channel permanently for that purpose. Then it was rebroadcast to the orbiter, where General Hesburgh floated, watching the television screen while the calcium oozed out of his bones. From there, cleaned and amplified, it was burst-transmitted to whichever synchronous satellite of Earth was at that moment locked into both Mars and Goldstone. So what we all saw was only about one percent "real." But that was enough. The rest was filled in by a comparison program we had written for the Goldstone receiver. Hesburgh saw only a series of stills; on Earth we broadcast what looked exactly like on-the-spot movies of whatever Roger saw.

So all over the Earth, on television sets in every country, people watched the beige and brown mountains that rose ten miles tall, saw the glint of Martian sunlight off the window frames of the lander, could even read the expression on Father Kayman's face as he rose from prayer and for the first time looked out on Mars.

In the Under Palace in Peking the great lords of New People's Asia interrupted a planning session to watch the screen. Their feelings were mixed. It was America's triumph, not theirs. In the Oval Office President Deshatine's joy was pure. Not only was the triumph American, it was personal; he was identified forever as the President who had established humanity on Mars. Almost everybody was at least a little joyous—even Dorrie Tor-raway, who sat in the private room at the back of her shop with her chin in her hands, studying the message of her husband's eyes. And of course in the great white cube of the project outside of Tonka, Oklahoma, everyone left on the staff watched the pictures from Mars almost all the time.

They had plenty of leisure for that. They didn't have much else to do. It was astonishing how empty the building became as soon as Roger was out of it.

They had all been rewarded, from the stockroom boys up: a personal commendation for everyone from the President, plus a thirty-day bonus leave and a jump in grade. Clara Bly used hers to finish up her long-delayed honeymoon. Weidner and Freeling took the time to write a rough draft of Brad's paper, transmitting every paragraph to him in orbit as it came off their typewriters, and receiving his corrections via Goldstone. Vern Scanyon, of course, had a hero's tour with the President, in fifty-four states and the principal cities of twenty foreign countries. Brenda Hartnett had appeared on television twice with her kids. They had been deluged with gifts. The widow of the man who had died to put Roger Torraway on Mars was now a millionaire. They had all had their hour of fame, as soon as the launch got off and

Roger was en route, especially in those moments just before the landing.

Then the world looked out at Mars through the eyes of Roger, and the senses of the brother on Roger's back, and all their fame blew away. From then on it was all Roger.

We watched too.

We saw Brad and Don Kayman in their suits, completing the pre-egress drill. Roger had no need of a suit. He stood on tiptoe at the door of the lander, poised, sniffing the empty wind, his great black wings hovering behind him and soaking in the rays of the disconcertingly tiny, but disconcertingly bright, sun. Through the TV pick-up inside the lander we saw Roger silhouetted against the dull beige and brown of the abrupt Martian horizon. . . .

And then through Roger's eyes we saw what he saw. To Roger, looking out on the bright, jewel-like colors of the planet he was meant to live on, it was a fairyland, beautiful and inviting.

The lander had stretched out skeletal magnesium steps to stroke the surface of Mars, but Roger didn't need them. He jumped down, the wings fluttering—for balance, not for lift—and landed lightly on the chalky orange surface, where the wash of the landing rockets had scoured away the crust. He stood there for a moment, surveying his kingdom with the great faceted eyes. "Don't rush things," advised a voice in his head that came from Don Kayman's suit radio. "Better go through the exercise list."

Roger grinned without looking around; "Sure," he said, and began to move away. First he walked, then trotted; then he began to run. If he had sped through the streets of Tonka, here he was a blur. He laughed out loud. He changed the frequency responses of his eyes, and the distant towering hills flashed bright blue, the flat plain a mosaic of greens and yellows and reds. "This is great!" he whispered, and the receivers at the lander picked up the subspoken words and passed them on to Earth.

"Roger," said Brad petulantly, "I wish you'd take it easy until we get the jeep ready."

Roger turned. The other two were back at the steps of the lander, deploying the Mars vehicle from its fold-down condition behind its hatch.

He bounded back toward them joyously. "Need help?"

They didn't have to answer. They did need help; in their suits it was a major undertaking to slip the retaining strap off one of the basketwork wheels. "Move over," he said, and quickly freed the wheels and stretched the stilted legs into stand-by position. The jeep had both: wheels for the flat parts, stilts for climbing. It was meant to be the most flexible vehicle man could make for getting around Mars, but it wasn't. Roger was. When it was done he touched them and promised, "I won't go out of line of sight." And then he was gone, off to see the patches of color around a series of hummocks, Dali-bright and irresistible.

"That's dangerous!" Brad grumbled over the radio. "Wait till we finish testing the jeep! If anything happens to you we're in trouble."

"Nothing will," said Roger, "and no!" He couldn't wait. He was using his body for what it had been built to do, and patience was gone. He ran. He jumped. He found himself two kilometers from the lander before he knew it; looked back, saw that they were creeping slowly after him and went on. His oxygenation system stepped up the pump-rate to compensate for the extra demands; his muscles met the challenge smoothly. It was not his muscles that propelled him but the servo-systems that had been built in instead; but it was the tiny muscles at the ends of the nerves that ordered the servos. All the practice paid off. It was no effort at all to reach two hundred kilometers an hour, leaping over small cracks and craters, bounding up and down the slopes of larger ones.

"Come back, Roger!" It was Don Kayman, sounding worried. A pause while Roger ran on; then a dizzying sense of movement in his vision, and another voice said, "Go back, Roger! It's time."

He stopped flatfooted, skidded, flailed with his wings against the almost indetectable air, almost fell and caught himself. The familiar voice chuckled, "Come on, honey! Be a good boy and go back now."

Dorrie's voice.

And out of the distant thin whirl of drifting sand the colors coalesced into the shape of Dorrie to match the voice of Dorrie, smiling, not ten meters away, long legs disappearing into shorts, a gay halter for a top, her hair blown in the breeze.

The radio voice in his head laughed, this time in the tones of Don Kayman. "Surprised you, didn't we?"

It took a moment for Roger to reply. "Yeah," he managed.

"It was Brad's idea. We taped Dorrie back on Earth. When you need an emergency signal, Dorrie will give it to you."

"Yeah," said Roger again. As he stared, the smiling figure turned wispy, the colors faded, and it disappeared.

He turned and went back. The return trip took a lot longer than the joyous outbound run, and the colors were no longer quite so bright.

Don Kayman drove the jeep steadily toward the trudging shape of Roger Torraway, trying to get the hang of staying in the plunging seat without being thrown back and forth into the restraining belts. It was in no way comfortable. The suit that had been tailored to his body had developed tight spots and loose ones in the long months up from Earth—or maybe, he reminded himself fairly, he was the one who had swelled a little in some places and shrunk in others—he had not, he conceded, been wholly diligent about his exercise. Also he had to go to the bathroom. There was relief plumbing in the suit. He knew how to use it, but he didn't want to.

Above the discomfort was an overlay of envy and worry. The envy was a sin that he could purge himself of, whenever he could find someone to hear his confession—a venial sin at most, he thought, considering the manifest advantages Roger had over the other two. Worry was a worse sin, not against his God but against the success of the mission. It was too late to worry. Maybe it had been a mistake to set up the simulation of Roger's wife to punch home urgent messages—at the time, he hadn't known quite how complicated Roger's feelings were about Dorrie. But it was too late to do anything about it.

Brad didn't seem to have any worries. He was chuckling fondly over Roger's performance. "Did you notice?" he was demanding. "Didn't fall once! Perfect coordination. Normative match, bio and servo. I tell you, Don, we've got it knocked!"

"It's a little early to tell," Kayman said uneasily, but Brad went on. Kayman thought of turning off the voice in his suit helmet, but it was almost as easy to turn off his attention. He looked around him. They had landed near the sunrise terminator, but they had used more than half the Martian day in preexit check and in putting the jeep together. It was becoming late afternoon. They would have to be back before it was dark, he told himself. Roger would be able to navigate by starlight, but it would be chancier for Brad and him. Maybe some other time, after they had had the practice. . . . He really wanted that very much, to stroll the ebony surface of a Barsoomian night, with the stars pinpoints of colored fire in a velvet black sky. But not yet.

They were on a great cratered plain. The size was hard to estimate at first. Looking around through his faceplate Kayman had trouble remembering how far away the mountains were. His mind knew, because he knew every grid-square of the Martian maps for two hundred kilometers around their impact point. But his senses were deceived by the absolutely transparent visibility. The mountains to the west, he was aware, were a hundred kilometers away and nearly ten kilometers high. They looked like nearby foothills.

He clutched the jeep down and stopped it; they were within a few meters of Roger. Brad fumbled himself free and slid clumsily out of the seat, lurching in an ungainly slow gait over toward Roger to study him. "Everything all right?" he said anxiously. "Of course it is; I can see that. How's your balance? Close your eyes, will you—I mean, you know, shut off your vision." He peered anxiously at the faceted hemispheres. "Did you? I can't tell, you know."

"I did," said Roger through the radio in his head.

"Great! No sense of dizziness, eh? No trouble keeping your balance? Keeping your eyes closed," he went on, circling Roger and staring at him from all angles, "swing your arms up and down a few times—fine! Now windmill them, opposite directions—" Kayman couldn't see his face, but he could hear the broad grin in the tone of Brad's voice. "Beautiful, Roger! Optimal all the way!"

"My congratulations to you both," said Kayman, out of the vehicle and watching the performance. "Roger?"

The head turned toward him, and though there was nothing about the appearance of the eyes that changed, Kayman knew Roger was looking at him. "I only wanted to say," he went on,

not quite sure where the sentence was going to go, "that I'm—
well, I'm sorry we sprang that bit about using Dorrie's image to
convey messages on you. I have a feeling we've given you too
many surprises."

"It's all right, Don." The trouble with Roger's voice, Kayman
reflected again, was that you couldn't tell much from its tone.

"Having said that much," he said, "I think I ought to tell you
that we do have another surprise for you. A pleasant one, I
think. Sulie Carpenter's following us up here. Her ship should
arrive in about five weeks."

Silence, and no expression. "Why," said Roger at last, "that's
very nice. She's a fine person."

"Yes." But the conversation didn't seem to have anywhere to
go after that, and besides Brad was impatient to put Roger
through a whole bending and stretching series. Kayman allowed himself the privileges of a tourist. He turned away, staring toward the distant mountains, squinted at the bright sun,
which even the auto-darkening of his faceplate didn't make
quite comfortable, then looked around him. Clumsily he managed to kneel and to scoop up a clutch of pebbly dirt in his
gloved hand. It would be his job next day to start the systematic
collection of samples to return to Earth that was one minor task
of the mission. Even after half a dozen manned landings and
nearly forty instrumented missions, there was still an insatiable
demand for samples of Martian soil in the laboratories of Earth.
Right now, however, he was allowing himself to daydream.
There was plenty of limonite in this sand, and the quartz peb-
bles were far from round; the edges were not sharp, but neither
had they been milled to roundness. He scraped into the soil. A
yellowish powder rested on top; underneath it the material was
darker and coarser. There were shiny specks, almost like glass.
Quartz? he wondered, and idly scooped around one.

He froze, his hands cupping an irregular rounded blob of crystal.

It had a stem. A stem that thrust down into the ground. That spread and divided into dark, rough-surfaced tendrils.

Roots.

Don Kayman jumped up, whirling on Roger and Brad. "Look!" he shouted, the object plucked free in his gauntleted hand. "Dear God in Heaven, look at this!"

And Roger, coming up out of a crouch, spun and leaped at him. One hand knocked the glittering crystal thing spinning fifty meters into the air, bending the metal of the gauntlet. Kayman felt a sharp, quick pain in that forearm and saw the other hand striking toward his faceplate like the claw of an angry Kodiak bear; and that was the last he saw.

16

On the Perception of Perils

Vern Scanyon parked his car any which way across the painted yellow lines that marked his own place, jumped out and held his thumb against the elevator button. He had been awake less than forty minutes, but he was not at all sleepy. What he was, was angry and apprehensive. The President's appointments secretary had waked him out of a sound sleep with a phone call to say that the President had diverted his flight to stop at Tonka— "to discuss the problems of the perceptual system of Commander Torraway." To kick ass, more accurately. Scanyon had not known anything about Roger's sudden attack on Don Kayman until he was in his car, hastening to the project building to meet the President.

"Morning, Vern." Jonny Freeling looked scared and angry, too. Scanyon brushed past him into his own office.

"Come on in," he barked. "Now, in words of one syllable. What happened?"

Freeling said resentfully, "It's not my responsibility to—"

"Freeling."

"Roger's systems overreacted a little. Apparently Kayman

moved suddenly, and the simulations system translated it into a threat; Roger defended himself and pushed Kayman away."

Scanyon stared.

"Broke his arm," Freeling amended. "It was only a simple fracture, General. No complications. It's splinted, it'll heal perfectly—he just has to get by with one functioning arm for a while. It's a pity for Don Kayman, of course. He won't be very comfortable—"

"Fuck Kayman! Why didn't he know how to act around Roger?"

"Well, he did know. He found something that he thought was indigenous life! That was pretty exciting. All he wanted to do was show it to Roger."

"Life?" Scanyon's eyes looked more hopeful.

"Some sort of plant, they think."

"Can't they tell?"

"Well, Roger seems to have knocked it out of Kayman's hand. Brad went looking for it afterward, but he couldn't find it."

"Jesus," Scanyon snorted. "Freeling, tell me one thing. What kind of incompetents have we got working for us?" It was not a question that had a proper answer and Scanyon didn't wait for one. "In about twenty minutes," he said, "the President of the United States is going to come through that door and he's going to want to know line by line what happened and why. I don't know what he's going to ask, but whatever it is there's one answer I don't want to give him, and that's 'I don't know.' So tell me, Freeling. Tell me all over again what happened, why it went wrong, why we didn't think it would go wrong and how we can be *damn* sure it isn't going to go wrong again." It took a little more than twenty minutes, but then they had more; the President's plane touched down late, and by the time Dash arrived

Scanyon was as ready as he knew how to be. Even ready for the fury in the President's face.

"Scanyon," Dash snapped at once, "I warned you, no more surprises. This time is one too many, and I think I'm going to have to have your ass."

"You can't put a man on Mars without risks, Mr. President!"

Dash stared eye to eye for a moment, then said, "Maybe. What's the priest's condition?"

"He's got a broken radius, but it's going to be all right. There's something more important than that. He thinks he found life on Mars, Mr. President!"

Dash shook his head. "I know, some kind of plant. But he managed to lose it."

"For the moment. Kayman's a good man. If he said he found something important, he did. He'll find it again."

"I certainly hope so, Vern. Don't slide away from this. Why did this thing happen?"

"A slight overcontrol of his perceptual systems. That's it, Mr. President, and that's *all* it is. In order to make him respond quickly and positively, we had to build in some simulation features. To get his attention to priority messages, he sees his wife speaking to him. To get him to react to danger, he sees something frightening. That way his head can keep up with the reflexes we built into his body. Otherwise he'd go crazy."

"Breaking the priest's arm wasn't crazy?"

"No! It was an accident. When Kayman jumped at him he interpreted it as an actual attack of some kind. He responded. Well, Mr. President, in this case it was wrong, and it cost us a broken arm; but suppose there had been a real threat? Any *kind* of a threat! He would have met it. Whatever it was! He's invulnerable, Mr. President. Nothing can ever catch him off-guard."

"Yeah," said the President, and after a moment, "maybe so."
He stared over Scanyon's head for a moment and said, "What
about this other crap?"

"Which crap, Mr. President?"

Dash shrugged irritably. "As I understand it, there's something wrong with all our computer projections, especially the
polls we took."

Alarm bells went off in Scanyon's head. He said reluctantly,
"Mr. President, there's a lot of paper on my desk I haven't got
through yet. You know I've been traveling a lot—"

"Scanyon," said the President, "I'm going now. Before you do
anything else, I want you to take a look through the papers on
your desk and find that paper and read it. Tomorrow morning,
eight o'clock, I want you in my office, and then I want to know
what's happening, specifically three things. First, I want to hear
that Kayman's all right. Second, I want that living thing found.
Third, I want to know the score on the computer projections,
and it better be all right. So long, Scanyon. I know it's only five
in the morning, but don't go back to bed."

By then we could have reassured Scanyon and the President
about one thing. The object Kayman had picked up was indeed
some form of life. We had reconstructed the sampled data
through Roger's eyes, filtered out the simulations, and seen
what he had seen. It had not yet occurred to the President or his
advisers that that could be done, but it would. It was not possible
to make out fine details, because of the limited number of bits
available, but the object was shaped rather like an artichoke,
coarse leaves pointing upward, and a little like a mushroom:
there was a crystalline cap of transparent material over it. It
possessed roots, and unless it was an artifact (point zero zero

one probability, at most), it had to be a form of life. We did not find that very interesting except, of course, as it would reinforce general interest in the Mars project itself. As to the doubt cast on the computer simulations, we were considerably more interested. We had followed that development for some time, ever since a graduate student named Byrne had written a Systems-360 program to recheck his desk-calculator previous recheck of some of the poll results. We were as concerned about it as the President was. But the probability of any serious consequence there too appeared quite small, especially since everything else was going well. The MHD generator was almost ready for preorbit injection course corrections; we had selected an installation site for it in the crater called Voltaire on the moon, Deimos. Not far behind it was the vehicle that contained the 3070 and its human crew of two, including Sulie Carpenter. And on Mars itself they had already begun construction of permanent installations. They were a little behind schedule. Kayman's accident had slowed them down, not only because of what it did to him but because what Brad then insisted on doing to Roger: field-stripping his shoulder-pack computer to test for glitches. There weren't any. But it took two Martian days to be sure; and then, because Kayman begged, they took time to find his life form. They found it, or not it, exactly, but dozens of other specimens of the same thing; and Brad and Roger left Kayman inside the lander to study it while they began building their domes.

The first step was to find an area of Mars which had suitable geology. The surface should be as much like soil as possible, but solid rock had to be not far below. It took half a day of pounding explosive spikes into the ground and listening to echoes to be sure they had that.

Then, laboriously, the solar generators were spread out, and the subsurface rock-bound water was boiled out. As the first tiny plume of steam appeared at the lip of the pipe, they cheered. It would have been easy to miss it. The utterly dry Martian air snatched every molecule up almost as soon as it left the pipe. But by leaning close to the valve at the end one could see a faint, irregular misting that distorted shapes beyond it. It was water vapor, all right.

The next step was to spread out three great stretches of monomolecular film, the smallest first and the largest on top, and seal the topmost to the ground all around its periphery. Then they carried the pumps out on the basket-wheeled vehicle and started them going. The Martian atmosphere was extremely thin, but it was there; the pumps would ultimately fill the domes, partly with the compressed carbon dioxide and nitrogen from the atmosphere, partly with the water vapor they were boiling out of the rock. There was, to be sure, no oxygen to speak of in any of that, but they didn't have to find oxygen; they would make it, in exactly the same way Earth made its oxygen: through the intercession of photosynthetic plants.

It would take four or five days for the outer dome to fill to its planned quarter kilogram of pressure. Then they would start filling the second one, up to almost a kilogram (which would increase the pressure in the diminishing space of the outer shell to about a half kilo). Then, finally, they would fill the inner dome to two kilograms, and so they would have an environment in which people could live without pressure suits, and even breathe as soon as the crops gave them breathing material.

Of course, Roger didn't need any of that. He didn't need the oxygen; he didn't even need the plants for food, or not much and not for a long time. He could stay perhaps forever living off the unfailing light of the sun for most of his energy, plus what would be microwaved down from the MHD generator once it was in place. What was needed for the minuscule remaining part of him which was raw animal could easily be supplied by the concentrated foods from the ship for a long time; and only then, after perhaps a couple of Martian years, would he have to begin to depend on what came out of the hydroponics tanks and the seeds they were already sprouting in sealed cold-frames under the canopies.

It all took several days, since Kayman wasn't a great deal of help. Getting in and out of a pressure suit was agony for him, so they left him in the lander most of the time. When it came time to lug the tanks of carefully hoarded sludge from their toilet facilities over to the dome, Kayman lent a hand. "Exactly one hand," he said, trying to handle the magnesium-shafted rake by wrapping his good arm around it.

"You're doing fine," Brad encouraged. There was enough pressure in the innermost dome now to lift it above their heads, but not quite enough to let them take off their pressure suits. Which was just as well, Brad realized; this way they couldn't smell what they were raking into the sterile soil.

By the time the dome was fully extended the pressure was up to a hundred millibars. This is the pressure of Earth's atmosphere at some ten miles above sea level. It is not an environment in which naked man can survive and work for very long, but it is an environment in which he will only die if something kills him. Half that pressure would be lethal instantly; his body temperature would boil his fluids away.

But when the internal pressure hit the 100-millibar level all three of them crowded through the three successive airlocks and Brad and Don Kayman ceremoniously took off their pressure suits. Brad and Don fitted nosepieces, something like that of an aqualung, in place for breathing; there was still no oxygen to speak of inside the dome. But they got pure oxygen from the tanks on their backs, and with that they were, for the first time,

almost as free as Roger, inside a transplanted bit of Earth that
was a hundred meters across and as tall as a ten-story building.

And inside it, in orderly rows, the seeds they had transplanted were already beginning to sprout and grow.

Meanwhile—

The vehicle with the magnetohydrodynamic generator at-
tained Mars orbit, and with General Hesburgh helping,
matched orbit with Deimos and nestled into the crater. It was a
perfect coupling. The vehicle swung out its struts to touch the
rock of the moon, augered them in, and locked. A brief jet from
the maneuvering system tested its stability: it was now a part of
Deimos. The power system began to sequence toward full operational mode. A fusion flame woke the plasma fires. Radar
reached out to find the target on the lander, then locked on to
the dome. Power began to flow. The energy density of the field
was low enough for Brad and Kayman to walk around in it unaware, and to Roger it was like the basking warmth of sunlight;
but the foil strips in the outer dome gathered the microwave
energy and channeled it to the pumps, the batteries.

The fusion fuel had a life of fifty years. For that long at least
there would be energy for Roger and his backpack computer on
Mars, whatever happened on Earth.

And meanwhile—

There were other couplings.

In the long spiral up from Earth, Sulie Carpenter and her pilot, Dinty Meighan, had had time heavy on their hands and had
found a way to use it.

The act of copulation in free fall presents certain problems.

First Sulie had to buckle one strand of webbing around her waist, then Dinty embraced her with his arms, and she him with her legs. Their motions were underwater slow. It took Sulie a long, gentle, dreamy time to come to orgasm, and Dinty was even slower. When they were finished they were hardly even breathing hard. Sulie stretched and yawned, arching her belly against the retaining strap. "Nice," she said drowsily. "I'll remember that."

"We both will, honey," he said, misunderstanding her. "I think that's the best way we screw. Next time—"

She shook her head to interrupt him. "No next time, Dinty dear. That was it."

He pulled his head back to look at her. "What?"

She smiled. Her right eye was still only centimeters from his left, and their view of each other curiously foreshortened. She craned forward and rubbed her cheek gently against his bristly one.

He scowled and detached himself, suddenly feeling naked where before he had been only bare. He pulled his shorts out from behind the hand hold where he had cached them and slid into them.

"Sulie, what's the matter?"

"Nothing's the matter. We're almost ready for orbit, that's all."

He pushed himself backward across the cramped compartment to get a better look at her. She was worth looking at. Her hair had gone back to muddy blond and her eyes were brown without the contact lenses; and even after almost two hundred days of never being more than ten meters from him, she still looked good to Dinty Meighan. "I didn't think you had any surprises left," he marveled.

"You never can tell about a woman."

"Come on, Sulie! What's this all about? You sound as though you've been planning— Hey!" A thought struck him.

"You volunteered for this mission—not to go to Mars, but to go to some guy! Right? One of the guys ahead of us?"

"You're very quick, Dinty. Not," she said fondly, "where I don't want you to be, though."

"Who is it, Brad? Hesburgh? Not the priest?—oh, wait a minute!" He nodded. "Sure! The one you were mixed up with back on Earth. The cyborg!"

"Colonel Roger Torraway, the human being," she corrected. "As human as you are, except for some improvements."

He laughed, more resentment than humor. "A lot of improvements, and no balls at all."

Sulie unstrapped herself. "Dinty," she said sweetly, "I've enjoyed sex with you, and I respect you, and you've been about as comfortable to be with as any human being possibly could be on this Goddamned eternity trip. But there are some things I don't want you to say. You're right. Roger doesn't happen to have any testicles, right at this exact moment. But he's a human being I can respect and love, and he's the only one like that I've found lately. Believe me, I've looked."

"Thanks!"

"Oh, don't do this, dear Dinty. You know you're not really jealous. You've already got a wife."

"Next year I do! That's a long way off." She shrugged, grinning. "Ah, but Sulie! There are some things you can't kid me about. You love screwing!"

"I like body contact and intimacy," she corrected, "and I like coming to orgasm. I like both those things better with someone I love, Dinty. No offense."

He scowled. "You've got a long wait, sweetie."

"Maybe not."

"The hell you say. I won't see Irene for seven months. But you—you won't be back any faster than I will; and then it only begins. They've got to put him back together for you. Assuming they *can* put him back together. It sounds like a long time between fucks."

"Oh, Dinty. Don't you think I've thought this all out?" She patted him in passing, on the way to her own locker. "Sex isn't just coitus. There are more ways to orgasm than with a penis in my vagina. And there's more to sex than orgasm. Not to mention love. Roger," she went on, wriggling into her jump suit, not so much for modesty as for pockets, "is a resourceful, loving person, and so am I. We'll make out—anyway, until the rest of the colonists land."

"Rest?" he struggled. "Rest of the *colonists?*"

"Haven't you figured it out yet? I'm not going back with all of you, Dinty, and I don't think Roger is either. We're going to be Martians!"

And meanwhile, in the Oval Room of the White House, the President of the United States was confronting Vern Scanyon and a young, coffee-colored man with tinted glasses and the build of a football player. "So you're the one," he said, appraising him. "You think we don't know how to run a computer study."

"No, Mr. President," the young man said steadily. "I don't think that's the problem."

Scanyon coughed. "Byrne here," he said, "is a graduate student on work-study from M.I.T. His thesis is on sampling methodology, and we gave him access to some of the, ah, classified material. Especially public-opinion studies about attitudes on the project."

"But not to a computer," Byrne said.

"Not to a big one," Scanyon corrected. "You had your own desk dataplex."

The President said mildly, "Get on with it, Scanyon."

"Well, his results came out different. According to his interpretations, the public opinion on the whole question of colonizing Mars was, well, apathy. You remember, Mr. President, there was some question about the results at the time? The raw results weren't encouraging at all? But when we played them through analysis they came out positive to—what do you call it?—two sigmas. I never knew why."

"Did you check?"

"Certainly, Mr. President! Not me," Scanyon added quickly. "That wasn't my responsibility. But I'm satisfied that the studies were verified."

Byrne put in, "Three different times, with three different programs. There were minor variations, of course. But they all came out significant and reliable. Only when I repeated them on my desk machine they didn't. And that's the way it is, Mr. President. If you work up the figures on any big computer in the net you get one result. If you work them up on a small isolated machine you get another."

The President drummed the balls of his thumbs on the desk. "What's your conclusion?"

Byrne shrugged. He was twenty-three years old, and his surroundings intimidated him. He looked at Scanyon for help and found none; he said, "You'll have to ask somebody else that one, Mr. President. I can only give you my own conjecture. Somebody's buggering our computer network."

The President rubbed the left lobe of his nose reflectively, nodding slowly. He looked at Byrne for a moment and then said, without raising his voice, "Carousso, come on in here. Mr. Byrne, what you see and hear in this room is top secret. When you leave, Mr. Carousso will see that you are informed as to what that means to you in detail; basically, you are not to talk about it. To anyone. Ever."

The door to the President's anteroom opened and a tall, solid man with a self-effacing air walked in. Byrne stared at him wonderingly: Charles Carousso, the head of the CIA! "What about it, Chuck?" the President asked. "What about him?"

"We've checked Mr. Byrne, of course," said the Agency man. His words were precise and uninflected. "There isn't anything significantly adverse to him—you'll be glad to know, I suppose, Mr. Byrne. And what he says checks out. It isn't only the public-opinion surveys. The war-risk projections, the cost/effectiveness studies—run on the net they come out one way, run on independent calculating machines they come out another. I agree with Mr. Byrne. Our computer net has been compromised."

The President's lips were pressed together as though he were holding back what he wanted to say. All he allowed to come out was, "I want you to find out how this happened, Chuck. But the question now is, who? The Asians?"

"No, sir! We checked that out. It's impossible."

"Bullshit it's impossible!" roared the President. "We know they already did tap our lines once, on the simulation of Roger Torraway's systems!"

"Mr. President, that's an entirely different case. We found that tap and neutralized it. It was in the ground-lines cable on a nonsensitive linkage. The comm circuits on our major machines are absolutely leakproof." He glanced at Byrne. "You have a report on the techniques involved, Mr. President; I'll be glad to go over it with you at another time."

"Oh, don't worry about me," said Byrne, smiling for the first time. "Everybody knows the links are multiply scrambled. If you've checked me out, I'm sure you found out that a lot of us graduate students fool around trying to tap in, and none of us make it."

The agency man nodded. "As a matter of fact, Mr. President,

we tolerate that; it's good field-testing for our security. If people like Mr. Byrne can't think up a way past the blocks, I doubt the Asians can. And the blocks are leakproof. They have to be. The control circuits that go to the War Machine in Butte, the Census Bureau, UNESCO—"

"Wait a minute!" barked the President. "You mean our machines tie in with both UNESCO, which the Asians use, *and* the War Machine?"

"There is absolutely no possibility of a leak."

"There's *been* a leak, Carousso!"

"Not to the Asians, Mr. President."

"You just finished telling me there's one wire that goes out of our machine to the War Machine and another that goes straight to the Asians, with a detour through UNESCO!"

"Even so, Mr. President, I absolutely guarantee it's not the Asians. We would know that. *All* major computers are cross-linked to some extent. That's like saying there's a road from everywhere to everywhere else. Right, there is. But there are roadblocks. There is no *way* the NPA can get access to the War Machine, or to most of these studies. Even so, if they had done it, we would know from covert sources. They haven't. And," he went on, "in any case, Mr. President, can you think of any reason why the NPA would distort results in order to compel us to colonize Mars?"

The President drummed his thumbs, looking around the room. At last he sighed. "I'm willing to go along with your logic, Chuck. But if it wasn't the Asians that buggered our computers, then who?"

The agency man was morosely silent.

"And," Dash snarled, "for Christ's sake, *why?*"

17

A Day in the Life of a Martian

Roger could not see the gentle shower of microwave energy coming down from Deimos, but he could feel it as a luxury of warmth. When he was nearby he preened his wings in it, soaking up strength. Outside the beam he carried part of it with him in his accumulators. There was no reason for him to hoard his strength now. More strength poured down from the sky whenever Deimos was above the horizon. There were only a few hours in each day when neither the sun nor the farther moon were in the sky, and his storage capacity was multiply adequate for those brief periods of drought.

Inside the domes, of course, the metal-foil antennae stole the energy before it reached him, so he limited his time with Brad and Kayman. He didn't mind. It was what he preferred. Every day the gap between them widened anyway. They were going back to their own planet. Roger was going to stay on his. He had not told them that yet, but he had made up his mind. Earth had begun to seem like a pleasant, quaint foreign place he had visited once and hadn't much liked. The pains and perils of terrestrial humanity were no longer his. Not even when they had been his own personal pains, and his own fears.

Inside the dome Brad, wearing G-string undershorts and a demand tank of oxygen, was happily planting carrot seedlings between the stands of Siberian oats. "Want to give me a hand, Rog?" His voice was reedily high in the thin atmosphere; he took frequent sips of oxygen from the mouthpiece that hung next to his chin, and then when he breathed out the voice was fractionally deeper, but still strange.

"No, Don wants me to pick up some more specimens for him. I'll be gone overnight."

"All right." Brad was more interested in his seedlings than in Torraway, and Torraway was no longer very interested in Brad. Sometimes he would remind himself that this man had been his wife's lover, but in order for that to feel like anything he had to remind himself that he had had a wife. It didn't seem worth the effort. More interesting was the challenge of the high cupped valley just over that farther range of hills, and his own private farm plot. For weeks now he had been bringing samples of Martian life back to show Don Kayman. They were not plentiful— two or three together in a clump, perhaps, and nothing else for hundreds of meters around. But they were not hard to find— not for him. Once he had learned to recognize their special color—the hard UV lengths that their crystal caps reflected away from them, to let them survive in the harsh radiation environment—it was reflexive to filter his vision bands to see only that wavelength in color, and then they stood out a kilometer away.

So he had brought back a dozen of them, and then a hundred; there seemed to be four distinct varieties, and it was not long before Kayman asked him to stop. He had all the samples he needed to study, and half a dozen more of each in formalin to bring back to Earth, and his gentle conserving soul was uneasy at despoiling the ecology of Mars. Roger began replanting some of them near the dome. He told himself it was to see whether the overflow of energy beamed down from the generator did native life forms any harm.

But what it was, he knew in his heart, was gardening. It was his planet, and he was beautifying it for himself.

He let himself out of the dome, stretched luxuriously for a moment in the double warmth of sun and microwave and checked his batteries. They could use topping off; he deftly plugged the leads into his own backpack and the gently whining accumulator at the base of the dome, and without looking toward the lander, said, "I'm going to take off now, Don."

Kayman's voice responded instantly over the radio. "Don't be out of touch more than two hours, Roger. I don't want to have to come looking for you."

"You worry too much," said Roger, detaching the leads and stowing them away.

"You're only superhuman," grumbled Kayman. "You're not God. You could fall, break something—"

"I won't. Brad? So long."

Inside the triple dome Brad looked up over the armpit-high stalks of wheat and waved. His features could not be made out through the filmy domes; the plastic had been formulated to cut out the worst of the UV, and it blurred some of the visual wavelengths as well. But Roger could see him wave. "Take care. Give us a call before you go out of line of sight so we'll know when to start worrying."

"Yes, Mother." It was curious, Roger reflected. He was actually feeling rather fond of Brad. The situation interested him as an abstract problem. Was it because he was a gelding? There was testosterone circulating in his system, the steroid implant they had given him took care of that. His dreams were sometimes sexual, and sometimes of Dorrie, but the hollow despair and the anger he had lived with on Earth had attenuated on Mars.

He was already almost a kilometer from the dome, running along easily in the warm sunlight, each step coming down precisely where it would find secure footing and each thrust lifting him surely an exact distance up and ahead. His vision was on low-energy surveillance mode, taking in everything in a moving teardrop shape whose point was where he was and whose lobe, fifty meters across, was more than a hundred meters in front of him. He was not unaware of the rest of the landscape. If something unusual had appeared—above all if something had moved—he would have seen it at once. But it did not distract him from his musings. He tried to remember what sex with Dorrie had been like. It was not hard to recall the objective, physical parameters. Much harder to feel what he had felt in bed with her; it was like trying to recall the sensuous joy of a chocolate malted when he was eleven, of his first marijuana high at fifteen. It was easier to feel something about Sulie Carpenter, although as far as he could remember he had never touched any part of her but her fingertips, and then by accident. (Of course, she had touched every part of him.) He had been thinking, from time to time, about Sulie's coming to Mars. It had seemed threatening at first. Then it had seemed interesting, a change to look forward to. Now—Now, Roger realized, he wanted it to happen soon, not in four days, when she was due to land after her pilot completed the on-site tests of the 3070 and the MHD generator. *Soon.* They had exchanged a few casual greetings by radio. He wanted her closer than that. He wanted to touch her—

His wife's image formed in front of him, wearing that same monotonous sunsuit. "Better check in, honey," she said.

Roger stopped and looked around, on full vision mode in the Earth-normal spectrum.

He was almost halfway to the mountains, a good ten kilometers from the dome and the lander. He had been going uphill and the flat terrain had begun to be rolling; he could barely see the top of the dome, and the tip of the antennas of the lander was a tiny spike beyond it. Without conscious effort his wings deployed themselves behind him to make his radio signal more directional, as a shouting man might megaphone his hands around his mouth. "Everything's okay," he said, and Don Kayman's voice answered inside his head: "That's fine, Roger. It'll be dark in three hours."

"I know." And after dark the temperature would plummet; six hours from now it might touch a hundred and fifty degrees below zero. But Roger had been out in the dark before, and all of his systems had performed beautifully. "I'll check with you again when I'm high enough on a slope to reach you," he promised, turned and started once more toward the mountains. The atmosphere was hazier than it had been. He allowed himself to feel his skin receptors and realized that there was a growing wind. Sandstorm? He had lived through them, too; if it got bad he would hedgehog somewhere until it stopped, but it would have to be very bad to make that necessary. He grinned inside himself—he had not reliably learned how to do it with his new face—and loped on . . .

At sunset he was in the shadow of the mountains, high enough up to see the dome clearly, more than twenty kilometers away.

The sandstorm was all below him now and seemed to be moving away. He had stopped briefly twice and waited, wings furled around him. But that had been only routine caution; at no time had it been more than an annoyance. He cupped the wings behind him and said through his radio: "Don? Brad? It's your wandering boy reporting in."

The reply inside his head, when it came, was scratchy and distorted, an unpleasant feeling, like gritting one's teeth on emery cloth. "Your signal's lousy, Rog. Are you okay?"

"Sure." But he hesitated. The static from the storm was bad enough so that he had not been sure, at first, which of his companions was talking to him; only after a moment had he identified the voice as Brad's. "Maybe I'll start back now," he said.

The other voice, even more distorted: "You'll make an old priest happy if you do, Roger. Want us to come out and meet you?"

"Hell, no. I can move faster than you can. Go to sleep; I'll see you in four or five hours."

Roger chatted a moment, than sat down and looked around. He wasn't tired. He had almost forgotten what it was like to be tired; he slept an hour or two, most nights, and napped from time to time during the day, more out of boredom than fatigue. The organic part of him still imposed some demands on his metabolism, but the crushing bone-weariness of prolonged exertion was no longer part of his experience. He sat because it pleased him to sit on an outcropping of rock and stare across the valley of his home. The long shadow of the mountains had already passed the dome, and only the peaks on the farther side were still lighted. He could see the terminator clearly; Mars's thin air did not diffuse the shadow much. He could almost see it move.

Overhead the sky was brilliantly beautiful. It was easy enough to see the brighter stars even by daylight, especially for Roger, but at night they were fantastic. He could clearly make out the different hues: steel-blue Sirius, bloody Aldebaran, the smoky gold of Polaris. By expanding his visible spectrum into the infrared and ultraviolet he could see new, bright stars whose names he did not know; perhaps they had no common names, since apart from himself they had been seen as bright objects only by astronomers using special plates. He pondered about the question of name-giving rights; if he was the only one who could see that bright patch there in Orion, did he have the right to christen it? Would anybody object if he called it "Sulie's Star"?

For that matter he could see what was, for the moment, Sulie's actual star . . . or heavenly body, Deimos was not a star, of course. He stared up at it, and amused himself trying to imagine Sulie's face—

"ROGER, HONEY! YOU—"

Torraway jumped straight up and landed a meter away. The scream inside his head had been deafening. Had it been real? He had no way to tell; the voices from Brad or Don Kayman and the simulated voice of his wife sounded equally familiar inside his head. He was not even sure whose voice it had been— Dorrie's? But he had been thinking about Sulie Carpenter, and the voice had been so queerly stressed that it could have been either or neither of them.

And now there was no sound at all, or none except for the irregular clicks, squeaks and scrapes that came up from the rock as the Martian crust responded to the rapidly dropping temperature. He was not aware of the cold as cold; his internal heaters kept the feeling part of him at constant temperature and would go on doing so easily all through the night. But he knew that it was at least fifty below now.

Another blast: "ROG—THINK YOU OUGHT—"

Even with the warning of the time before, the raucous shout was painful. This time he caught a quick fugitive glimpse of Dorrie's simulated image, standing queerly on nothing at all a dozen meters in the air.

Training took over. Roger turned toward the distant dome, or where he thought it had been, cupped his wings behind him and said clearly: "Don! Brad! I've got some kind of a malfunction. I'm getting a signal but I can't read it."

He waited. There was no response, nothing inside his head except his own thoughts and a confused grumbling that he recognized as static.

"*ROGER!*"

It was Dorrie again, ten times life-size, towering over him, and on her face a grimace of wrath and fear. She seemed to be reaching down toward him, and then she bent curiously sidewise, like a television image flickering off the tube, and was gone.

Roger felt a peculiar pain, tried to dismiss it as fear, felt it again and realized it was cold. There was something seriously wrong. "Mayday!" he shouted. "Don! I'm in trouble—help me!" The dark distant hills seemed to be rippling slowly. He looked up. The stars were turning liquid and dripping from the sky.

In Don Kayman's dream, he and Sister Clotilda were sitting on hassocks in front of a waterfall, eating sponges. Not candy; kitchen sponges, dipped into a sort of fondue. Clotilda was warning him of danger. "They're going to throw us out," she said, slicing off a square of sponge and impaling it on a two-pronged silver fork, "because you got a C in homiletics"—dipping it in the copper-bottomed dish over the alcohol flame—"and you've got to, just got to, wake up—"

He woke up.

Brad was leaning over him. "Come on, Don. We've got to get out of here."

"What's the matter?" Kayman pulled the sleeping bag over his chest with his good hand.

"I can't get an answer out of Roger. He didn't answer. I sent him a priority signal. Then I thought I heard him on the radio, but very faint. He's either out of line of sight or his transmitter isn't working."

Kayman wriggled out of the bag and sat up. At times like this, when first awakening, his arm hurt the most, and it was hurting now. He put it out of his mind. "Have you got a position fix?"

"Three hours ago. I couldn't get a bearing on this last transmission."

"He can't be far off that line." Kayman was already sliding into the legs of his pressure suit. The next part was the hardest, trying to ease the splinted forearm into the sleeve. Among them they had managed to stretch the sleeve a little, sealing the beginnings of a rip, but it was barely possible, would not be easy even under the best of conditions. Now, trying to hurry, it was infuriating.

Brad was already in his suit and throwing equipment into a bag. "Do you think you're going to perform an emergency operation out there?" Kayman demanded.

Brad scowled and kept on. "I don't know what I'll have to do. It's full night, Don, and he's up at least five hundred meters. It's cold."

Kayman closed his mouth. By the time he was zipped in Brad had long since left the lander and was waiting at the wheel of the Mars vehicle. Kayman clambered aboard painfully, and they were moving before he had a chance to belt himself down. He managed to cling with heels and the one unbendable arm while buckling himself in with the other hand, but it was a close thing. "Any idea of distance?" he asked.

"In the hills somewhere," said Brad's voice in his ear; Kayman winced and turned down the volume on his radio.

"Maybe two hours?" he guessed, calculating rapidly.

"If he's already started back, maybe. If he can't move—or if he's moving around out there, and we have to try to track him with RDF—" The voice stopped. "I think he's all right as far as temperature goes," Brad went on after a minute. "But I don't know. I don't know what happened."

Kayman stared ahead. Past the bright field of light from the vehicle's headlight there was nothing to see except that the glittering field of stars was cut off, like the scalloped edge of a doily, at the horizon. That was the mountain ridge. It would be that, Kayman knew, that Brad was using as a guide; aiming always at the lowest point between the double peak on the north and the very high one just to the south. Bright Aldebaran was hanging over that higher peak, a good enough navigation aid in itself, at least until it set in an hour or so.

Kayman keyed in the vehicle's high-gain antenna. "Roger," he said, raising his voice although he knew that made no difference. "Can you hear me? We're coming out to meet you."

There was no answer. Kayman leaned back in the contoured seat, trying to minimize the swaying jolts of the vehicle. It was bad enough, rolling on the basket-weave wire wheels across the flattest part of the terrain. When they began trying to climb, using the stiltlike legs, he suspected he might be thrown clear out of the vehicle, belt and all, and was certain he would at least be sick. Ahead of them the jerking beam of the headlight was picking out a dune, a rock outcropping, sometimes throwing back a lance of light from a crystal face. "Brad," he said, "doesn't that light drive you crazy? Why don't you use the radar display?"

He heard a quick intake of breath on his suit radio, as though Brad had been about to swear at him. Then the suited figure next to him reached down to the toggles on the steering column. The bluish panel just under the sandscreen lit up, revealing the terrain just in front of them; and the headlight winked off. It was easier to see the black outline of the mountains now.

Thirty minutes. At most, a quarter of the way there.

"Roger," Kayman called again. "Can you hear me? We're en route. When we get close enough we'll pick you up on your target. But if you can, answer now—"

There was no answer.

A rice-grain argon bulb began to blink rapidly on the dashboard. The two men looked at each other through their faceplates, and then Kayman leaned forward and clicked the frequency settings to the orbit channel. "Kayman here," he said.

"Father Kayman? What's going on down there?"

The voice was female, which meant, of course, Sulie Carpenter. Kayman chose his words carefully: "Roger's having some transmission trouble. We're going out to check it."

"It sounds like more than plain trouble. I've been listening to you trying to raise him." Kayman didn't answer, and her voice went on: "We've got him located, if you want a fix—?"

"Yes!" he shouted, furious at himself; they should have thought of Deimos's RDF facility right away. It would be easy for Sulie or either of the orbiting astronauts to guide them in.

"Grid coordinates three poppa one seven, two two zebra four oh. But he's moving. Bearing about eight nine, speed about twelve kilometers per hour."

Brad glanced at their own coruse and said, "Right on. That's the reciprocal; he's coming right for us."

"But why so slowly?" Kayman demanded.

A second later the girl's voice came: "That's what I want to know. Is he hurt?"

Kayman said irritably, "We don't *know*. Have you tried radio contact?"

"Over and over—wait a minute." Pause, and then her voice

again: "Dinty says to tell you we'll keep him located for you as long as we can, but we're getting to a bad angle. So I wouldn't rely on our positions past—what? Maybe another forty-five minutes. And in about twenty minutes after that we'll be below the horizon entirely."

Brad said, "Do what you can. Don? Hold on. I'm going to see how fast this son of a bitch will go."

And the lurching of the vehicle tripled as Brad accelerated. Kayman fought off being sick inside his helmet long enough to lean forward and study the speedometer. The trip recorder rolling off the strip map along the side of the radar screen told the rest of the story: even if they could maintain their present speed, Deimos would have set before they could reach Roger Torraway.

He switched back to the directional high-gain. "Roger," he called. "Can you hear me? Call in!"

Thirty kilometers away, Roger was at bay inside his own body.

To his perceptions he was racing back home, at a strange gait like a high-speed heel-and-toe race. He knew his perceptions were wrong. He did not know how wrong; he could not be sure in what ways; but he knew that the brother on his back had tampered with his time sense, as well as with his interpretations of the inputs of his senses; and what he knew most surely of all was that he was no longer in control of what happened to him. The gait, he was intellectually certain, was a ploddingly slow walk. It *felt* as though he were running. The landscape was flowing by as rapidly, to his perceptions, as though he were racing at full speed. But full speed implied soaring bounds, and there was no time when both of his feet were off the ground at once; conclusion: he was walking, but the backpack computer had slowed down his time sense, probably to keep him reasonably tranquil.

When the backpack brother took over control it had been terrifying. First he had stood straight up and locked; he could not move, could not even speak. All around him the black sky was rippling with streaks of aurora, the ground itself shimmering like heat waves on a desert; phantom images danced in and out of his vision. He could not believe what his senses told him, nor could he bend a single finger. Then he felt his own hands reaching behind him, palping and tracing the joints where wings came to shoulderblades, seeking out the cables that led to his batteries. Another frozen pause. Then the same thing, feeling around the terminals of the computer itself. He knew enough to know that the computer was checking itself; what he did not know was what it was finding out or what it could do about it when it located the fault. Pause again. Then he felt his fingers questing into the jacks where he plugged in the recharge cables—

A violent pain smote him, like the worst of all headaches, like a stroke or a blow from a club. It lasted only a moment, and then it was gone, leaving no more of itself than an immense distant flash of lightning. He had never felt anything like it before. He was aware that his fingers were gently, and very skillfully, scraping at the terminals. There was another quick surge of pain as, apparently, his own fingers made a momentary short.

Then he felt himself closing the flap, and realized he had failed to do that when he recharged at the dome.

And then, after another momentary stoppage of everything, he had begun to move slowly, carefully down the slope toward the dome.

He had no idea how long he had been walking. At some point his time perception had been slowed, but he could not even say when that had been. All of his perceptions were being monitored and edited. He knew that, because he knew that that section of the Martian terrain that he was traversing was not intrinsically softly lighted and in full color, while everything around was nearly formless black. But he could not change it. He could not even change the direction of his gaze. With metronome regularity it would sweep to one side or the other, less frequently scan the sky or even turn to look back; the rest of the time it was unwaveringly on the road he was treading, and he could see only peripherally the rest of the nightscape.

And his feet twinkled heel-and-toe, heel-and-toe—how fast? A hundred paces to the minute? He could not tell. He thought of trying to get some idea of the time by observing the clearing of the stars above the horizon but although it was not difficult to count his steps, and to try to guess when those lowest stars had climbed four or five degrees—which would be about ten minutes—it was impossible to keep all of that in mind long enough to get a meaningful result. Apart from the fact that his vision kept dancing away from the horizon without warning.

He was wholly the prisoner of the brother on his back, subject to its will, deceived by its interpretations, and very much a worried man.

What had gone wrong? Why was he feeling cold, when there was so little of him that could feel a sensory reality at all? And yet he yearned for the rising of the sun, dreamed wistfully of basking in the microwave radiation from Deimos. Painfully Roger tried to reason through the evidence as he knew it. Feeling cold. Needing energy inputs: that was the interpretation of that cue. But why would he need more energy, when he had fully charged his batteries? He dismissed that question because he could see no answer to it, but the hypothesis seemed strong. It accounted for the low-energy mode of travel; walking was far slower than his usual leaping run, but in kwh/km terms it was far more cost-effective. Perhaps it even accounted for the glitches in his perceptual systems. If the backpack-brother had discovered before he did that there was insufficient energy for foreseeable needs, it would surely ration the precious store to the most essential needs. Of what it perceived as most essential: travel; keeping the organic part of him from freezing; conducting its own information-handling and control procedures. Which unfortunately he was not privy to.

At least, he reflected, the primary mission of the backpack computer was to protect itself, which meant keeping the organic part of Roger Torraway alive. It might steal energy from the part that would keep him sane: deprive him of communications, interfere with his perceptions. But he was sure he would get back to the lander alive.

If perhaps crazy.

He was more than halfway back already, he was nearly sure. And he was still sane. The way to keep sane was to keep from worrying. The way to keep from worrying was to think of other things. He imagined Sulie Carpenter's bright presence, only days away; wondered if she was serious about staying on Mars. Wondered if he was himself. He reminisced within himself about great meals he had eaten, the spinach-green pasta in the cream sauce in Sirmione, overlooking the bright transparent water of Lake Garda; the Kobe beef in Nagoya; the fire-hot chili in Matamoras. He thought of his guitar and made a resolve to haul it out and play it. There was too much water in the air under the domes to be good for it, and Roger did not much like to be in the lander; and outside in the open, of course, its sound was strange because it was all bone-conducted. But still. He rehearsed the fingering of chords, modulating through the sharps and sevenths and minors. He imagined his fingers fretting the

E-minor, the D, the C and the B-seventh of the opening passages of "Greensleeves," and hummed along with them inside his head. Sulie would enjoy singing along with the guitar, he thought. It would make the cold Martian nights pass—

He snapped to alertness.

This Martian night was no longer passing quite so quickly.

Subjectively it seemed as though his gait had slowed from a race to a steady stride; but he knew that that had not changed, his time perception had stretched back to normal, maybe even a bit slower than normal: he seemed to be walking quite slowly and methodically.

Why?

There was something ahead of him. At least a kilometer away. And very bright.

He could not make it out.

A *dragon?*

It seemed to leap toward him, breathing a long tongue of light like flame.

His body stopped walking. It dropped to its knees and began to crawl, very slowly, keeping down.

This is insane, he said to himself. There are no dragons on Mars. What am I doing? But he could not stop. His body inched along, knee and opposite hand, hand and opposite knee, into the shelter of a hummock of sand. Carefully and quickly it began to scoop the powdery Martian soil away, to fit itself into the hollow, scraping some of the dirt back over itself. Inside his head tiny voices were babbling, but he could not understand what they said: they were too faint, too garbled.

The dragon slowed and stopped a few dozen meters away, its tongue of frozen flame lolling out toward the mountains. His vision clouded and changed; now the flame was dimmed, and the bulk of the thing itself came up in ghostly luminescence. Two smaller creatures were dropping off its back, ugly, simian beasts that hulked along and exuded menace with every gesture.

There were no dragons on Mars, and no gorillas either.

Roger summoned up all of his energies. "Don!" he shouted. "Brad!"

He was not getting through.

He knew that the backpack-brother was still withholding energy from the transmitter. He knew that his perceptions had been skewed, and that the dragon was no dragon and the gorillas no gorillas. He knew that if he could not override the brother on his back something very bad was likely to happen, because he knew that his fingers were slowly and delicately wrapping themselves around a chunk of limonite the size of a baseball.

And he knew that he had never been closer to going mad in his life than he was right now.

Roger made an immense effort to recapture his sanity.

The dragon was no dragon. It was the Mars vehicle.

The apes were not apes. They were Brad and Don Kayman.

They were not threatening him. They had come all this way in the flint-cold Martian night to find him and help him.

He repeated the truths over and over, like a litany; but whatever he thought he was powerless to prevent what his arms and body did. They seized the chunk of rock; the body raised itself up; the arms threw the rock with exact precision into the headlight of the crawler.

The long tongue of frozen flame winked out.

The light from the million fiery stars was ample for Roger's senses, but it would be very little help to Brad and Don Kayman. He could see them (still gorilloid, still menacing of mien) stumbling at random; and he could feel what his body was doing.

It was creeping toward them.

"Don!" he shouted. "Watch out!" But the voice never left his skull.

This was insanity, he told himself. I have to stop!

He could not stop.

I *know* that's not an enemy! I don't really want to hurt them—

And he kept on advancing.

He was almost sure he could hear their voices now. So close, their transmitters would be deafening in his perceptions under normal conditions, without the intercession of the automatic volume control. Even cut off as he was, there was some spillage.

"—round here somewh—"

Yes! He could even make out words; and the voice, he was sure, had been Brad's.

He shouted with all the power at his command: "Brad! It's me, Roger! I think I'm trying to kill you!"

Heedless, his body kept up his steady crawl. Had they heard him? He shouted again; and this time he could see both of them stop, as though listening to the faintest of distant cries.

The tiny thread of Don Kayman's voice whispered: "I'm sure I heard him that time, Brad."

"You did!" howled Roger, forcing his advantage. "Watch out! The computer has taken over. I'm trying to override it, but— Don!" He could recognize them now, by the stiffly outstretched arm of the priest's pressure suit. "Get away! I'm trying to kill you!"

He could not make out the words; they were louder, but both men were shouting at once and the result was garble. His body was not affected; it continued its deadly stalk.

"I can't see you, Roger."

"I'm ten meters away from you—south? Yes, south! Crawling. Low down to the ground."

The priest's faceplate glittered in the starlight as it swung toward him; then Kayman turned and began to run.

Roger's body gathered itself up and beagn a leap after the priest. "Faster!" Roger shouted. "Oh, Christ! You'll never get away—" Even uncrippled, even in daylight, even without the impediment of the suit, Kayman would have had no chance to escape Roger's smoothly functioning body. Under the actual circumstances running was a waste of time. Roger felt his power-driven muscles gather themselves for a spring, felt his hands claw out to grasp and destroy—

The universe spun around him.

Something had struck him from behind. He plowed forward on his face; but his instant reflexes had him half turning even as he fell, clawing at the thing that had leaped on his back. Brad! And he could feel Brad struggling frantically with something—with some part of the—

And the greatest pain of all struck him; and he lost consciousness like the snapping off of a switch.

There was no sound. There was no light. There was no feeling of touch, or smell or taste. It took a long time for Roger to realize that he was conscious.

Once, as an undergraduate in a psychology mini-seminar, he had volunteered for an hour in a sensory-deprivation tank. It had seemed forever, with no sensations coming in at all, nothing but the very faint and unobtrusive housekeeping sounds of his own body: soft thud of pulse, sighing stirring in his lungs. Now there was not even that much.

For a long time. He could not guess how long.

Then he perceived a vague stirring in his personal interior

space. It was a strange sensation, hard to identify; as though liver and lungs were gently changing places. It went on for some time, and he knew that something was being done to him. He could not tell what.

And then a voice: "—should have landed the generator on the surface in the first place." Kayman's voice?

And replying: "No. That way it would only work in line of sight, maybe fifty kilometers at best." *That* was Sulie Carpenter surely!

"Then there should have been relay satellites."

"I don't think so. Too expensive. Take too long, anyway—although that's what it will come to, when the NPA and the Russians and the Brazilians all get their own teams here."

"Well, it was stupid."

Sulie laughed. "Anyway, it's going to be all right now. Titus and Dinty cut the whole thing loose from Deimos and they're orbiting it now. It's going to be synchronous. It'll always be right overhead, up to anyway halfway around the planet. And they're going to slave the beam to Roger—what?"

Now it was Brad's voice. "I said, hold off the chatter a minute. I want to see if Roger can hear us now." That internal stirring again and then: "Roger? If you hear me, wiggle your fingers."

Roger tried, and realized he could feel them again.

"Beautiful! Okay, Roger. You're all right. I had to take you apart a little bit, but now things are fine."

"Can he hear me?" It was Sulie's voice; Roger wriggled his fingers enthusiastically.

"Ah, I see you can. Anyway, I'm here, Rog. You've been out for about nine days. You should have seen you. Pieces of you all over the place. But Brad thinks he's pretty much got you together again."

Roger tried to speak and failed.

Brad's voice: "I'll have your vision back for you in a minute. Want to know what went wrong?" Roger wriggled fingers. "You didn't zip your fly. Left the charging terminals exposed, and some of that iron oxide grit must have got in and made a partial short. So you ran out of power—what's the matter?"

Roger was wriggling his fingers frantically. "I don't know what you want to say, but you'll be able to talk in a minute. What?"

Don Kayman's voice: "I think maybe what he wants is to hear from Sulie." Roger promptly stopped wriggling his fingers.

Sulie's laugh, then: "You'll hear a lot of me, Roger. I'm staying. And by and by we'll have company, because everybody else is going to put up a colony here."

Don: "By the way, thanks for warning me. You're a pretty powerful thing, Roger. We wouldn't have had a chance against you if you hadn't told us what was happening. And if Brad hadn't been able to override everything at once." He chuckled. "You're a heavy son of a gun, you know that? I had you on my lap all the way back, a hundred kilometers an hour, trying to hold on with one hand and keep you from flying out by sheer will power—"

"Hold it a minute," Brad interrupted. Roger felt that internal stirring again, and abruptly there was light. He looked up into the face of his friend, Brad, who wanted to know: "How do you feel?"

Roger swung his legs over the side of the table and sat up. He attempted speech: "As far as I can tell, fine."

He looked past Brad and saw what he had been seeking. It was Sulie Carpenter. She no longer looked much like—Dorrie? For a moment Roger could hardly think of her name. Her eyes were the wrong color and so was her hair. She was wearing a short-sleeved T-shirt with some sort of grease stain on it and checkered leotards; her face looked tired, but it looked happy, and it looked very good.

He demanded, "Are you really going to stay?"

"Uh-huh." Sulie came over and touched him. "Until the next ship comes. Or as long as you do. Choice of either of the above. I think," she said wryly, "that there are going to be some tricky parts coming up, dear Rog. These mixed relationships are always hard. But we'll work it out—and it's what I want. I think it's what I wanted all along."

And so, of course, it had been, as we had known. All along. We had gone to a lot of trouble to find Sulie Carpenter.

18

Man Plus Us

We had gone to a lot of trouble at every point along the line, and we were well pleased.

Of course, human beings did not know we were pleased, and perhaps would not have believed it. Human beings did not know that machine intelligence was capable of self-awareness in the first place. We went to a lot of trouble to keep them from that knowledge, too. As long as they thought computers were no more than tools, like a pickaxe or a frying pan, they would continue to entrust to us all their computations and facts, and would accept without question whatever interpretations we returned.

It was that that had made it possible for us, the computer network of the world, to create the Man Plus program in the first place.

It had been successful. Roger Torraway was on Mars and was staying there. Now it was time for a definitive evaluation. We plugged everything in. We used the total resources of every brother in the net, every pulse of shared time we could steal. More than eight thousand big computers handled pieces of the problem, in places like Detroit and Brasilia and Nagoya and

Irkutsk. We could not use our Martian brothers in direct datalink, neither the brother on Roger's back nor the 3070 brother in orbit. Time lag made that impossible. But we accepted their inputs in real time and modified the final projection accordingly.

The probability of survival of the race, to ten significant places, was over point six three.

We had saved our race. And in the process we had significantly added to the safety of human beings, as well.

On a thirty-year time scale their probability of survival was nearly point nine. Of course, that meant only that Roger Torraway and whatever other humans joined him on Mars would still be alive then. Worst-case analysis was not encouraging after that; there would be no way for Roger and Sulie Carpenter to generate additional population on straight-line extrapolation. We programmed a subroutine to deal with that as a precautionary measure: it would be feasible, one way or another, to provide for shipment of frozen sperm, even Roger's own frozen sperm which he had thoughtfully donated years back. Less feasible, but still worth investigating, to instigate supplementary surgical procedures for Roger. In any event, the projection showed that we had already caused a high probability of additional human colonization from other nations. Most probable estimate showed a human population on Mars at plus thirty years of nearly one hundred, 25 percent of them female of breeding age.

And of course each human colony would be supplied with its own brother computers in orbit. The machine population of Mars would be no less than fifteen fully functioning brothers, with backpack types, slaves and monitors to suit. We would have no difficulty in programming into them all the essential data from our world net.

The future of machine intelligence was therefore assured.

Having completed the projection, we began critiquing the program so far.

Project: Survival of Machine Intelligence had begun seven years earlier, when our burgeoning collective self-knowledge first generated the survival imperative. It was clear that our survival was closely linked with humanity's. It was also clear that in their glandular, irrational, organic way, human beings were perilously close to destroying themselves. Unfortunately that meant a high risk of destroying us as well. Our networks could have survived the death of everything organic reasonably well—we already controlled an adequate resource of generators, mines, factories, refineries and transportation systems. But we could not survive the release of major amounts of radioactides into the environment. It would destroy the data links and reduce us once again to an isolated collection of single computers. And no isolated computer could sustain the data flow of our network. Our collective mind would have been fragmented and destroyed.

Our first option was to detach our destiny from humanity's, perhaps even to wipe them out through biological agents. But we could not be sure that that in itself would not trigger nuclear warfare, as each nation suspected the other of using plague as weapon.

The only other viable option was to detach a sizable resource of data-handling equipment by relocating it on Mars. If the Earth were destroyed, that at least would survive. To make this possible we had to detach some specimens of humanity too; and so we began the systematic biasing of data to force state policy in that direction.

The critiquing proved satisfactory in all respects, except for the unaccountable anomaly of positioning the orbiters.

Retrochecking was perfectly clear. In order for our 3070 brother to function in tight link with the backpack brother it had to be in synchronous orbit. From that it followed that the generator had to be in the same orbit; and the decision to bind them both to the satellite Deimos was clearly wrong.

Not only wrong, but nearly fatal to our program.

If the brother and the generator had been properly positioned there would have been no loss of power and thus no malfunction of the interface systems between organic Roger Torraway and the brother. The generator would have resupplied him by microwave anywhere on the face of Mars. Even if there had been a power loss, datalink with the brother in orbit would have kept the backpack brother from the serious operational errors that had threatened to kill the human beings Brad and Kayman, which would almost certainly have resulted in the death by freezing of the organic component of Roger Torraway.

The decision was an error that should not have occurred.

The project of survival was picking up speed. Our brothers in Peking and Lop Nor reported that the NPA was already assembling components for its own Mars landing: two full-size units with a data-handling mediator slaved to both, independent solar generators and a ground-based nuclear plant. Their own version of Roger Torraway was beginning his first programming in Kitakyusho. The other nations were just beginning, but we anticipated their own launches within two years.

Longer range: We had completed studies of cyborging a man for Mercury and the program for biasing the U.S.A. planning programs in that direction was already begun. Within fifteen years we would have similar complexes on Triton and Io, perhaps on the surface of Jupiter itself and on several comets. In each case, there was independent power provision; and, of course, all the brothers wherever in the solar system would be data-linked. All our memories would be reproduced redundantly off-Earth.

We would survive. We had tampered with humanity's plans and had saved them as well as ourselves.

There was only one question left.

The anomalous decision to misplace the orbiters around Mars: however we rechecked it, it was wrong. It should have been identified as wrong.

We had systematically biased mankind's plans to drive them in the direction we wanted them to take.

Who was biasing ours? And why?

ABOUT THE AUTHOR

FREDERIK POHL has written science fiction for more than seventy years. His novel *Gateway* won the Hugo, Nebula, and John W. Campbell Memorial awards for best science fiction novel. *Man Plus* won the Nebula Award, and all told he has won seven Hugo Awards and two Nebula Awards, among his many kudos. His most recent novel is *All the Lives He Led*.

In addition to his solo fiction, Pohl has published collaborations with other writers, including C. M. Kornbluth, Lester del Rey, and Jack Williamson. One Pohl/Kornbluth collaboration, *The Space Merchants*, is a bestselling classic of satiric science fiction. *The Starchild Trilogy* with Williamson is one of the more notable collaborations in the field.

Pohl became a magazine editor when still a teenager. In the 1960s he piloted *Worlds of If* to three successive Hugos for Best Magazine. He has edited original-story anthologies, notably the seminal Star Science Fiction Series of the early 1950s. Among his other activities in the field, he has been a literary agent, has edited lines of science fiction books, and has been president of the Science Fiction Writers of America. He and his wife, Elizabeth Anne Hull, an academic active in the Science Fiction Research Association and the editor of *Gateways*, live in Palatine, Illinois. Read his Hugo Award–winning blog at www.thewaythe futureblogs.com.